# TRIGGERS

By Stephen Leather

## ALSO BY STEPHEN LEATHER

Pay Off, The Fireman, Hungry Ghost, The Chinaman, The Vets,
The Long Shot, The Birthday Girl, The Double Tap, The Solitary
Man, The Tunnel Rats, The Bombmaker, The Stretch, Tango One, The
Eyewitness, Penalties, Takedown, The Shout, The Bag Carrier,
Plausible Deniability, Last Man Standing, Rogue Warrior, The
Runner, Breakout, The Hunting, Desperate Measures, Standing Alone,
The Chase, Still Standing
*Spider Shepherd* thrillers:
Hard Landing, Soft Target, Cold Kill, Hot Blood, Dead Men, Live
Fire, Rough Justice, Fair Game, False Friends, True Colours, White
Lies, Black Ops, Dark Forces, Light Touch, Tall Order, Short Range,
Slow Burn, Fast Track, Dirty War
*Spider Shepherd: SAS* thrillers:
The Sandpit, Moving Targets, Drop Zone, Russian Roulette
*Jack Nightingale* supernatural thrillers:
Nightfall, Midnight, Nightmare, Nightshade, Lastnight, San
Francisco Night, New York Night, Tennessee Night, New Orleans
Night, Las Vegas Night

# Table of Contents

# CHAPTER 1

Eighteen years ago.

MARIANNE turned her back to the bedroom door and curled up into a tight ball, her eyes firmly shut. 'Please, no. Please, no. Please, no,' she whispered as she clutched her teddy bear to her stomach.

Her father was downstairs. She had heard him walk along the hall to the kitchen, and heard him open and close the fridge. Then she had heard the hiss of a can of lager being opened, and his footsteps as he went back to the sitting room. It was his third can, and it was after his third can that he usually came upstairs. She would smell the lager the moment he opened the door. Lager and cigarettes and sweat. He would open the door and stand looking at her. What happened then depended on whether or not he switched on the light.

If the light stayed off he would take off his clothes and get into bed with her. He would touch her and caress her and she knew from experience that there was nothing that she could say that would stop him.

Bad as it was, if he switched on the light it would be worse. He would make her get out of bed and he would make her dress and then he would take her downstairs. There would be a van outside and she would have to get into the back. There would be another man driving the van and her father would get in the back with her. She never cried. If she cried he would slap her so she would just curl up into a ball and wait for it to be over.

Sometimes he took her to a house. Sometimes to a hotel. Once he took her to a castle. A real castle with suits of armour in the hall. But no matter where he took her, bad things happened to her. Things that she shouldn't bear to think about, things that she tried to blot out

'Woody, please. Please, Woody. Can you do it for me? Please.'

She hugged her teddy bear tighter and kept her eyes firmly closed.

'Woody, I need you. Please.'

Marianne couldn't take the abuse any more. It was more than she could bear. But Woody could. Woody was strong, like wood. Woody was tough, Woody could take whatever was done to him. He was smart and he was brave and he was resilient, he was everything that Marianne wasn't.

She sniffed. 'Please, Woody. Do this for me.'

The door handle turned. She hugged her bear tighter and buried her face in its fur.

'Please.'

The door creaked as it slowly opened.

Tears ran down her face and onto the pillow.

*'It's okay, Marianne. I'm up.'*

The light flicked on.

# CHAPTER 2

Present day

JASMINE smiled as she saw him walk into the club, just as she was starting her second set. Boris Morozov. Russian oligarch and gangster. He was a big man, with a shaved head that glistened in the candlelight and a Savile Row suit cut to emphasise his broad shoulders and weight lifter forearms. She allowed her eyes to hold his gaze for a couple of seconds, she gave him the faintest of smiles, then looked over at her pianist. He was a young guy, barely in his twenties, but he was one of the best jazz pianists she had sung with. He knew every song that she threw at him and was able to follow her whenever she improvised. His name was Ben and he played with her most weekends. During the week he taught music at a North London private school so Jasmine's accompanist Monday to Friday was much older and less talented. She came to the end of the song and mouthed 'You don't know what love is.' He smiled and nodded and immediately started to play.

It was one of the sexiest songs in her repertoire, written by Don Raye and Gene de Paul. It became a jazz classic when Miles Davies recorded an instrumental version in 1954 and Dinah Washington released the definitive vocal version the following year. Jasmine, though, based her rendition on the style of the late great Billie Holiday.

She waited until the third verse before she looked over at the Russian again. He was sitting at a table close to the entrance, his back to the wall. There were two men sitting with him, a few years younger but just as big. One was bearded with thick-lensed glasses, the other had a wicked scar across one cheek. On the table in front of them was a bottle of Cristal champagne in an ice bucket and Ronnie the maitre d' was pouring for them. The Russian smiled at her and she smiled back, holding eye contact for a couple of seconds before looking around the room, sharing the love.

She could feel his eyes on her, taking in the soft swell of her breasts and the slit down the side of the red dress she was wearing.

There were two other men sitting at another table close to Morozov. One had come into the room before the Russian, the other, tall and thin with a drooping moustache, had followed the group in. Both had watchful eyes and were drinking water. Bodyguards.

She waited until she had sung two more songs before allowing her glance to settle back on his table. He was drinking champagne and listening to something the bearded man was saying. Morozov was nodding but his eyes were on her. She smiled and he raised his glass and smiled back. A gold tooth glittered at the side of his mouth. She held his glance, then started to work the room again. Even though she didn't look back at his table she could feel his eyes staring at her, taking it all in.

Eventually she finished her set to enthusiastic applause. She took a bow and Ben waved, then as the clapping died down she headed over to the bar. She slid onto a stool and Lucian the barman handed her a glass of water with a squeeze of lemon. She sipped it gratefully. Ben continued to play the piano softly. Background music.

Ronnie appeared at her side. 'Beautiful performance as always, princess,' he said. He was in his fifties, stick thin with grey hair, teeth and fingernails discoloured from a lifetime of smoking.

'Thanks, Ronnie.'

'Mr Morozov would like you to join him at his table.'

'Which one is he?'

'The Russian by the door. Big money, princess. And a big tipper.'

'Russian mafia?'

Ronnie chuckled. 'Maybe. But he has a Bentley and a huge house in Mayfair and when he's in a good mood he spends thousands.'

'So you want me to put him in a good mood?'

'I'm sorry, princess. Just sit at his table and have a drink with him then make your excuses and leave. You'd be doing me a big favour.'

4

She sipped her water and flashed him a smile. 'It's okay, Ronnie. I'm a team player.'

'I know that, princess.' He took her hand and kissed the back of it. 'I owe you one.'

She took her hand back and slid off the stool. 'Tits and teeth,' she whispered to herself. 'Tits and teeth.'

She forced a smile and held her head high as she walked over to the Russian's table. He watched her with hungry eyes as he sipped champagne. The two men he was with stood up and moved to another table. The one with the beard clicked his fingers to attract the attention of a waitress.

Morozov waved his glass at her. 'Sit,' he said, as if he was talking to a dog.

Jasmine sat on his right. He pushed an empty glass in front of her and poured champagne into it. Ronnie hurried over to help but Morozov shook his head and the maitre d' backed away. Morozov finished pouring the champagne and put the bottle back into the ice bucket. He raised his glass. 'To a wonderful performance,' he said.

Jasmine picked up her glass and clinked it against his. 'You're very kind,' she said.

'Your name is Jasmine?'

'It is, yes.'

'But that is not your real name, is it? Jasmine is a stage name?'

'Why do you say that?'

Morozov's eyes narrowed. 'You don't look like a Jasmine.'

'Really?'

He chuckled. 'Really.'

'What do I look like?'

He shrugged. 'I'm not sure. But not a Jasmine.'

She sipped her champagne. 'And what about you? What's your name?'

5

'Boris.'

'And is that your real name?'

'Why would I lie?'

'Oh, everybody lies.'

'Do they?'

'In my experience, yes.'

They both sipped their champagne.

'So what do you do, Boris?'

'Import, export. I buy and sell.'

'Are you an oligarch?'

He laughed. 'I am, yes. But one of the good ones.' He reached over and patted her knee. 'This dress, where did you get it from?'

'Camden market.'

'You would look good in Armani. Or Dior. I should take you shopping.'

'Shopping? Really?'

'We could go to New Bond Street. Maybe have lunch in Petrus. Have you been to Petrus?'

'I don't think so.'

'It's a Gordon Ramsay restaurant. It has a Michelin star.'

'I'm vegan.'

'I'm sure they serve vegan food. Though I can never understand why anyone would deprive themselves of the joy of eating a Kobo steak.' His hand moved slowly up her thigh and he squeezed gently. 'Meat is good.'

Jasmine looked down at his hand. 'That's a nice watch,' she said.

Morozov took his hand off her thigh and showed her the watch. 'It's a Patek Philippe,' he said. 'It cost more than a quarter of a million pounds.' He looked at her left wrist. 'You don't have a watch?'

'I've never worn one,' she said. 'I always know the time. Night or day, I know to within a minute or two what time it is. Even when I wake up, I know straight away what time it is.'

'That's a gift,' he said. 'But a watch isn't about telling the time. It makes a statement.'

'And what statement does your watch make?'

Morozov laughed. 'That I'm richer than God,' he said. He drained his glass. 'Do you want to see my house?'

'Your house?'

'It's not far. Mayfair. We can have another drink there and we can discuss our shopping expedition.'

'So we're definitely going shopping, are we?'

'That's up to you, Jasmine. So is that a yes?' His hand moved back to her thigh. 'I'll make it worth your while.'

She drained her glass and flashed him a smile. Tits and teeth. 'Sure,' she said. 'Why not?'

# CHAPTER 3

JASMINE looked up at the house as the gate rattled open. Morozov had called it a house but it was clearly a mansion, with four brick-faced storeys and a garage block to the right. There was a large courtyard in front of the house, with a green Lamborghini, a red Porsche and a white Aston Martin SUV on display. Two men in black suits were standing by the front door. More bodyguards.

'Do you like cars?' asked Morozov. His hand was back on her thigh. They were sitting in the back of a black Bentley. The driver was a Russian heavy in his thirties with slicked-back hair and a crucifix tattoo on his neck. The two men who had been drinking with Morozov had stayed behind, but the two bodyguards were behind them in a BMW SUV.

'I'm more of a cyclist,' she said.

'Not in a dress like that,' he said, giving her thigh a squeeze. 'Are you wearing underwear?'

Jasmine laughed but didn't answer the question.

As soon as the gate was fully open, the driver edged the Bentley into the courtyard and pulled up next to the Porsche. The BMW followed them in and parked in front of the garage.

The Bentley driver got out and opened the door for Morozov. Jasmine opened her own door and climbed out. The two bodyguards stayed in their vehicle as the gate rattled closed.

Morozov waved for Jasmine to join him and together they walked to the front door. It was opened by a grey-haired man in a butler's uniform. He stepped to the side and bowed his head as they walked into the house.

'This is Robert, he used to work for Prince William,' said Morozov.

'Hello, Robert,' she said.

'Good evening, madam,' said the butler. His voice was deep and rich and made her think of Morgan Freeman. He closed the door behind them.

Jasmine stopped and looked around. They were in a huge double-height hall with a wide marble staircase that wound around a massive crystal chandelier that descended from the ceiling high above like a shimmering waterfall. Several black doors led off the hall. One of them opened and two heavies appeared. Big men wearing black suits. As they stepped into the hall, the jacket of one opened to reveal a gun in an underarm holster.

Morozov dismissed them with a wave of his hand and they went back through the door.

'Are they butlers, too?' asked Jasmine.

'They are my security.'

Jasmine frowned. 'Why do you need security?'

'When you have nice things, there are always people who want to take them from you,' said Morozov. 'Let's go upstairs, shall we?'

Jasmine put up her hands. 'Hey, steady on, Boris. I said I'd come back for a drink, I didn't say anything about visiting your bedroom.'

Morozov frowned in confusion, then he shook his head and grinned. 'The sitting room is upstairs. The ground floor is for staff. The bedrooms are at the top of the house.' He patted her on the arm. 'Just a drink,' he said. He looked over at the butler who was standing by the main door. 'A bottle of Cristal, Robert. And caviar. Lots of caviar.'

'Yes, sir,' said the butler, and he headed to the kitchen.

'I have the best Russian caviar,' said Morozov. 'It is harvested from a rare albino sturgeon in the south Caspian Sea. One teaspoon costs more than a hundred pounds. You will love it.'

'I'm a vegan, remember?'

'It's fish eggs. That's vegan, right?'

Jasmine shook her head. 'No,' she said. 'It's not.'

'More for me, then,' said Morozov. He held out his hand. Jasmine took it and they walked up the stairs together. The stairs opened onto a hallway that ran both sides of the house. There were two more bodyguards there. One of them stepped forward to open a pair of double doors. As he stepped back, Jasmine caught a glimpse of a gun in a holster under his left arm.

The doors opened into a huge room overlooking a garden at the rear of the house. There were two large leather sofas at one end, and a baby grand piano at the other.

'It's a Steinway,' said Morozov as Jasmine went over to it.

'Do you play?'

He shook his head. 'No.'

'So why do you have it?'

'It was here when I moved in.'

'The owner left it behind?'

Morozov shrugged. 'He died.'

Jasmine walked over to look at a painting on the wall. She stood staring at it, her arms folded. Morozov walked over to stand next to her. He was so close that she could smell the sickly sweet scent of his aftershave. 'You like it?' he asked.

'It's pretty. Who painted it?

'No idea. It came with the house.'

She turned to look at him. 'So you bought the house with everything in it?'

He grinned. 'I didn't actually buy it. But it's all mine.' He slipped his arm around her shoulder but she twisted away and walked back to the piano. She tapped on the keys. 'Can you play?' he asked.

'I'm just a singer.'

'You're not just a singer. You have an amazing voice.'

'Thank you.'

'I mean it. You sing from the heart. You've had a rough life, haven't you?'

She turned to look at him. 'Why do you say that?'

'Great artists have always suffered. Suffering is like a forge. The hotter the forge, the harder the steel.'

'What about you Boris? Have you suffered?'

He nodded. 'It applies to business, too. The best businessmen come from nothing. Hardship makes you work harder.'

'But you're not suffering now, are you?'

He chuckled and put his arm around her again and pulled her close. He kissed her on the cheek before she slipped out of his grasp. He followed her, like a lion after its prey. 'Now I make others suffer,' he said. He reached for her again but was interrupted by the doors opening. It was the butler, carrying a tray. He carried it over to a table and laid out a bottle of champagne in an ice bucket, two crystal flutes and a dish filled with caviar. He opened the champagne with barely any sound and poured some in to both flutes. When he had finished, the butler nodded at Morozov and left the room, closing the doors behind him.

Morozov went over to the table. He picked up a silver spoon, plunged it into the pile of caviar, and thrust it into his mouth. He groaned with pleasure, then took another spoonful and offered it to her. Jasmine shook her head. 'Vegan, remember?' she said.

He sneered and licked the caviar off the spoon before putting it back in to the dish. He picked up one of the champagne flutes and toasted her. 'Champagne and caviar,' he said. 'Nectar of the Gods.' He drained the glass and refilled it. 'Take off your dress,' he said.

'Say what now?' said Jasmine.

'You heard me. I want to see you naked.'

'That's not going to happen, Mr Morozov.'

'We both know why you're here.'

'I'm here because my boss said I should be nice to you.'

'So be nice to me. Take off the fucking dress and come over here and get on your knees. Let's see what else you can do with that mouth other than sing.' He drained his glass again and put it down on the table.

'I'm leaving,' said Jasmine. She walked towards the doors but Morozov moved to intercept her. She tried to get around him but he blocked her way.

'You're not going anywhere, you fucking bitch,' he said, and grabbed her by the shoulder, so hard that she winced in pain.

'*Sofia,*' said Woody. '*You're up.*'

# CHAPTER 4

SOFIA grabbed Morozov's wrist and twisted it savagely. He released his grip on her shoulder. Morozov yelped in pain but Sofia kept the pressure on and forced him back.

He grunted in pain and she laughed. 'Who's the bitch now?' she said, in Russian.

His eyes widened in surprise but before he could say anything she twisted his arm in the opposite direction and forced him backwards. He stumbled over a leather armchair and she let go of him and he fell to the floor. He roared as he got to his feet and charged towards her like an angry bull. Sofia stepped to the side and stuck out her foot, catching his right leg. He sprawled forward and crashed onto a glass coffee table. It shattered under his weight and he fell on to the broken glass.

He lay there groaning. Sofia walked over to him but stopped when the doors flew open. She looked over as the two bodyguards rushed into the room. 'Mr Morozov fell over,' she said. 'Help him, please.'

The two men rushed over to their boss. Sofia walked quickly over to the double doors and locked them.

As the bodyguards helped Morozov to his feet, he began to cough and splutter. There were cuts on his face from the broken glass. He shook the bodyguards away and pointed at Sofia. 'Get the bitch!' he shouted in Russian.

The two men moved towards Sofia. She kicked off her high heels and waited for them to get close. They didn't pull out their guns. They probably figured she was just a little girl who wouldn't take much handling. Big mistake. 'Please don't hurt me,' she said, but they didn't get the sarcasm. One of them reached out to grab her. She caught him by the wrist and twisted it until she heard it crack. She twisted the arm again and as he doubled over she brought her knee into his stomach. The breath exploded from his lungs and she let go of his arm. She took a half step back and punched him in the temple, putting all her weight behind the blow. He fell face forward, his eyes rolling back into his head.

The second bodyguard reached for his gun but before he could pull it out, Sofia slashed him across the throat with the flat of her hand, splintering his larynx. He pulled out his gun as he staggered back and Sofia grabbed it and twisted it from his hand. His breath was coming in ragged gasps and his eyes were wide and fearful. She smiled at him and smashed the gun against the side of his head. He fell to the floor and Sofia stepped back.

Sofia checked out the gun. It was a Glock 17, beloved by law enforcement agencies around the world. There were only 33 parts, including the polymer magazine which held seventeen 9mm rounds. It had high muzzle energy and packed a punch, and in the hands of an expert it was accurate up to twenty five metres. Sofia was a fan. She aimed at Morozov's face. 'I think maybe you're the one who should get on his knees,' she said, in fluent Russian.

'Who the fuck are you?' he asked.

'*Okay, Marianne,*' said Woody. '*You're up.*'

# CHAPTER 5

MARIANNE glared at Morozov. 'You really don't remember me?' she said. 'After everything you did to us, you don't remember?'

Morozov frowned and his eyes narrowed. He said something in Russian and Marianne shook her head. 'I don't speak Russian,' she said.

'Yes you do. You spoke Russian before.'

'Speak English,' said Marianne. 'Do you remember me?' She kept the gun pointed at his face but it was heavy and it began to waver.

'What are you talking about, bitch? I met you for the first time tonight.'

Marianne shook her head. 'No. We met years ago. You raped me. I was different then. I've changed a lot. But I remember you and I remember everything you did to me.'

Morozov swore at her in Russian. 'You are fucking crazy,' he said.

'I was nine years old!' Marianne shouted.

The Russian's jaw dropped, then he tilted his head on one side as he scrutinised her face.

'You were staying in a big house, almost as big as this one. My father drove an hour to get to you.'

'Who are you?'

'You raped me. You paid my father so that you could do whatever you wanted. And you did a lot, Boris. You did everything. Afterwards I was bleeding and I couldn't walk. My father had to carry me to the van. I couldn't go to school for a week. My parents told the school that I had chickenpox.'

'It was a long time ago.'

'So now you remember?'

Morozov shook his head.

'I think about it every day. Every single day. I remember the smell of you. I remember the blackheads all over your nose. And that gold tooth. I remember everything.' The gun was getting heavier and Marianne's hands were shaking.

'Your parents pimped you out and you're blaming me?' He sneered and cursed in Russian.

'Do you remember what you did?'

'It was a long time ago.'

'And you fuck a lot of children, is that it?'

'You need to talk to your parents about this.'

'They're dead.'

'So you're an orphan? That's tough.'

'You think this is funny?'

'I think you're upset and confused. And I think you have no idea how to handle a gun.' His right hand flashed out, catching the gun and pushing it to the side. He stepped forward, raised his other hand and slapped Marianne across the face. Her head span and she staggered back, the gun tumbling from her nerveless fingers. 'Stupid bitch!' Morozov shouted. He slapped her again and she fell to the floor, sobbing.

'I'll show you how to use a gun, you stupid bitch,' said Morozov. He bent down and picked up the Glock.

'*Sofia*,' said Woody. '*You're up.*'

# CHAPTER 6

SOFIA grinned as she saw Morozov walk over to her. His finger tightened on the trigger. She rolled to the left and the bullet thwacked into the floor, right where her head had been. The Russian cursed and fired again but Sofia continued to roll and his second shot also missed. She lay on her back, grunted, and pulled her knees up to her chest. She placed her hands on the floor, and pushed at the same time as she kicked out with her feet. She arched her back and straightened up the second her feet touched the floor. In less than a second she was facing Morozov, who was so shocked by the move that he froze, giving Sofia more than enough time to drop down and sweep his feet from under him.

He fell and hit the floor hard, knocking the wind from him. He kept a grip on the Glock so Sofia moved quickly, walking over to him and stamping on his arm. He screamed and his hand opened, releasing the gun. Sofia bent down, picked it up, and took a step back.

Someone began to bang on the door. More bodyguards. There were shouts outside in the hallway. Sofia ignored them and she pointed the gun at Morozov's groin. She pulled the trigger and Morozov screamed in pain. A red stain spread across his trousers. The smell of cordite made Sofia's eyes water.

'Please, don't...' he said, holding out his hands, fingers spread wide.

'Burn in hell,' said Sofia, in Russian. She shot him in the stomach, then as his hands dropped she put a round between his eyes and he went still.

The doors shuddered and there was the sound of splintering wood. She turned. The doors shuddered again but the lock held. Just. She moved towards a large leather armchair, knelt down behind it, and aimed at the doors. There were more shouts from the corridor and then the door flew open.

A man staggered into the room, off balance after his kick. He was holding a Glock in his right hand but it was pointing at the ground. He stared at Morozov lying on the carpet and Sofia had all the time in the world to put two rounds in his chest. As he slumped to the floor, a second bodyguard came into the room. He was one of the men who had been at the club, the tall, thin one with a moustache. His eyes scanned the room and he kept low but long before he spotted Sofia she had shot him in the face and blood, brain and skull fragments splattered over the wallpaper.

Sofia walked quickly into the hall. The butler was standing with his back to the wall, his hands clasped together as if in prayer. 'How many more men are downstairs, Robert?' she asked.

'Seven, madam,' he said.

'And upstairs?'

'None, madam.'

'Thank you, Robert. You have a nice evening.' She headed up the stairs.

'You, too, madam.'

She heard a door open and peered over the bannister. A heavy ran in to the hall and peered up, a gun in his hand. He brought the gun to bear on Sofia but he was too slow and she put two rounds in the man's chest. Blood smeared along the wallpaper as he slid to the floor. 'I'm sorry about the mess, Robert,' she said.

'It's not a problem, madam.'

Sofia ran up the stairs. She had just reached the second floor when a volley of shots screeched past her and thudded in to the ceiling. She crouched down and squinted over the bannister. Two more heavies were running up the stairs. A bullet thwacked into the bannister but she didn't flinch, she shot the first man in the head and put two shots in the chest of the second man.

She ran up the final flight of stairs. She heard shouts from down below. She looked over the bannister. Two more heavies were coming up the stairs, their backs pressed against the wall, guns at the ready. One of them spotted her and took a shot. She pulled her head back and the bullet smacked into the wall behind her. She moved a few feet along the bannister, popped up and fired two quick shots but they were moving and she missed.

She looked over her shoulder. There were half a dozen doors, presumably bedrooms. There were more shots from down below and the chandelier shattered. Pieces of broken glass tinkled down to the floor, far below. There were more shouts. Robert had said there were seven men downstairs. Assuming he wasn't lying there were four men still alive, two of them on the floor below her. That meant that going downstairs wasn't an option.

She headed for the nearest door and opened it. A bullet whizzed past her and buried itself in the jamb close to her head. She span around in a crouch, the gun in both hands. One of the bodyguards was standing at the top of the stairs. He had fired one-handed which is probably why the round had gone wide. Even professionals made mistakes. Sofia wasn't a professional but she rarely made a mistake. She fired twice and both shots hit the man in the chest. His arms flailed and he staggered backwards, knocking into the man behind him. Sofia hurried across the hall. The man behind the one she'd hit tried to bring his gun up but he was off balance. He cursed in Russian. Sofia aimed at him but she couldn't get a clear shot.

The two men hit the wall and as the one with the bloodstained chest slumped forward she fired twice, catching the second heavy in the neck and then the face. Blood splattered across the wall behind him and he slid down on top of his colleague.

There were more shouts from down below and Sofia ducked and swivelled around. She ran back to the door and into the bedroom. There was a king size bed, a sitting area and a door leading to an en suite. She closed the door and slid a bolt across it, then grabbed a chair and jammed it against the door handle. It would hold them for a while, but they'd get in eventually. She padded over to the window and opened it. The cool night air blew in and she shuddered. She looked out of the window and the wind whipped at her hair. Her head span as she realised just how high up she was. She could see the cars far below, and her heart lurched as the ground appeared to rush up at her. She leaned back in the room, breathing heavily. 'I hate heights,' she muttered. 'I've never been good with heights.' She heard rapid footsteps in the hallway and something thudded against the bedroom door.

'*Jim*,' said Woody. '*You're up.*'

# CHAPTER 7

JIM sniffed and wiped his nose with the back of his hand. He smelled the cordite on the gun and he looked at it as if seeing it for the first time. A gun was of no use to him but he was reluctant to throw it away. He pulled at the dress and tucked it into the bra but winced when he realised that the barrel was hot. He pulled the gun out and frowned. There was no way that he'd be able to climb down with the gun in his hand. There was a loud thud as if someone had kicked the door. The chair would keep them at bay for a while but not forever. He leaned out of the window. There was a triple garage to the left, brick built with a flat roof. To the right was a line of bushes against a brick wall. He tossed the gun at one of the bushes and it crashed through the branches and fell to the ground.

There was another thud at the door. Jim reached for the sides of the window, put his foot on the sill and heaved himself up. There was a small balcony outside the window directly below him. He turned around so that he was facing the room. The door shuddered as it was kicked again and the chair moved slightly.

Jim took a deep breath and let go of the window. Time slowed down as it always did when he was in parkour mode. All his senses were in overload as he started to fall. The balcony was about three feet wide, more than enough room for him to land and flex his knees to absorb the shock, providing he stayed upright. The bricks flashed past as gravity pulled him down. He put his arms to his side and felt the air rush over his skin. He looked down. The balcony was rushing towards him. He pointed his toes down. Parkour in bare feet was never a good idea but he didn't have a choice. He wouldn't be able to roll to absorb the impact but it was a twelve foot drop at most so his knees would do the job.

The bricks changed to glass and then his feet hit the balcony. He let his knees bend and then he tightened his muscles, keeping his back straight so that he didn't pitch forward against the window. He grunted but there was no real pain, just a stinging sensation that quickly faded. He turned around. He was on the second floor now, and he could probably drop down onto one of the parked cars without hurting himself, but it was a risk and if he twisted his ankle he'd be a sitting duck.

There was another balcony to his left, a twin of the one he was standing on, but it was closer to the garage block. It was ten feet away. Doable.

He backed up as far as he could go, took a breath, exhaled, then sprang forward. It was two steps to the side of the balcony, he jumped and planted his right foot on the railing, leant forward and pushed off with all his might. As he soared through the air he put his hands out, fingers splayed, ready to grab the railing of the balcony opposite.

He had judged the jump perfectly and managed to get both feet onto the balcony as he grabbed at the railing. He paused for a second before springing over the bar and landing on the balcony. He was breathing slowly and evenly as his eyes swept the ground below. There were two men in suits down below, looking at the front door. They had obviously heard the shots inside but made no move to enter so they were probably drivers rather than bodyguards.

He moved over to the side nearest the garage block. He stopped when he realised that the curtains were wide open but it was clear that the room was in darkness so he carried on. He bent over the railing and peered down at the garage. The roof looked solid enough. It was about ten feet from the balcony and the drop was about twelve feet and there was plenty of room for a forward roll. Then an eight foot drop to the ground. But then what? The metal gates were closed and he wasn't sure how fast or how far he could run in bare feet.

He heard shouts from above and realised that he had to get moving. He jumped up onto the railing, steadied himself, then threw himself off. He brought his knees up and kept his arms out to the side to maintain his balance, then just before he made contact with the roof he lowered his legs and powered forward, turning the downward motion into a forward roll. His feet hit the roof and almost immediately he went down on his shoulder, rolled, and came up, facing the cars. He ran forward, jumped off the roof and landed in the courtyard. He heard more shouts from the top of the house.

The two men standing by the front door turned to look at Jim. He sprinted towards them, then barged into the older of the two, knocking him to the ground. He whirled around and punched the other man in the face, wincing with pain as he made contact. The man staggered back, blood pouring from his nose and collapsed against the door. Jim bent down next to the older man and quickly went through his pockets. He pulled out a key fob and looked at the logo. It had a bull on it, below the name of the make. Lamborghini.

He straightened up. As he did, a bullet screeched off the tarmac and he flinched. One of the cars was a low slung green Lamborghini and he ran towards it. As he ran, he pressed the key fob and the driver's door opened, pointing skywards. He climbed in and dropped down into the driving seat. He was surprised at how low to the ground he was. It was like being at the controls of a racing car. He held the key fob in his hand and frowned. 'I can't drive,' he said. 'I can't fucking drive.' He slapped the steering wheel in frustration.

'*Liz, you're up,*' said Woody.

# CHAPTER 8

LIZ scanned the instruments in front of her. It was a Lamborghini Sian, a limited edition hybrid that cost close to three million pounds. But money wasn't enough to buy the supercar - only 63 were ever made and the company only sold them to a favoured few. It had a top speed of 217 mph and could do zero to 60mph in less than three seconds. 'Right my little beauty, let's see what you can do,' whispered Liz.

She pulled the handle to close the door, then lifted the rose gold cover off the start/stop button. She pressed the button and the engine burst into life and growled like an angry lion. 'Oh sweetie, you're making me wet,' she whispered. She looked through the windscreen at the black metal gates barring her way and blipped the accelerator. She wasn't sure how the carbon fibre bodywork would react to the metal gate, but then she saw the remote control clipped to the sun visor. She reached up and pressed it and the gate rattled open. As soon as there was enough space she put the beast into gear and pressed her bare foot on the accelerator. The engine roared and the car sped through the gap. Liz immediately put the car into a tight turn to the right and accelerated. The car sped down the road. There were a set of red lights ahead of her but she ignored them, taking a hard right turn that had the tyres squealing on the tarmac. She accelerated and took a quick look in the rear view mirror. There didn't seem to be anyone following her.

She took a quick left turn, accelerated by a black cab that was picking up a fare. There was a queue of cars waiting at a red light ahead of her and she slowed. As the engine noise lowered to a throaty growl, she heard the sound of turbines above her. A helicopter. She looked up but the sun roof was opaque. She pressed a button on the dashboard and almost immediately the sun roof became crystal clear. About eight hundred feet above her was a helicopter.

'Come on sweetie, time to show what you can do,' Liz murmured. She pulled out into the right hand lane and jammed her foot on the accelerator. There was a Prius heading towards her but she kept accelerating,. The Prius swerved to the side and went up onto the pavement as she sped through the red light. She pulled a hard left. The road ahead was clear. She headed towards another set of lights, also on red, and again she powered through regardless, this time turning right on to Piccadilly. She glanced up through the sun roof. The helicopter was still there. Her eyes flicked to the rear view mirror. She wasn't being followed.

She took the Lamborghini up to eighty. On her left Fortnum and Mason flashed by, then the Ritz Hotel. She reached Green Park and took a hard right, heading north and going against the traffic. Horns were blaring and cars were swerving to get out of her way. She needed to find somewhere to bail, but it was going to be difficult to escape the eye in the sky. They had infra red cameras that would be able to track her by her body heat. There would be nowhere to hide. Somehow she would have to lose the helicopter, but she doubted that even the supercar would be able to outrun it.

There was a black Range Rover parked at the side of the road ahead of her. She pulled out to overtake it but cursed when a figure appeared and threw something across the tarmac. It was a stinger, a highly effective tyre deflator with stainless steel spikes embedded in a nylon polymer strip. She braked but there was no time to stop or swerve to avoid it. The steering wheel bucked in her hands as she drove over the spikes and the Lamborghini slowed to a crawl. There were two more black Range Rovers ahead of her. They hadn't been following her, the helicopter had obviously been radioing in her route and they had driven to intercept the Lamborghini. She switched off the engine, took a deep breath, steadied herself, then opened the door. She climbed out, faced the two black Range Rovers and raised her hands above her head. 'Okay, I'm giving myself up!' she shouted.

Four men piled out of the vehicles. They were dressed in black. Liz frowned as she realised they were wearing ski masks. She looked up at the helicopter which was hovering a hundred feet or so above her head. A searchlight flared and she squinted into the light. The downdraft tugged at her hair and her eyes began to water.

She looked back at the men in ski masks. One of them was holding a gun in his right hand. 'Don't shoot!' she shouted above the roar of the turbines. 'Please don't shoot!'

The man stopped, aimed the gun at her chest and pulled the trigger. Liz had less than a second to realise that she had been tasered, but then she went into spasm and fell to the ground, her whole body twitching.

# CHAPTER 9

MARIANNE fought to control the mounting panic that threatened to grip her heart and tear it from her chest. She kept her eyes closed and concentrated on her breathing, keeping it slow and even. She had to keep a tight grip on her imagination because she kept flashing back to when she was a child. Sometimes her father had put a bag over her head when he had taken her out at night, making her lie on the back seat of his van and threatening to hit her if she cried. The bag would stay on until they had arrived at their destination. He would grab her hand roughly and make her walk, cursing her every time she missed her footing. Doors would open and close, sometimes she would be taken up stairs, sometimes down into a basement.

The bag would always be removed eventually. If she was lucky there would be just one man there and it would be over quickly. Sometimes there would be a group, women as well as men, and then the abuse would go on for hours. Sometimes all night.

She was in a van now, with two other people. They didn't speak so she had no way of knowing if they were men or women. For the first couple of minutes she had been unable to move but then the effects of the taser had worn off. She had asked them who they were and what they wanted but they hadn't responded.

She was lying in the floor of the van, curled up on her side.

The van turned to the right and she heard a horn blare that sounded as if it was a bus or a truck, something big. The driver cursed.

They slowed, then stopped, then started again.

Marianne still had her eyes closed. It was always more frightening when she opened her eyes. With her eyes closed she could imagine that she was at home, in her bed.

Who were they? She hadn't seen any uniforms so she didn't think they were police. And they hadn't chased her in police cars. Maybe they were Morozov's heavies. But she hadn't seen them follow her from the mansion, they had picked her up along the road. And there's no way the Russian could have a helicopter at his command, surely? And why would Morozov's men use a taser? They had been trying to kill her in the mansion, it made no sense to use a taser in the street.

Panic gripped her heart and she concentrated on breathing slowly and evenly. Nothing bad would happen until the bag was taken from her head. She knew that from experience.

The van stopped for a while, presumably at a traffic light, then made several turns, then slowed. She heard something rattle, a gate, maybe. Then the exhaust sound changed and she realised that they were inside a building. A car park maybe. An underground car park.

The van came to a stop and the van door slid back. She was helped out and then they gripped her arms and something was fastened around her neck, then she felt something brush against her legs. 'No, leave me alone!' she shouted.

'Lift your left leg.'

She did as she was told and she felt them pull something up her leg and then put something soft on her foot.

'Now your right leg.'

She lifted her right leg and material glided up it. Again they put something on her foot. They pulled her arms and pushed them into whatever it was they were making her wear. She heard the sound of a zip being pulled up and then they gripped her arms again.

'Walk,' said a man gruffly.

They pulled her forward. They walked for a while and then they took her into a lift. They went up for a few seconds and then the lift doors opened and they made her walk again. A door opened and she was moved forward and then pushed down onto a chair. She heard whispered voices. She couldn't make out what they were saying.

She heard several people moving around, then the door opened and closed and there was only silence. 'Is anyone there?' she asked.

28

'Keep quiet,' growled a man. 'Speak only when you are spoken to.'

Marianne blinked away tears but then closed her eyes again. She tried to imagine that she was sitting in a park and that birds were singing in the distance.

The door opened and closed and she heard footsteps, the click-clack of high heels on the tiled floor. There was a scraping sound, and the bag was taken off. She kept her eyes closed.

'Are you okay?' asked a voice. A woman.

Marianne opened her eyes. Sitting opposite her, on the other side of a metal table, was a blonde-haired woman with pale blue eyes and a snub nose sprinkled with freckles. She was wearing a dark blue suit and a white shirt and around her neck was a small gold cross hanging from a thin chain. The woman smiled showing white, even teeth. The lights hurt Marianne's eyes and she closed them again.

'I thought you might like some water,' said the woman,

Marianne opened her eyes and the woman passed a bottle of Evian across the table. 'Would you like anything else? Coffee? Tea? Coke?' She smiled. 'The soft drink I mean, obviously. Not the drug.'

Marianne opened the bottle and sipped some water. She looked down and saw that she was wearing a paper suit, the sort that forensic detectives wore on cop shows. And there were matching paper shoe covers on her feet.

'Are you hungry?' asked the woman.

'I feel sick. I can't eat. You tasered me.'

'We were worried you might hurt someone.'

Marianne looked around the room. 'Where am I?' There was a large man standing at the door behind her, his arms folded. He was wearing black jeans and a black bomber jacket and a black ski mask. There was a gun in a holster on his hip.

'That doesn't matter. Look, my name is Samantha. But you can call me Sam. What's your name?'

29

'I want to go home,' said Marianne, turning back to look at the woman.

'And where is home?'

Marianne shook her head and stared at the table.

'Can you at least tell me your first name?' asked Sam.

Marianne put down the bottle of water and folded her arms. 'I want to go home now.'

'I'm sure you do,' said Sam. 'But there are things we have to talk about first. You killed a lot of people in that house. Eight in all. And two more who are in ICU.' She opened the file in front of her and took out a print-out of a driving licence, which she slid across the table.

Marianne started down at the print-out but didn't say anything.

'Well, that's your picture, obviously,' said Sam. 'But the name on the licence, Briana Callaghan, that's not real. Well, it's real, but it's not you, is it?' Sam smiled. 'And that's not your date of birth, is it? Though it looks about right. You do look twenty three.' She reached over and took the sheet of paper back and looked at it. 'The thing is, Briana Callaghan was a cot death baby. Passed away when she was just three months old, poor thing.' Sam took another sheet of paper from the file and pushed it towards Marianne. 'The same birth certificate was used to apply for a passport. Using your photograph.'

Marianne stared down at the passport with unseeing eyes.

'Did you do that yourself, or did someone do it for you?' asked Sam.

'I want to go home.'

'You have to talk to me first. We ran your fingerprints through the system but they're not on record. And we're analysing your DNA as we speak, but I'm assuming we won't find a match. You're off the grid, clearly. And that's the problem because we can't let you go home until we know who you are and where your home is. You can understand that, surely?'

Marianne slowly closed her eyes and sighed.

'*It's okay,*' said Woody. '*I'm up.*'

# CHAPTER 10

WOODY leaned back in the chair. 'I think I will have a coffee,' he said. 'One sugar and just a splash of milk.'

'We can get that for you,' said Sam.

'And something to eat. I haven't eaten for almost twelve hours.'

'What would you like?'

'A club sandwich.'

'I'm sure we could get you a club sandwich. Or if not, a ham and cheese.'

'I'd prefer a club sandwich. With real bacon. It's never the same with processed ham. Or that ridiculous turkey bacon. And do you think I could have chips with it? French fries, I mean, not crisps. Real chips.'

Sam looked over at the man at the door. 'Could you get us a club sandwich and French fries and a coffee, please. One sugar, just a splash of milk.'

The man nodded and let himself out.

'Can I see your warrant card?' asked Woody after the door had closed.

'No,' said Sam. 'This isn't that sort of interrogation.'

'So we're not subject to the Police And Criminal Evidence Act?'

'You're just here to answer a few questions.'

'Helping you with your enquiries?'

'Exactly.'

'So I'm free to leave at any time?'

Sam flashed him a tight smile. 'I'm afraid not.'

'So I'm being detained. But not arrested?'

'We just need you to answer some questions. And I'd like to start with your name and address.'

Woody looked around the room. 'Where are we?'

'That's not important.'

'This room looks official. You've got two CCTV cameras so the session is being recorded, but there's no tape recorder and they are standard in police interrogation suites. Also there's no alarm rail, you know, that thing that runs along the wall that sounds an alarm if you push it. In case it kicks off. So this isn't a police station which means you're not police.'

'It doesn't matter who I am.'

'Well, it does actually. So I'm thinking MI5 or MI6. Or some other shady government department. If you were MI5 or MI6 then you'd probably take me to a safe house. A safe house might well have a room like this but I doubt it would have a cook on tap to turn out a club sandwich and French fries this late at night. So not a safe house. I don't think we crossed the river so we're not in MI6's HQ. Time-wise we could be in Thames House, and I guess they would have a canteen.'

'Time-wise?'

'It took eight minutes to drive here so late at night that means we drove about two and a half miles. That would fit with Thames House on Millbank.'

'How do you know how long it took you get here? You were tasered and there was a bag over your head.'

Woody smiled. 'Tasers don't knock you out, they incapacitate you. Recovery is a matter of seconds. I was awake when your men swabbed my mouth for a DNA sample and pressed my fingers against a mobile fingerprint scanner.'

'But you don't have a watch.'

Woody's smile widened. 'It's easy enough to keep track of time, Sam. One hippopotamus, two hippopotamus, three hippopotamus. So we could be in Thames House, but I don't think you'd take me there, even if you did work for MI5, because I don't think this is official. This is off the books, right?'

'You're not the one here to ask questions,' said Sam.

'So just tell me where we are, then I won't have to play Sherlock Holmes.'

'As I said, it doesn't matter where we are, I just need you to answer a few questions about what happened tonight.'

'I did think we drove past a park on the way here, on our left. That could have been Hyde Park which would fit in with Thames House. Or it could have been Regent's Park.'

He grinned when he saw her eyes widen a fraction. 'Right, so Regent's Park it is. Which would mean that we're now in Regent's Park Barracks, London home to the SAS.' His smile widened. 'Deny it all you want, Sam, but I can see from your micro expressions that I'm right.'

He twisted around in his chair and smiled at the man in the ski mask. 'So, who dares wins, huh?' he chuckled.

'Please don't talk to him,' said Sam. 'Talk to me.'

Woody turned around to look at her. He reached up and felt the collar around his neck. It was loose enough so that he could breathe easily, and there wasn't much weight to it. It felt as if it was made of nylon and there were two bulges, one on either side of his neck, each about the size and shape of an AA battery. 'What is this?' he asked.

'Nothing to worry about,' said Sam. 'It's a GPS tracker, so that we don't lose you.'

'Why not put it on my wrist or ankle, then?'

'It'd be too easy for you to remove it,' said Sam. 'You'll barely notice it after a while.'

'You're seriously putting a shock collar on me?'

The smile stayed on Sam's face but her eyes went hard. 'There's no need to over react,' she said.

'And if I do, you'll zap me?'

'It won't come to that.'

'You realise that this breaks God knows how many laws and rides roughshod over my human rights?'

'It's a matter of trust,' said Sam. 'Until we can trust you, we need to take precautions. Or we could simply hand you over to the police and let them charge you with the murders in Mayfair. It's your call.'

Woody smiled. 'If you were seriously going to charge me, I'd be in a police custody suite already.'

'Can you at least tell me your name?'

'I'll tell you mine if you tell me yours.'

'I told you. Sam. So who are you?'

Woody folded his arms and studied her for a few seconds. 'If I was being polite I'd say you were in your mid forties but hand on heart I reckon you're closer to fifty. Forty nine maybe. So what would be the most popular names back when you were born? What would the doting aspirational parents call their baby girl?'

'Aspirational?'

'You went to university, clearly. You have the look. Probably Oxbridge. Just the way you hold your chin up and look down your nose at me tells me that. You've polished your accent, not all the way, I can still hear the Mancunian in it, so you're not ashamed of being from Manchester but you wanted to fit in with the London set. You were probably the first member of your family to go to university. A working class hero, right? You left Manchester and never really went back. So yes, aspirational. So, what names now? Samantha, yes, that was popular then. But I can't see you telling me your real name. Helen and Karen were popular but a bit common, right? And I don't see them calling you Lisa, or Emma, or Nicola. Sarah? Yes. Sarah, would work.' Woody smiled. 'Ah, but wait. You were very quick with that "call me Sam" remark. You're used to shortening your name.'

Woody's smile widened. 'Charlotte,' he said. 'Charlotte but "call me Charlie" is what you usually say.' Woody grinned triumphantly. 'And I can see by the look on your face that I'm right. Charlie it is. But I'll still call you Sam if that's what you want.'

Sam's eyes narrowed. 'Where's your accent from?'

'Why don't you try to guess?'

'When you first spoke I thought East London. Essex maybe. But now I'm thinking the Midlands. Birmingham, perhaps.'

'Not from Bonnie Scotland, then?' said Woody in a thick Scottish brogue.

'No, Midlands,' said Sam. 'But of course you could be putting it on.'

'You think I'm that devious?'

'Oh yes, I'm starting to think you are.'

Woody laughed. 'You're the one who gave me a made up name.'

'Why won't you tell me yours?'

'Because you don't need to know my name. Eventually you're going to have to let me go. You can't keep me here for ever.'

'You killed eight men. You're not going anywhere.'

'So charge me. Present your case to the CPS. Put me on trial.'

'Is that what you want?'

'I just want to go home.'

'Except you won't tell me where home is.'

Woody shrugged but didn't answer.

'Tell me this, then. Why did you kill Morozov?'

'He attacked me. I defended myself.'

'Really? He attacked you? He's twice your size.'

'He made a bad call.'

'You met him in a club in Mayfair, not far from his house. You were singing.'

Woody shrugged.

'Hell of a singer by all accounts. You joined him at his table. What were you talking about?'

'Jazz. Bitcoin. Racehorses. Chit chat.'

'And then you left with him. To go to his house.'

'He invited me,' said Woody. 'It would have been impolite to have refused.'

'You go back home with every man who offers?'

'It depends.'

'On what?'

'On lots of things.'

Sam sat back in her chair. 'When he walked into the club, did you know who he was?'

Woody frowned. 'What do you mean?'

'It's a simple enough question. Did you know who he was?'

'I think someone might have told me that he was a rich Russian, yes.'

'And at what point did you decide you were going to kill him?'

There was a knock on the door and the door opened. It was the man with Woody's food. He placed the tray on the table and went back to stand by the door. Woody looked down at the club sandwich and French fries. 'Look at that,' he said. He picked up one of the chips and showed it to Sam. 'They used real potatoes. None of that oven chip nonsense. They peeled a potato and sliced it up and cooked it in oil. That's a quality chip, right there.' He put the chip down on the plate and opened up the sandwich. 'And look at that. Real bacon. Cooked to perfection. And the egg is just the way I like them.' He replaced the bread and picked up one half of the sandwich. 'Would you like the other half?' he asked. 'I'm happy to share.'

'I'm good,' said Sam.

Woody took a bite of the sandwich, chewed, and moaned with pleasure. 'Oh, that's good. Really, Sam, you should try it.'

'No, I'm fine. But thank you.'

Woody picked up his coffee and sipped it. 'It's real coffee, too,' he said. 'None of that instant rubbish. You definitely have a cook here. This is the sort of food to keep squaddies going. So I'm right about Regent's Park Barracks, aren't I?'

'Eat your sandwich,' said Sam.

'Yeah. I'm right,' said Woody. He took a large bite of his sandwich and grinned.

# CHAPTER 11

MARIANNE opened her eyes. For a second or two she thought she was back in her own bed but then realisation hit her and she moaned. She was in a grey box with no windows, just an LED light set into a plastic panel in the ceiling, controlled by a dimmer switch by the door. The bed was a concrete block topped with an inch-thick blue plastic mattress. They had given her a grey blanket and a pale blue pillow, both in sealed plastic bags. There was a small shower room without a door, with a stainless steel toilet, a matching sink, and a small shower. Above the sink was a square of polished stainless steel to use as a mirror.

There was a sprinkler in the middle of the ceiling, and two CCTV cameras, one of which covered the doorway to the bathroom. Next to the dimmer switch was a stainless steel intercom unit, set into the concrete.

Two men in ski masks had put a bag over her head and marched her to the cell after she had finished eating. She had turned the light down to a warm glow and had fallen into a deep dreamless sleep.

She stood up and turned the light full on, then went through to the bathroom and splashed water on her face. She stared at her reflection. She looked tired, there were dark patches under her eyes and most of her make-up had gone.

She peered at the black nylon collar around her neck. She touched it and then ran her fingers along it but couldn't find anyway to remove it.

She heard bolts being drawn back and the door opened. A man in grey overalls and a black ski mask stood in the hallway, holding a plastic tray. Behind him was another masked man, this one holding a taser.

The man with the tray walked over to the bed and put it down. On it was a croissant, an apple and a banana, with a bottle of water and a smaller bottle of orange juice. 'You need to be ready in thirty minutes,' he said. He turned to the man in the hallway who handed him a carrier bag. 'Wear these,' he said, tossing the bag onto the bed. He left and she heard the bolts slam home.

She opened the carrier bag and peered inside. There was a dark blue Adidas tracksuit and Nike training shoes. She took out the shoes. They were her size. There was a Nike sports bra, also her size, and shorts, and a white t-shirt. At the bottom of the bag was a small black plastic bag with a zipper. She unzipped it. Inside was a folding toothbrush, a small tube of Colgate toothpaste, a bar of soap wrapped in plastic, and a bottle of shampoo. There was no comb, she realised.

She brushed her teeth, showered and dried herself with the single towel they'd left in the bathroom. The clothes fitted perfectly. She folded up the paper suit and put it by the pillow.

She sat on her mattress and ate her breakfast. She was just finishing her banana when the door opened. It was the same two men. This time the man who'd given her the tray was holding a black hood. She took a step back and put up her hands. 'You don't want to fuck about,' he growled. 'My friend here has been told to taser you if you give us any problems. That means you'll probably piss yourself and we only have the one set of clothes for you.'

Marianne lowered her hands and let him put the hood over her head. He gripped her arm and took her out into the corridor. 'Where are we going?' she asked.

'You'll find out soon enough,' said the man.

They went along a corridor then she heard a door opening and they went through.

She heard lift doors open and he pulled her forward. He pushed her so that her back was against the wall and she heard the other man come in. The doors closed and they went up. After thirty seconds or so the lift stopped and the doors opened. They went down another corridor and then she heard a door open and he took her through. She heard voices. Men talking. And movement. Footsteps. Then a man laughed harshly. She could tell from the echoes that they were in a large room. There was a dull, thudding sound coming from somewhere ahead of her.

The man tightened his grip on her arm and brought her to a stop. He pulled the hood from her head and she blinked as the bright lights irritated her eyes. There were a dozen or so men in tracksuits to her left. They were in a gymnasium. At the far end there were several punch bags of different sizes and styles. A man in boxing shorts was pounding at a bag with bare fists, his chest bathed in sweat. The ceiling was twenty metres high and there were three thick climbing ropes hanging from a steel beam that ran the length of the room.

'So this is our wonder girl,' growled a man behind her. Marianne resisted the urge to look around. She stared at the floor, her hands clasped in front of her. The man in boxing shorts continued to hit the bag. Thump, thump, thump.

'Cat got your tongue, girl?' A short, stocky man with a five o'clock shadow moved to stand in front of her. He was in his forties, with a square chin and pale blue eyes. He was wearing black tracksuit bottoms and a baggy beige sweatshirt.

'I just want to go home,' said Marianne quietly.

'That's not going to happen for a while yet,' said the man.

'Who are you?'

'You can call me Jock, most of my friends do.'

'You're not my friend.'

'No, I'm not. But you can still call me Jock.'

Marianne looked around. Most of the men had gathered around to look at her though the boxer continued to pound at his bag. Thump, thump, thump.

'She doesn't look like much,' said one of the men. 'A gust of wind would blow her away.'

'Looks can be deceiving,' said Jock. 'Apparently this little lady took care of a house full of bodyguards, most of whom were former Spetsnaz.'

'Bullshit,' growled another man.

'I'm just telling you what I was told,' said Jock. 'She killed the principal, ripped through the bodyguards and parkoured her way out of the house like a world class gymnast.'

'Come on, sweetheart. Let's see you do a backflip,' said one of the men.

'I just want to go home,' said Marianne. Tears welled up in her eyes. 'You can't keep me here.'

'You're not going anywhere,' said Jock.

Marianne sniffed. 'What do you want?'

'We want to see what you can do,' said Jock.

'What do you mean?'

'You've got skills, right? We're here to assess those skills.'

She shook her head. 'I don't have any skills.'

'You're too modest,' said Jock. He reached out and prodded her shoulder. 'Come on, show me what you've got.'

'I don't have anything,' said Marianne.

Jock prodded her again, harder this time. 'Come on. Throw a punch. Try to hit me.' The men around her laughed and she stared at the floor, blinking away tears.

*'It's okay, Marianne,'* said Woody. *'I'm up.'*

# CHAPTER 12

WOODY took a deep breath, then stared at Jock as he slowly exhaled. 'You get a kick out of threatening a woman, do you?' he said. 'Trying to put the fear of God into a girl half your age. That makes you feel good about yourself does it? Makes you feel like a man?'

Jock's jaw dropped, but then he regained his composure. 'No one was threatening you.'

'You prodded me, and trust me, Jock, you prod me again and I'll break off your finger and shove it up your arse.'

Several of the men laughed and Jock's cheeks reddened.

The gymnasium doors opened but Woody didn't look to see who had arrived. He knew who it was as soon as he heard the high heels clicking on the wooden floor. 'What's going on?' asked Sam.

'I was just explaining what we're doing,' said Jock. 'There appears to be some resistance.'

Sam smiled at Woody. 'Is there a problem?' She was wearing a dark blue pantsuit over a white linen shirt and had the look of an estate agent set to go on a viewing.

'Your friend Jock seems to think he has carte blanche to lay his hands on me,' said Woody. 'I was just explaining the error of his ways and what will happen if he does it again.'

'I'm sorry if you're upset by what's happening, but you did rather bring it upon yourself,' said Sam.

'So call in the cops and let them handle it,' said Woody.

'Is that what you want, to spend the rest of your life behind bars?'

'I think you overestimate the British criminal justice system. Look at me, and look at Morozov. As you said before, he was twice my size. I'm a young girl, he was a vicious Russian thug.'

'You shot him. Guns are great equalisers.'

'You have the gun, do you?' Sam's jaw tightened and Woody smiled. 'I thought not. I'm guessing the bodyguards who weren't indisposed would have got rid of all the weapons. They were pros. So with no guns and no CCTV inside the house, what do you have? Not a lot, obviously. Now if you'd done the smart thing and swabbed me for gunshot residue yesterday then you might just have found evidence that I fired a gun, but you didn't and you haven't.' He held up his hands. 'Nice and clean.' He grinned. 'So what do you have, Sam? Video of me fleeing the house in fear of my life? Why? Because someone in said house was on a killing spree. I had a lucky escape, that's what that video shows. I was a victim.'

'A victim who then drove through London at high speed in a stolen car?'

'I wanted to put as much distance as I could between me and the house. Sam, any time you want to hand me over to the police is fine by me. I'm sure they'll see my side.' He faked a frown. 'Oh, but wait. If you do get the police involved then you'll have to explain where I've been for the past twelve hours. And I'm sure you don't want to do that, do you?'

'I assume that question is rhetorical?'

'As I know the answer, yes. Of course. The question that isn't rhetorical is what you'll do to me if I don't cooperate.'

'Let's cross that bridge when we come to it, shall we?'

'Because the way I see it, you have only two options. Option one is that you simply let me go and we both move on with our lives.'

'And option two?'

'You know what option two is, Sam. The question is, who you'd get to carry it out.' He nodded at Jock. 'Is Jocky here up for a job like that?'

44

'Please, can we just take this one step at a time. There's no point in either of us jumping to conclusions at the moment. We just want to assess your abilities.'

'You're testing me? Is that it?'

'It's about assessing your skill levels,' she said. 'We saw some pretty dramatic gymnastic skills as you left the mansion in Mayfair, and obviously you can drive like Lewis Hamilton. But we don't know exactly what went down inside the house, other than that eight men died and two more are in intensive care.'

'Why do you care what my skill set might or might not be?'

'Can we leave the explanations for later?'

'One step at a time?'

'Exactly.'

Woody's smile widened. 'Why not?'

*'Sofia, you're up.'*

# CHAPTER 13

SOFIA flexed her arms and rolled her neck, then linked her fingers and cracked her knuckles. She smiled at Sam. 'So how do we go about assessing my skill levels?'

'I'm just an observer,' said Sam. 'Jock will be doing the assessment.'

Sofia turned to look at Jock. 'I'm all yours, honey,' she said.

'We'll start with some unarmed combat,' said Jock.

'My favourite sort. Shall I just hit you, would that work?'

He smiled thinly. 'I need to study your technique so I'll have to pass.'

'So you'll be an observer, too?' She sneered with contempt and shook her head.

'I'll take her on, Sarge,' said one of the onlookers. He was big, well over six feet tall, with broad shoulders and a wide chin that looked as if it could take a good punch. He was wearing a black sweatshirt and blue tracksuit bottoms and the fact his feet were bare suggested he had an affinity for martial arts, probably karate or taekwondo.

'Let's rumble, big boy,' said Sofia, turning to face him.

'Stand down, Toby, I want to try her against someone her own size,' said Jock.

'Size isn't everything, Jock,' said Sofia.

'Andy, you have a go,' said Jock.

'Happy to, Sarge,' said a guy in a Nike tracksuit and gleaming white trainers.

'Don't hurt her,' said Jock. 'And no punches to the face, we don't want her marked.'

'Roger that, Sarge,' said Andy. The rest of the onlookers moved away and Sam and Jock went to stand by the wall, giving Sofia and Andy plenty of room.

Sofia smiled at Andy and she could see him gritting his teeth to kill the reflex to smile back. He had his game face on but his heart wasn't in it. He didn't see her as a threat. Most men didn't. She was fifty kilos dripping wet, perky breasts and long legs, model cheekbones and pearly white teeth. Men wanted to fuck her, fighting her was the last thing on their minds.

Andy was five ten, probably weighing in at eighty-five kilos, fit, for sure, but with none of the muscle bulk that came from steroids or lifting weights. He had sandy hair, cut short, and pale green eyes.

'I like your eyes, Andy,' she said. 'Like a cat's.' He had no tattoos so probably not MMA, no damage to his face so not a boxer. Hair was neither short nor long but it wasn't a military cut, so probably SAS if he was a Brit or a Navy SEAL if he was a Yank. 'Are you ready, honey?' she asked.

He didn't reply but he smiled just enough to reveal his teeth and she figured he was a Brit. Americans always had ridiculously white, slab-like teeth. This guy's teeth were small and uneven and off white. So he was probably SAS, which meant he'd done a lot of unarmed combat training with a sprinkling of Krav Maga. He'd probably spent more time practising self defence than attacking. That's what most fight training was for the military and for the cops - they trained to block attacks and to counter attack. Sofia was only interested in attack moves. She wasn't in the business of protecting herself.

Krav Maga was great for defending against an attacker but once they'd done the block and counter they then had to wait to see what their attacker would do next. It was all about reacting.

'So what do you want me to do, Jock?' Sofia asked, her eyes fixed on Andy.

'Just show me what you can do,' said Jock.

'No limits?'

Jock frowned. 'What do you mean?'

'Can I kill him?'

The man's companions laughed. 'She's feisty,' said one. Another Brit. He grinned at her. 'I like feisty birds.'

Sofia smiled at him, then looked over at Jock, waiting for an answer. Jock locked eyes with Sofia. Initially Jock's eyes were flint hard but as the seconds ticked by, Sofia could see the uncertainty slowly appear. Sofia raised an eyebrow. 'Your call,' she said.

'Don't kill him,' said Jock quietly.

'Are you fucking kidding me?' said one of the men standing by the wall. Shaved head, big muscles, broken nose. A bruiser.

Sofia looked over at him. 'Do you want to take a shot, big guy?' she asked.

He licked his lips suggestively and grabbed at his own groin.

'Can you focus on the job at hand,' said Sam.

Sofia looked back at her. 'So what are the rules?'

'Just spar with him. Like Jock said, we just want to see what you can do.'

'I'm not an exhibition boxer,' said Sofia.'I don't do this for fun.'

'We just want to know what you're capable of.'

Sofia laughed. 'So what are the rules? I can't kill him. how about I put him in a wheelchair?'

'What is she on?' said the bald guy. 'Someone needs to give her a slap.'

Sofia turned and walked towards the man. He was still laughing and he shook his head as she walked up to him.

'You are one dopey…' he began but she smacked him across the throat with the flat of her hand and he staggered back, gasping for breath. He put both his hands up to his throat so she dropped down and punched him in the solar plexus - left, right, left - three tight jabs that paralysed the nerve bundle. She stepped back and straightened up and grinned at his distress. She could see the panic in his eyes, now. Panic and the realisation that he had underestimated her.

The two men standing behind the bald guy moved towards her. She stepped back, considering her options. The one on the right had his right hand back so he was going to punch but his left hand was forward, fingers open so he was probably hoping to grab as well. But that move depended on her moving towards him so he was waiting to see what she would do. The one on the right had moved his left leg forward and his right back. His weight was on his right leg so any attack was going to need effort and she would see it coming. He was shuffling forward, his jaw clenched and his eyes fixed on hers. Probably done some karate which meant he'd have practised attacking but it also meant he'd spent most of his time pulling his punches and kicks which was never a good thing when it came to combat.

She turned slightly, took a quick half step and planted a side thrust kick into his stomach. extending her leg fully and putting all her weight behind the kick. He saw it coming and managed to tense his stomach but the blow still sent him staggering back. The onlookers cheered.

Sofia kept moving, faked a low kick to his groin that made him drop his hands, then she leapt up and caught his neck in a scissor grip with her legs. She squeezed tightly as she shifted her weight so that he staggered backwards. He clawed at her legs with his hands but there was no way he could release her grip. They fell and she broke her fall by slapping her left arm as she hit the floor. The man was fighting to breathe, his face reddening. Sofia squeezed tighter. And tighter. His attempts to pry her legs from around his neck grew weaker and weaker. The onlookers were shouting at him to fight back but Sofia knew there was nothing he could do. She had cut off the blood flow to his brain and he was growing weaker by the second. If she kept the hold on long enough he would be dead.

She looked over at Jock and grinned. 'This is the best you've got?'

Jock didn't look happy but he didn't reply. Sofia tightened her legs even more and after a few seconds the man tapped on her thigh. Sofia didn't usually let people go just because they tapped out, but this was an unusual situation so she released her grip on his neck and rolled away. He lay gasping for breath, his hands on his throat, as Sofia stood up and smiled at Jock.

'Where did you learn that move?' asked Jock.

Sofia grinned. 'YouTube.'

'I've seen the scissor take down done before but outside the movies I've never seen it done to the neck like that.'

'Well you live and learn, Jock. Hopefully.'

'Let me have a go, Sarge,' said Toby.

Jock looked over at Sam and she nodded. Jock gestured at Toby to approach Sofia and his face broke into a grin.

'Come on, big boy, give it your best shot,' said Sofia. She wiggled her shoulders and flexed her fingers.

Toby hitched up his tracksuit bottoms and walked towards her.

Sofia bobbed up and down on the balls of her feet. He was slightly pigeon toed, probably the result of years of karate, where a strong stance was key to a winning punch. 'Let's go, Toby,' she said. 'Don't keep me waiting.'

Toby took a quick breath and his right hand closed and he pulled it back as he sprang forward. The move telegraphed his attack and she had plenty of time to step to the side and hit him three times over the kidney before jumping back. One punch with all her weight behind it would probably have burst his spleen, but rules were rules.

Toby snarled as he turned to face her. She'd hurt him but he tried not to show it. His friends were cheering him on, which seemed a bit unfair considering he was twice her size. He shuffled towards her, bobbing from side to side. He grunted and transferred his weight onto his left leg, a sure sign that he was about to kick with his right. She stayed where she was so that he didn't realise that she knew what he was going to do, but the moment that he started the kick she moved to the side and hooked her left arm under his leg. He was trapped and she pushed him backwards to put him off balance, before slamming her right elbow against his chin. It wasn't a killing blow but his eyes rolled back into his head and he collapsed onto the floor.

There were gasps of amazement from the onlookers and a fair amount of swearing.

The guy at the punchbag had stopped and was looking at her, his hands on his hips. Sofia walked over to him.

'Wanna spar, honey?' she asked.

He grinned at her. He was in his twenties with a shock of ginger hair and freckles running across his shoulders and down his arms. 'Sure.'

He held out his fists and she prodded them with her fists, then put them up in front of her face. Boxers were the easiest to fight. All you had to do was to kick them between the legs and they went down. Restricting combat to fists only meant it was a sport rather than a martial art, but the guy seemed pleasant enough so Sofia only planned to have some fun with him.

He threw a slow roundhouse at her but it wasn't a serious punch so she let it bounce off her hands. Next he threw a couple of half hearted jabs, but he was just testing her. She took the blows on her arms, bunching her fists in front of her face. She jabbed with her left and when he blocked it she sprang forward and punched him twice in the solar plexus, then jumped back before he could react. He grinned and nodded at her. 'Nice,' he said, but it was clear that she'd hurt him.

The next few punches were harder and faster but he was still testing her out and she took them on her arms. He was trying to get a feel for her technique but she was learning just as much. His left hand jabs were fast and instinctive but when he used his right hand for anything other than a jab he tended to tighten his jaw, just a fraction. And his guard was low on his left side.

She smiled. 'Ready to take it up a notch?' she asked.

'Sure.'

She nodded, jabbed twice at his face, left, right, then stepped to the side and threw an uppercut to his left cheek. His block was too slow and her fist glanced off his face but she was already dropping down

51

and she jabbed him twice in the stomach with her left hand. The breath exploded from his lungs and his hands dropped just as she straightened up and punched him on the chin with her right fist. His head snapped back and he fell hard, his shoulders hitting the floor with a thud that echoed around the gymnasium.

She stood over him, her fists at the ready, but his eyes stayed closed. She cursed and dropped down on one knee but as she did he took a breath and she smiled. 'Not dead yet,' she said.

'Girl, you pack a punch,' he mumbled, his eyes still closed.

She patted him on the shoulder. 'And you can take one,' she said.

She straightened up. Jock was hurrying over, a look of concern on his face. 'He's okay,' she said.

Toby was sitting up at the other side of the gymnasium. Two of his colleagues helped him unsteadily to his feet.

Jock knelt down next to the boxer, who had now opened his eyes. 'You okay, Terry?'

'I will be when the room stops spinning, Sarge,' he said.

Jock glared up at Sofia. 'You could have killed him,' he said.

'Could have, would have, should have,' she said. She walked up to the men standing around Toby. 'Anyone else?' she said.

'What is your fucking problem?' asked one of the men.

'I'm just showing the Sarge what I can do.'

'A couple of lucky punches doesn't mean shit,' said the man. He was short and stocky, only a few inches taller than Sofia, with a crew cut and a square chin. He was wearing a t-shirt and baggy camouflage pattern trousers. His dog tags were hanging outside his shirt.

Sofia waggled her fingers at him. 'Come on then, show me what you've got.'

Two more men joined him and the three of them lunged at her. She stepped to the side and kicked the man on the right in the knee. It snapped with the sound of a twig breaking. He screamed and fell to the floor.

The guy in the camouflage trousers grabbed her hair and swung her around. She tried to get her hand to his face but he kept her off balance and she clawed at empty air. The other man grabbed her legs and lifted her off the ground. 'Let's get the bitch!' he shouted.

Sofia kicked out but his grip was too strong. She put her hands up to her head and grabbed one of the fingers that was clutching her hair. She twisted it back savagely and heard it crack. The man holding her screamed and let go and Sofia's shoulders hit the floor. She was still being held by her legs and the man holding her was shouting abuse at her. She bent at the waist and tried to grab him but he began pulling her along the floor and she fell back. He let go and moved to kick her in the side but she rolled away and got to her feet. He ran at her and tried to grab her throat but she sidestepped and slammed her elbow into his solar plexus. He roared in pain and bent double and she chopped the side of her hand down on the back of his neck. He still didn't go down so she stepped behind him and grabbed his head with both hands.

'No!' shouted Jock.

Sofia ignored him. She took a breath, gritted her teeth and prepared to break the man's neck by twisting his head savagely but then a bolt of electricity seared through her neck and she let go, staggered back and fell to the floor.

# CHAPTER 14

MARIANNE opened her eyes and groaned. Sam was looking down at her. 'Are you okay?' asked Sam.

'What happened?' said Marianne.

'You were going to kill him, I could see it in your eyes.'

'You're crazy.'

'I had to stop you. I'm sorry.'

Marianne reached up to touch the collar around her neck. 'You can't do this to me. I'm not an animal.'

'I couldn't let you kill him.'

Marianne closed her eyes. 'I want this to stop,' she said. 'Please, Woody, get them to stop.'

'Who's Woody?' asked Sam.

'*It's ok, Marianne,*' said Woody. '*I'm up.*'

# CHAPTER 15

WOODY opened his eyes. He sat up and then slowly got to his feet. 'You've no right to do that to me,' he said.

'You were going to kill him.'

'They attacked us.'

'Us?'

'You saw what they did. They grabbed me by the hair, they lifted me off the ground and then threw me down. How was that a fair fight?'

'They weren't going to kill you.'

'You don't know how far they would have gone.' He shook his head. 'I don't understand why the stick is your default position. You get much better results with carrots.'

'I understand what you're saying, but Jock had already asked you to stop and it was clear you weren't listening to him.'

'I didn't hear him. I would have heard you if you had shouted.'

'You were going to kill him, weren't you?'

'Sam, you're the one who wants to assess my abilities.' He grinned. 'Breaking necks happens to be one of my abilities.'

'You mentioned carrots. What carrots would work for you?'

'My freedom, for a start. I want out of here.'

'We're working towards that. One step at a time.'

'And what's the next step?'

Sam looked over at Jock. He smiled thinly. 'How are you with knives?'

'*Sofia,*' said Woody. '*You're up.*'

# CHAPTER 16

SOFIA looked at the knife in Jock's hand. It was about a foot long with a serrated edge on one side and at first sight looked lethal until she realised it was made of rubber. 'Are you serious?' she said. 'A rubber knife?'

'I wouldn't want to cut you,' he said.

She laughed, then lunged forward and grabbed his wrist with her left hand. The move caught him by surprise and as he tried to pull his arm away she slapped his groin with the flat of her hand. He yelped in pain and she twisted his arm around, jerked him down and then pulled the knife out of his grasp. She stepped back as Jock bent over, gasping for breath.

'That was impressive,' said Sam. 'But not really fair.'

Sofia swished the knife back and forth. 'Life's not fair, honey,' she said. 'You think I should have waited for him to attack me? That's the wrong mindset. If you wait for the attack then all you're ever doing is reacting defensively. A better test would be for Jock to try to take the knife off me. Or better still, for me to attack him with it.'

Jock straightened up, still breathing heavily.

'What do you think, Jock?' asked Sam. 'Do you want to give it a go?'

Jock nodded. 'I don't see why not.'

Sofia hefted the knife in her hand. 'The balance is off,' she said. 'It's not realistic.'

'It's for exercises,' said Jock.

'I get that,' said Sofia. 'But in the real world, a knife this big, I'd throw it at your throat. Job done.'

'Let's assume that's not an option,' said Sam. 'See how else you can use it.'

Sofia nodded. She looked over at Jock, who had dropped into a crouch, both hands forward, chin down against his chest. She couldn't help but smile. 'I guess you're ready,' she said.

'Give her what for, Sarge!' shouted one of the onlookers.

Sofia jabbed at him with the knife. It wasn't a serious attack, she just wanted to see how he'd react. Her question was answered when he jumped back. Purely defensive and it didn't get him any closer to taking the knife off her. She smiled and tossed the knife from her right hand to her left. It was clear from the way he frowned that the move had confused him. Only ten per cent of people were left handed so soldiers like Jock spent most of their time learning to defend themselves against right handed attacks. She jabbed with the knife again and he made an attempt to grab it but he was too slow and she slashed the blade across the back of his arm, just below the elbow. He nodded, acknowledging that if the knife had been real she would have dealt him a disabling blow.

She kept the knife moving. His eyes stayed on the blade, which was a mistake. She jabbed slowly at his right shoulder and he moved both hands to intercept her hand. As he moved his left leg forward she kicked out with her right foot catching his ankle and sweeping his leg out.

He gasped in surprise as he lost his balance and she stepped behind him and brought the knife up under his chin, forcing his head back. 'Gotcha!' she said. She grinned at Sam as she held the knife tight against Jock's neck.

'Okay, that'e enough,' said Sam. 'You've made your point.'

Sofia took the knife away and released her grip on Jock. He walked away, rubbing his throat.

'Now what?' asked Sofia.

Sam motioned at two men in tracksuits. One of them was holding a black hood. 'We need to take you to a different room,' she said.

'You don't have to cover my head.'

'We'd rather that you didn't know your way around just yet,' said Sam.

'You don't trust me?'

'Trust has to be earned,' said Sam. She nodded at the man with the hood and he carefully placed it over Sofia's head. She didn't resist. There was no point.

'*Okay, Sofia,*' said Woody. '*I'm up.*'

# CHAPTER 17

WOODY started counting his steps the moment they took him out of the gymnasium. Eighteen paces straight ahead, then five paces to the right. Then a lift. Judging distance in a lift was difficult but there was a slight difference in sound as they passed by a floor and so far as Woody could tell they went down two floors. The doors opened and they walked forward seven paces before turning right. There was a man each side, holding him by the upper arm. Sam's high heels clicked on the tiled floor behind them. They took four paces to the right then he heard a door open. Almost immediately he smelled cordite.

They walked forward. He heard muffled voices ahead of him. The doors closed and the hood was removed. To the left was the range with a dozen targets hanging from wires. Behind the targets was a wall of sandbags. There were three men standing in front of Woody, all wearing desert camouflage fatigues. The man in the middle was in his late forties, grey haired and wearing glasses. His companions were taller and younger. All three had Glocks in nylon holsters on their thighs.

Between the men and the targets were open booths with a selection of weapons laid out. Woody wasn't an expert when it came to weapons, but he knew someone who was.

'*Sofia*,' he said. '*You're up.*'

# CHAPTER 18

Sofia looked at the line of guns and smiled. 'Please don't get any ideas,' said Sam from behind her. 'Don't forget you're still wearing the collar.'

Sofia turned. Sam was holding up a fob. At least she had the grace to smile. Sofia smiled back. 'Please don't press that again,' she said.

'So long as you behave, I won't have to.'

Sofia's eyes hardened. 'If you do press it again, I'll kill you,' she said coldly.

'I don't think you're in a position to be issuing threats,' said Sam.

'Skazannoye slovo ne vorobey,'

'What is that, Russian?' asked Sam.

'A spoken word is not a sparrow,' said Sofia. 'Once it flies out – it cannot be caught. Be careful what you say. You accuse me of making threats, but it's quite clear that I'm the one being threatened here.'

Sam put the fob away. 'You're right. Trust is a two way street.'

Sofia nodded. 'I will not shoot you, or your men,' she said. 'You have my word.'

'Thank you.' She gestured at the grey-haired man. 'This is Murray. He wants to put you through your paces.'

Sofia looked back at Murray. 'Okay, honey, let's do this.'

'How familiar are you with small arms?' Murray asked.

Sofia grinned at him and walked to the nearest booth. There were three semi-automatics on the shelf and half a dozen filled magazines. She gestured at them with her chin. 'Heckler and Koch HK45, Beretta Model 92FS, Glock 17. If you want a .45 then the HK is the way to go.

Less recoil than most .45s. Thirty one ounces unloaded, takes a ten round magazine. The frame is polymer and the slide is forged steel. Available in black, olive drab and tan.' She nodded at the gun in the middle. 'The Beretta is a nice double-stack 9mm, reliable and accurate but I've never really been a fan of Italian guns. It has a capacity of fifteen plus one which beats the Glock's ten plus one, but I always value quality over quantity, you know? Plus the extra rounds add to the weight so the Glock is a full half pound lighter. The thing is, we girls do like something smaller in our hands, despite what you might have heard - and the Beretta is so big that you have no choice other than to use both hands. There are times when you can only use the one and that's when you'll be glad it's a Glock.'

Murray nodded. 'You know your guns.'

'Yes, I do,' said Sofia. She picked up the HK45. Murray tensed but she kept the barrel pointed down the range and he relaxed. She ejected the magazine and quickly and efficiently broke the gun down into its seven components which she laid out on the shelf - the barrel, slide, recoil spring, recoil spring guide rod, frame, slide stop and the magazine. She smiled at Murray. 'Oh dear, I seem to have broken it.'

Murray grinned and shook his head, then looked over at Sam. 'She knows her handguns.'

Before he had finished speaking, Sofia had picked up the Glock and broken it down into its component parts, in this case just five - the barrel, slide, frame, magazine, and the recoil-spring assembly.

Murray chuckled. 'Please stop doing that,' he said.

'Your wish is my command,' said Sofia.

'Can you reassemble them as quickly as you broke them down?'

'Sure. Fancy a race? I'll let you have the Glock.'

'A race?' He looked over at Sam, and then nodded. 'Sure, why not?'

'Eyes closed or eyes open?'

'Are you serious?'

'Sure.'

'It'll have to be eyes open.'

'Chicken,' said Sofia. 'I tell you what, you can keep yours open but I'll close mine.' Before he could reply, she closed her eyes and reached for the pieces. Her hands moved quickly and efficiently as she began to put the gun together. Murray cursed and hurried over to the booth. He started to assemble the Glock but he was barely halfway done before Sofia slapped the magazine into the HK45 and stepped back. She put her hands in the air and opened her eyes. 'Done!' she said.

It took Murray another few seconds to finish his Glock. He put it down on the shelf and stepped back and looked at Sam.

'Let's see if she's as good at firing them as she is at assembling them,' she said. Murray nodded.

One of Murray's assistants went over to the wall and took down two sets of orange ear defenders. He gave a pair to Sam and offered a pair to Sofia. She shook her head. 'I never use them,' she said.

'They protect your hearing,' said Murray, putting on a pair.

'Then when you fire a gun without them, you flinch at the noise,' said Sofia. 'Better to get used to it.'

The two men with Murray put on their defenders and stood next to Sam. Sofia realised they were there to guard her.

'Which gun do you want?' asked Murray.

'You choose.'

'Well you've made it clear that you don't like the Beretta, so why not go with the HK45?'

'Okay,' she said. She picked up the handgun and chambered a round.

Murray pointed at the target, 25 metres ahead of her. The target was in the shape of a man with a large bullseye in the centre of the chest and a smaller one in the middle of his head. 'Head or chest, whichever you prefer,' said Murray.

'From here?'

'That's how we do it on the range,' said Murray.

Sofia wrinkled her nose and looked at the target. 'Okay,' she said.

'In your own time.'

Sofia nodded, raised the gun with both hands and sighted on the target. She widened her stance, took a breath, and began to pull the trigger. She fired ten shots and then ejected the magazine. She slotted in a full one. 'Let's check the target,' said Murray.

'No problem,' said Sofia, putting the gun back on the shelf.

Murray pressed a button on the side of the booth and the target whizzed towards them, suspended by two wires. Murray stopped it when it was a metre away and studied the holes. 'One in the inner bullseye at the head, two in the outer. Four in the inner bullseye in the chest and five in the outer. Three outside the bullseyes but still on the target. That's quite good, especially when you were firing an unfamiliar weapon.' He looked over at Sam. 'She's okay. Not bad.'

'I shoot better when I'm moving,' said Sofia.

Sam and Murray looked at her. 'What do you mean?' asked Sam.

Sofia picked up the HK45 with her left hand, and the Glock with her right. She walked around the booth so that there was nothing between her and the line of targets.

'We have to stay this side of the booths,' said Murray. 'Health and…'

Before he could finish, Sofia started to walk alongside the booths. She raised the guns and fired with both hands at the second target. Bang bang. She kept moving and fired two shots at the third target. Bang bang. And the fourth. Bang bang. She increased the pace and began to run, firing so quickly that it sounded as if the guns were firing on fully automatic. She continued to fire two shots at each target until both magazines were emptied, then she stopped and smiled over at Murray, who was watching her in amazement.

Sam walked over to join Murray and together they went over to the line of targets. The target in the second lane had two holes in it. One in the centre of the bullseye in the head, the other in the middle of the chest bullseye. The target in the third line was the same. And the next one. Sam and Murray walked down the range. Every target was the same. Two perfect shots.

Sofia went back to the booth and put the guns back on the shelf. There were two guns in the next booth, an Uzi and a MAC-10, and several filled magazines. 'Do you want me to fire these?' she asked.

# CHAPTER 19

WOODY stood still as one of the men opened the door. They had put the hood over his head and walked him from the firing range back to the lift. There were two men, one each side, and Sam was behind them. He had heard her high heels clicking behind them all the way.

He had concentrated on the sound the lift made as it ascended and he was fairly sure that they had gone up three floors. Then they had walked two paces out of the lift and then turned left for eight paces and then turned right for six paces. He was pushed forward and he stepped into the room. They took him three paces into the room as he heard the door close. He heard the sound of a chair scraping against carpet. 'Sit,' growled the man on his right.

Woody did as he was told. He heard another chair scrape against the carpet and then the hood was taken from his head.

He was sitting at a polished mahogany table which had been set for lunch. Sam was sitting opposite him. It was a meeting room, there was a pristine whiteboard on one wall and a clock on another. There were windows to his right but the blinds had been closed and he couldn't see out. The two men who had brought him there stood with their backs against the door. There was an opened bottle of Perrier water on the table and two glasses. Sam poured water into them both and passed one to Woody. He thanked her and took a sip.

'So, I'm told we can have Dover sole, steak, or vegetable lasagna,' said Sam.

'I'd love a steak,' said Woody. 'The rarer the better.'

Sam smiled and looked over at the men at the door. 'A rare steak, and a sole,' she said. 'Ideally off the bone.'

One of the men let himself out. Woody looked around the room. 'Well this is very civilised,' he said.

'I thought you deserved a treat,' she said. 'After your stunning performances in the gym and the firing range.'

'I try to please,' said Woody. 'So are we finished?'

'Not quite.'

'I've shown you I can fight, and shoot, so what next? A trip to the swimming pool?'

'Are you a good swimmer?'

'I get by. The question I'm asking is how much longer this is going to go on?'

'We're almost there.'

'Almost where?'

She smiled and sipped her water. 'Just a few more tests.'

'What sort of tests?'

'This afternoon we'll have a doctor look at you, and then we need to run a few psychological tests on you.'

Woody frowned. 'What sort of psychological tests?'

'Oh, nothing invasive. Most of it is on a computer. You'll answer a few questions and hopefully that will allow us to understand what makes you tick.'

'And then? When the testing is finished?'

'One step at a time,' she said.

'You must have some idea of where we're headed. You're obviously working to some sort of plan.'

'A lot depends on how you perform in the tests,' said Sam.

'And if I'd failed the fighting test? Or failed to hit the targets in the range? What then? You wouldn't be proceeding with the psychiatric tests, would you?'

'Probably not.'

'So here's a question for you. Have you done this to other people?'

'Done what, exactly?'

'Locked them in a cell and treated them like lab rats. I can't imagine I'm the first.'

'There have been others, yes. Not many.'

'And what happened to those who failed?'

'Failed?'

Woody smiled. 'You know what I mean, Sam, don't be coy. When someone doesn't meet your standards, what happens to them?'

Sam shrugged. 'It varies.'

'How many of them are still alive?'

Sam's jaw dropped. 'Why would you ask that?'

'I just want to know what my options are.'

'So far you've passed every test with flying colours,' said Sam. 'I don't think you need to worry.'

'You're avoiding answering my question,' said Woody.

Before Sam could reply, the door opened. It was the man returning with their food on a tray. Woody switched his knife and fork around as the man carried the tray over to the table. He placed a plate in front of Sam. There was a filleted grilled Dover sole with boiled potatoes and asparagus. 'Oh this looks delicious,' she said.

Woody's plate had a sirloin steak, chips, and peas. He looked at the man and smiled. 'Would you have any mustard? Coleman's, if you have it.'

The man's jaw tightened, then he looked at Sam. 'Please get some mustard for our guest,' she said. The man nodded and left the room. 'I hope your steak tastes as good as it looks,' said Sam.

Woody picked up his knife and fork and cut into the steak. 'Perfect,' he said. He popped a piece into his mouth and chewed. It was good meat and cooked perfectly.

'So, how come you're so handy with guns?' Sam asked.

Woody shrugged. 'YouTube.'

Sam laughed. 'I don't think so. You've had a lot of practice, clearly.'

'I suppose so.'

'But not in the UK, obviously. Civilians aren't allowed to handle guns in this country. That must mean that you went overseas.'

Woody smiled and put a chip in his mouth.

'But we haven't found a record of the Briana Callaghan passport being used.'

Woody shrugged and continued to eat.

'So I'm guessing that you have another passport, in a different name.' She smiled. 'I suppose we all have our secrets, don't we?'

Woody swallowed. 'So what's your secret, Sam?'

'Well now, if I were to tell you that, it wouldn't be a secret, would it?'

'Exactly,' said Woody.

'But telling me where you got your weapons experience, that's not really letting me in on a secret, is it?'

'Sam, you're keeping me a prisoner, you move me around with a hood over my head, and I sleep on a plastic mat in a cell with no windows. I'm not going to tell you anything.'

'The more you tell me, the more I'll trust you.'

Woody smiled tightly. 'You don't trust me already?'

'Of course not, no.'

Woody stood up so quickly that his chair tipped over and crashed against the floor. He rushed around the table and stood behind Sam, his knife against her throat. The man at the door grabbed his gun and pointed it at Woody. 'Drop the fucking knife!' he shouted.

Sam sat calmly, her knife and fork in her hands. 'Don't shoot,' said Sam.

'You talk about trust, but you have to understand that I can kill you any time I want to,' said Woody. 'With a knife or without it.'

'I mis-spoke,' said Sam.

'Yes, you did, I'm not the one who has to earn trust,' said Woody. 'I've shown you that I can be trusted. It would have been the easiest thing in the world to have shot you on the range. You and Murray and the rest of them. Bang, bang. Bang, bang. Remember that?'

'I do,' said Sam. 'I will.'

The door opened. It was the man returning with the mustard. As soon as he saw what was happening he pulled his Glock from its holster and pointed it at Woody.

'It's okay, it's okay!' said Sam.

Woody stepped away from her, holding the knife in the air. 'I was just proving a point,' he said.

The two men moved towards Woody, their guns aimed at his face.

Sam stood up and held her hands up. 'No, please, put your guns away. I'm in no danger. We were having a discussion about trust, that's all.'

Woody backed away until he was standing next to the wall, his knife above his head.

'Are you sure, ma'am?' asked the guy with the mustard.

'I'm sure,' said Sam. She turned to look at Woody. 'We don't have a problem, do we?'

'Not now that I've got my Coleman's,' said Woody.

'Then why don't you get back to your steak?'

# CHAPTER 20

WOODY counted seven paces from the lift until they stopped. They had travelled up one floor from where he had eaten his lunch with Sam. It had been an excellent steak and the chips had clearly been double fried, the mark of a chef who cared about his craft. Sam had offered him dessert, which was a nice surprise, and an excellent tiramisu had arrived shortly afterwards, along with a cup of freshly brewed coffee.

He hadn't protested when they had put the hood back on his head and taken him from the room, he had just stayed quiet and counted his paces. He hadn't heard Sam's high heels so figured that she had stayed behind.

They stopped and Woody heard a door being opened. 'In you go,' said one of the men. Mustard Man. He had spent the entire lunch glaring at Woody with undisguised hatred. Woody had just smiled back and once had offered him a chip.

Woody stepped into the room. He moved his head as he listened but he couldn't hear anything. He was pushed forward, then to the side, then Mustard Man hissed 'sit.'

Woody sat. He heard one of the men move behind him and then heard the door close. Then the hood was pulled off his head and he blinked. There were two bright fluorescent lights overhead and the walls were white. He was facing a large monitor and there was a keyboard on the table in front of him.

'What do I call you?' said a man's voice. Woody looked to his right. The man was sitting at a glass and chrome table. He was in his forties, his black hair flecked with grey. He had pale green eyes and designer stubble and was wearing what looked like a Hugo Boss suit. He peered at Woody over the top of black-rimmed glasses.

71

'Subject A,' said Woody.

'Does the A stand for something?'

'Apple. Anteater. Antipodean. It stands for lots of things.'

'But you don't want to tell me your name.'

'You know what they're doing to me, right? They lock me in a cell and put a bag over my head when they move me. I don't owe them, or you, anything.'

'Would it hurt to tell me your name?'

'Why don't you tell me yours?'

'Of course. Dr Simon Carter.'

'Really? You don't look like a Simon. You don't look like a Carter, either.'

'What do I look like?'

Woody chuckled. 'I reckon you have a three syllable surname, but that would be a guess. Carpenter, maybe. Close enough to Carter that you won't forget it.' He studied the man's face but there was no reaction so he shrugged. 'You're 45 years old, 46 maybe, 47 at a push. So what were the most popular names for boys 45 years ago? David? Christopher? Andrew? John? James? Craig?' He smiled. 'Ah, Craig, maybe. You do look like a Craig,'

'That's a neat trick.'

'What is?'

'Saying possible names and then seeing how I react. You're good at reading people, aren't you?'

Woody's eyes narrowed, then he grinned. 'You faked it.'

'Faked what?'

'When I said Craig you smiled, just a bit, but it wasn't a micro expression, it was you doing it deliberately. I should have seen it but you did it so well that I fell for it. So you're a psychiatrist?'

'I am, yes. Briana is the name on your passport, but I gather that she died. So you're not Briana, obviously.'

'Do I look like a Briana?'

'No, you don't. So what if I use your little trick. You're what, 23 or 24? What were the most popular girls names when you were born?' He frowned and rubbed his chin, then leaned forward and tapped on his keyboard. He studied the screen, sat back, and smiled at Woody. 'So, Chloe? Emily? Megan? Charlotte? Jessica? Lauren? Sophie? Olivia? Hannah? Lucy?' He laughed and threw up his hands. 'Looks like I'm wasting my time. I'm either wrong or you can hide your micro expressions.'

'You can't hide micro expressions,' said Woody. 'That's the point.' He sighed and looked around the room. 'So why am I here?'

'Well that's the ultimate question, isn't it? Why are we here? Why are any of us here.''

Woody's eyes narrowed. 'You think this is funny?'

'I was just trying to lighten the moment.'

Woody touched the collar around his neck. 'Have you seen this? They've put a shock collar on me, like I was a dog that needs to be disciplined.'

'That wasn't my idea.'

'So whose idea is it? Charlie's?'

'She felt it was necessary and I'm afraid she's in charge here.'

Woody resisted the urge to smile. At least now he knew Sam's real name. 'This is no way to treat a human being,' he said.

'I couldn't agree with you more.'

'But you're part of it,' said Woody. 'You could get me out of here if you wanted to.'

'It's not as simple as that.'

'Just tell the police what's going on.'

Dr Carter shook his head. 'The police wouldn't be able to help.'

'The Government, then. Tell an MP. Go to the papers.'

'An MP couldn't help you, and neither could a journalist. You're in a very grey area at the moment. In limbo, as it were.'

'You can't keep me here for ever.'

'Well, the jury's out on that, isn't it? Not that there is a jury, of course. But they can certainly keep you here for as long as they want.'

Woody shook his head in disgust. 'How do you live with yourself?'

'I'm just here to help understand you. I want to find out what makes you tick, and once we've done that we can see about getting you out of here.'

'Yeah, well I won't be holding my breath. So how do we do this? Are you going to make me do the Rorschach inkblot test?'

'Have you done it before?'

Woody shrugged but didn't answer.

'I'm not a fan of projective tests,' said Dr Carter. 'It's too easy to fake, especially if someone is familiar with the test. You know how it works, do you?'

Woody sighed. 'Sure. You show me an ambiguous, meaningless image and my mind will do its best to impose some sort of meaning on that image. That meaning will give you an insight into how my mind works. But as you say, if I lie then you're none the wiser.'

'Why would you lie?'

'Why would I lie? Because if I tell you what you want to hear, there's more chance you'll let me go.'

Dr Carter frowned. 'You're worried that if I get a true insight into your thought processes, we'll keep you here?'

'I didn't say that. Can we just get on with this?'

Dr Carter stood up and walked around his desk. He leant across Woody and clicked the mouse. A small box appeared with SUBJECT NAME on it. 'Just type in your name,' he said. 'A will do, if that's what you want. Then hit ENTER and the program will run. It's self explanatory.'

Woody typed in A and then tapped the ENTER button as Dr Carter walked back to his desk.

The first set of questions were general knowledge, the sort of questions that would be asked in a pub quiz. There were a hundred, most of which Woody had no problem answering. The second set of a hundred questions were more like an IQ test, and again Woody flew through them. The third set seemed to be geared towards revealing his personality. Each question gave him two choices and he was asked to agree or disagree. The first one was 'I prefer to read a book to playing sport.' Woody went for agree, which was true. He didn't see any point in lying. After the first fifty questions there were another fifty, which were the reverse of the first set. So this time he was asked to agree or disagree with 'I prefer playing sport to reading a book.' He smiled to himself. The repetition was to detect dishonesty. If the subject took longer to complete the second half it would suggest that he was having to remember his first answers.

The next sets were more complex. One he recognised as the Hexaco Personality Inventory-Revised test, a tool used by psychologists to define six personality traits - Extroversion, Agreeableness, Conscientiousness, Negative Emotionality, Open-Mindedness and Honesty-Humility. Woody took more care over that test.

'Is everything okay?' asked Dr Carter from his desk.

'It's quite tiring,' said Woody.'

'You're almost done,' said Dr Carter, and Woody realised that he was watching him in real time on his own computer.

'Good to know,' said Woody. He kept a smile on his face as he looked at the latest test. He knew it was a version of the Minnesota Multiphasic Personality Inventory, and he needed to be careful. It was used to assess symptoms of mental illness and inappropriate behaviour. It was used as a test to evaluate applicants for public safety jobs, and by forensic teams looking for sociopaths and psychopaths. It consisted of 567 true-false questions, including questions designed to show how the subject felt about taking the test, and questions set up to show whether the subject was being deceptive.

Among the first questions were - No One Seems To Understand Me. I Would Like To Be A Singer, I Feel That It is Certainly Best To Keep My Mouth Shut When I'm In Trouble, and Evil Spirits Possess Me At Times. Some of the questions seemed ridiculous, but Woody knew that the test did work so he took care to make sure he answered the right way - letting Dr Carter know exactly how his thought processes actually worked would only end badly. Most people took between sixty and ninety minutes to complete the MMPI-2 - Woody made sure he took seventy-five minutes.

When he'd finished, Dr Carter put a sensor on Woody's index finger on his left hand. 'What's this for?' asked Woody.

'Just to monitor your pulse,' said Dr Carter. 'The computer will show you some images and you'll be asked to say how much you like or dislike the images on a scale of one to ten.' He gestured at the screen. 'It's self-explanatory.'

Dr Carter walked back to his desk as Woody clicked on the mouse to start the program. There followed a brief set of instructions. He would be shown a series of images and he was to press a number on the keyboard, 1 if he hated the image, 10 if he loved it, and any number in between. He clicked YES to say that he understood, and the first image flashed up onto the screen. A sunset. Woody pressed 5. The next picture was a cat, playing with a ball of string. Woody pressed 6. Then there were several short videos of cute animals. But then the videos and pictures became darker. Clips of war atrocities, injured animals and murder victims, interspersed among pastoral scenes and plates of delicious food. Woody realised pretty quickly what was going on - what mattered was how he reacted to the gory images. It wasn't hard to give Dr Carter the results he'd want to see.

The program ran for almost half an hour, after which Dr Carter removed the sensor. 'Okay?' he asked.

'Sure,' said Woody. 'All good.'

The final test was a series of pairs of photographs with small differences between them. His task was to use the mouse to click on as many differences as he could find. With several of the pictures he wasn't able to find any differences - he wasn't sure if that was because they were a trick or if he had simply failed.

When he'd finished he sat back and rubbed his eyes. According to a clock on the wall he'd spent almost four hours on the tests.

'Okay?' asked Dr Carter.

'How did I do?'

'I won't know until I've been through the results,' said Dr Carter. 'Before then, we need to give you a check up. A physical.'

Woody shrugged. 'Okay. What's involved?'

'Some running. A few sit ups. Press ups. Things like that. So we can get an idea of how fit you are.'

'Can't you tell by looking at me?'

Dr Carter laughed. 'Yes, you look fit. Stunning, in fact. But it would be helpful to know how strong you are.'

'No problem,' said Woody.

*'Okay, Jim. You're up.'*

# CHAPTER 21

JIM followed Dr Carter through a set of double doors into another white room. The two heavies followed. There were several exercise machines, a set of weights, and a treadmill next to a bank of monitors. There were no windows in the room, but cold air streamed in from an air conditioning unit.

An Asian nurse stood by the treadmill, holding a chest strap and various sensors.

'We'll try you on the treadmill first,' said Dr Carter. 'Lisa here will fix you up.'

'No problem,' said Jim. He held his arms to the side as the nurse attached the sensors and fitted the chest strap.

'Have you done this before?' asked Dr Carter as he studied the monitors.

'No,' said Jim.

'We call it an exercise stress test,' said Dr Carter. 'Basically we see how your heart functions as we increase your workload.'

The nurse attached a blood pressure cuff to Jim's left arm and then gestured for him to get on the treadmill. 'Okay, so your resting heart rate is sixty, which is good,' said Dr Carter. 'We'll start you walking, and then we'll put in a slight incline. Let's see how you go.'

The treadmill kicked into life and Jim began to walk. After a couple of minutes there was a grinding sound and the treadmill inclined. One degree. Then two. Then three.

'That's good,' said Dr Carter. 'Your heart rate is sixty-five now. We'll just increase the speed a little.'

The treadmill started to go faster and Jim began to jog. Dr Carter studied the monitor and then increased the incline to five per cent. Jim continued to jog.

'That's excellent,' said Dr Carter. 'Your pulse is at seventy.'

The cuff tightened on Jim's arm as the blood pressure monitor kicked in. The nurse walked over to stand next to Dr Carter. She murmured something to him and he nodded. 'Your blood pressure is excellent,' said Dr Carter. 'One hundred and ten over seventy. And your pulse is holding steady at seventy. Are you a runner?'

'I can run,' said Jim.

'But do you seriously? Like every day?'

'No. Not every day.'

'Because most marathon runners would kill for readings like this.'

'I've never seen the point of the marathon,' said Jim. 'If it's that far, call an Uber, right?'

Jim looked down at the treadmill's screen. It was showing six kilometres an hour and he was jogging comfortably, despite the incline.

Dr Carter increased the speed. Seven kilometres an hour. As it moved to eight kilometres an hour, Jim transitioned from jogging to running. Carter watched the monitors and increased the speed. Nine, ten, eleven, and finally twelve kilometres an hour.

The cuff tightened again and Dr Carter and the nurse looked at the results, and then looked at each other. The nurse whispered to Dr Carter and Dr Carter shook his head.

'Is something wrong?' asked Jim. He was running smoothly and breathing easily.

'No, everything is fine. Better than fine. Perfect, I'd say. Your pulse is holding steady at seventy and your blood pressure is still a hundred and ten over seventy. These are the sort of results I'd expect to see from an Olympic athlete. Are you okay to keep going?'

'Sure.'

Dr Carter took the treadmill up to fourteen kilometres an hour. Jim adjusted his pace accordingly. His legs were starting to burn a little but it was an irritation rather than discomfort. Dr Carter continued to monitor the readings, and after a couple of minutes he slowed the treadmill and Jim was soon back to walking pace. Eventually it stopped and Jim stepped off. The nurse removed the blood pressure cuff.

'You're not sweating,' said Dr Carter.

'I'm not tired,' said Jim.

'You should be. You say you don't run regularly, but with the sort of results you demonstrate, you could be a world class marathon runner. Do you work out, in the gym?' He removed the chest strap and pulled off the sensors.

'Not really. Parkour is my thing.'

'Parkour? Ah, right. Free running we used to call it. That'll keep you fit. What about strength stuff? Do you lift weights?'

'Not a fan,' said Jim.

'Let me see you do press ups.'

'How many?'

'How many can you do?'

'I've never tried.'

'Would you try now?'

Jim grinned. 'Sure.' He dropped down onto his knees, put his hands flat on the floor, then pushed himself up. He began a series of fast push ups. Dr Carter counted them off. When he reached twenty, Jim started to clap between push ups. He did that for a count of twenty, then went back to regular push ups.

Dr Carter counted him up to sixty, then told him to stop. Jim got to his feet and rubbed his hands together.

'You're not even breathing heavily,' said Dr Carter. 'You can do chin-ups?'

'Sure.'

'Let me see.'

Jim walked over to a horizontal bar, rolled his shoulders, then jumped up and grabbed it. He hung by his arms for a few seconds, then began doing chin ups. Dr Carter watched him and counted them off. Five. Ten. Fifteen. Twenty. Twenty-five. Jim let go off the bar, dropped to the floor, and grinned at Dr Carter.

'Tired?' asked Dr Carter.

'Bored,' said Jim.

'Sorry about that,' said Dr Carter. 'We're almost done. How are you with weights?'

'I get bored easily, if that's what you mean.'

Dr Carter chuckled and pointed at a set of weights and a bench. 'Those sort of weights, is what I mean,' he said. 'How much can you lift?'

Jim wrinkled his nose. 'I've never tried.'

'Let's try. Lie down on the bench.'

Jim did as he was told and Dr Carter put weights on to a bar. 'Try that,' he said.

Jim took hold of the bar, tensed, and pushed up. The bar wouldn't move. He gritted his teeth, took a breath, and tried again. After a few seconds he groaned and gave up.

'Too heavy?' said Dr Carter.

Jim nodded. Dr Carter took a weight off each side of the bar. 'Try again.'

This time Jim was able to lift the bar off its rest and he managed two lifts before his arms began to tremble. Dr Carter helped him put it back on the rest. 'That's interesting,' he said.

Jim sat up. 'What is?'

'Well, your stamina is amazing. And the chin ups and press ups show that you have great upper body strength. But you can't lift. I mean, I can lift more weight than you.'

'You do look fairly strong.'

Dr Carter laughed. 'I do go to the gym several times a week. Most of my work is office based so I need to exercise when I can. But I certainly don't have your stamina. Or your blood pressure.'

'I guess I have good genes.'

'Were your parents athletes?'

Jim frowned.

'*Okay, Jim,*' said Woody. '*I'm up.*'

# CHAPTER 22

WOODY smacked his lips. 'Can I have some water?' asked Woody. 'I'm parched.'

'Yes, of course,' said Dr Carter.

The nurse went over to a glass-fronted fridge and took out a bottle of water, which she gave to Woody. He thanked her, unscrewed the top, and drank deeply.

'I guess you don't want to talk about your family,' said Dr Carter.

'You guess right,' said Woody.

'You had a tough childhood?'

Woody wiped his mouth with the back of his hand. 'Which part of "I don't want to talk about it" didn't you understand?'

'I'm sorry, it's my job,' said Dr Carter.

'And who is your employer?'

'What do you mean?'

'I mean, who is paying you to go rooting around my psyche? You say you have a job, that means you have a boss.'

Dr Carter looked pained. 'That's confidential, I'm afraid.'

'The Government? MI6? Some off the books NGO?'

'I really can't say.'

Woody took another drink of water. 'So what are your conclusions?'

'My conclusions?'

'All these tests, you must have some thoughts.'

'As I said, I'll need to go through the results. I won't be rushing to any conclusions. But we'll talk again tomorrow.'

He waved over at two men by the door and the one with the hood walked towards them.

Woody held up a hand. 'I don't want the hood.'

'It's procedure, I'm afraid.'

'Whose procedure?' asked Woody. 'Yours, or Sam's?' He looked up at the CCTV camera in the corner of the room. 'Is the hood your idea, Sam? Because it's pissing me off.'

'It's only while we move you between locations,' said Dr Carter.

Dr Carter turned to look at him. 'So is it your idea, or Sam's? Is she doing it to keep me in the dark about where I am, or is it some psychiatrist's trick to keep me off balance?'

'It's not a trick.'

'No, but it's a way of demonstrating that you have power over me. It puts me in a subservient position.'

'If that was the idea we'd be doing other things, too.'

Woody touched the collar around his neck. 'Like this, you mean?'

'I argued against that,' said Dr Carter. 'I said that was crossing a line, but no one would listen to me.'

'By no one, you mean Sam.'

'I said it was a mistake, especially in view of...' He held up his hands. 'Forget it.'

'In view of what?'

'It doesn't matter. But I said there was no way you would ever trust us if we put a shock collar on you. If you treat someone like an animal you can't be surprised if they act like an animal.'

'So none of this is your doing?'

Dr Carter shook his head. 'I'm interested in what makes you tick. And if you need help, maybe I can help you.'

'Why do you think I need help?'

Dr Carter smiled. 'You have issues, clearly. What you did in that house in Mayfair. That's not normal, you know that. You killed a lot of people.'

'Ah, so you think I'm a serial killer?'

'Strictly speaking, you're a spree killer.'

Woody grinned. 'Unless I've done it before.'

'Have you?'

Woody wagged a finger at him. 'That's for me to know,' he said.

'Okay, but how about telling me this. Did you have a reason for killing the Russian? Or was it random?'

'Why do you ask that?'

'Because if you didn't have a reason, then maybe you are a stone cold serial killer who kills for the thrill of it.'

'And if I am, you can help me?'

'If there's a reason you became a serial killer, then yes, there might be treatments available.'

'And if it wasn't random?'

'Well then a lot would depend on what the reason was. It was personal, right? You had a personal reason for killing the Russian and you killed anyone who got in your way.'

Woody's smile tightened. 'I'm ready for the hood now.'

# CHAPTER 23

MARIANNE opened her eyes and stared at the ceiling. She had turned the lights down to a dull glow. She had slept surprisingly well, despite the fact she didn't know who was holding her prisoner or what they wanted from her. At least they hadn't tried to hurt her. She smiled ruefully as she remembered that Sam had actually hurt her, she had activated the shock collar without a second thought. It was Sofia who had borne the brunt of the pain, but Marianne had felt it.

There was a rattle at the door and it opened. There were two men there. She didn't know if they were the same men from the previous day, but this time they weren't wearing ski masks. She didn't know if that was significant or not. One of them was holding a plastic tray and he handed it to her. On it were small bottles of water and orange juice, a croissant, two hard boiled eggs and a banana. 'Be ready in half an hour,' he growled as she took the tray from him.

She sat down on the bed as they closed and locked the door. She wasn't hungry but she knew that she needed to keep up her strength so she drank the orange juice and ate the croissant and the banana. She showered and put her tracksuit on, then studied herself in the mirror. She looked tired and there were dark patches under her eyes. She sighed. 'I want to go home,' she said to her reflection.

She sat down on the bed and waited. Eventually the door was unlocked again. One of them stepped into her cell, holding the hood. 'Time to go,' he said.

'Please, don't make me wear the hood again,' she said as tears welled up in her eyes.

'Do as you're told,' said the man by the door, his hand reaching for his taser.

'*It's okay Marianne,*' said Woody. '*I'm up.*'

# CHAPTER 24

'Does that make you feel good, threatening a girl?' said Woody, glaring at the man with the taser.

'Just do as you're told.'

'You're SAS, right? The best of the best. So do you get a hard on hurting girls?'

'Don't make this more difficult than you have to.'

Woody smiled, but his eyes stayed hard. 'You know, I could take that taser off you and shove it so far up your arse that sparks will be flying out of your mouth.'

'You wanna try?'

'Leave it, Mitch,' said the other man. 'You're being wound up.'

'Yeah, Mitch, get back in your box. I didn't see you getting busy in the gym yesterday. Discretion the better part of valour, yeah?'

Mitch's hand gripped his taser.

'You pull that taser out and you'll regret it,' said Woody calmly. It wasn't a threat, it was a statement of fact.

The other man put his hand on Mitch's shoulder. 'Stand down,' he said. 'We're not here to get physical.'

Woody started making cluck-cluck-cluck noises and Mitch's face hardened.

'*Sofia*,' said Woody. '*You're up.*'

# CHAPTER 25

SOFIA stepped forward and slapped Mitch across the throat with the back of her hand. He staggered back into the corridor, gasping for breath, his eyes wide and fearful.

The other man dropped the keys he was holding and grabbed her arm. She slammed her other elbow into his face, breaking his nose. He kept his grip on her arm despite the blood spurting down his face. She used her right leg to sweep his feet out from under him and he finally released his grip on her. He hit the floor hard but almost immediately he tried to get to his feet. She dropped down on top of him, her legs straddling his chest, and punched him in the face, left, right, left, three stinging punches that jerked his head from side to side. He was unconscious after the second punch but she continued with the third to be sure.

Mitch was groping for his taser. Sofia jumped to her feet and rushed towards him. He managed to get his finger on the trigger but as he pulled it she slapped his hand to the side and the two prongs shot down the corridor, trailing their wires after them. She used her elbow again, smashing it into the side of his head, then brought her knee into his groin. He yelped in pain and as he bent double she hit him on the back of his neck with the side of her hand and he went down onto his knees. He was still conscious so she punched him in the side of the head with her right fist and he went down, face first.

Sofia looked up and down the corridor but there was no one to be seen. There was a CCTV camera pointing at the door so she figured that reinforcements wouldn't be long.

She grabbed Mitch's feet and dragged him into the cell. She put him next to his colleague, then bent down and picked up the set of keys.

'Okay Sofia,' said Woody. 'I'm up.'

# CHAPTER 26

WOODY stepped out of the cell and locked the door. He tossed the keys down the corridor, walked to the lift and pressed the button to open it. The doors opened immediately and he stepped inside. The button for -2 was glowing. He pressed the button for -1 and the doors closed. He looked up at the CCTV camera and grinned. He didn't know if they were looking at him or not. He didn't care.

The lift rode up one floor, and the doors opened again. He counted off the steps as he walked away from the lift, turned left and continued counting. The count took him to a door with INTERVIEW ROOM stencilled on it. He opened the door and walked in. It was the room they had taken to him the first time he had been in the building. He sat down on the chair with his back to the door, linked his fingers together, and waited.

The door opened a few minutes later and two men in desert fatigues rushed in brandishing guns. They moved to the corners of the room, pointing their guns at his face. 'Hands in the air, now!' shouted the taller of the two. He was in his twenties, with blond hair and a small scar across his left cheek. He had both hands on his gun and his finger was on the trigger.

Woody slowly raised his hands.

'Get down on the floor now!' shouted the other man. He was older, in his thirties, with receding hair and a sweeping moustache. Both men were suntanned, presumably from time spent in a sunny trouble spot.

'There's no meed for that,' said Dr Carter as he walked into the room holding a manila file and an iPad. 'You can put your guns away.'

'Tell that to our two guys on the way to hospital,' said the man with the moustache.

'You can see there's no threat here,' said Dr Carter. 'You need to stand down.'

'Do as you're told, lads,' said Woody. 'That's what you do, isn't it? Obey orders?'

The two soldiers continued to point their weapons at Woody's chest. He smiled amiably and slowly lowered his hands.

Dr Carter sat down on a chair facing Woody and placed the file and iPad on the table. 'Gentlemen, please. Any threat that there was has clearly now passed. Please stand by the door so I can continue this interview.'

The two soldiers stared at Woody, then they slowly holstered their weapons and walked over to the door. They stood with their backs to it, their arms folded. Woody grinned at them. 'Good dogs.' He turned to look at Dr Carter. 'Maybe reward them with a biscuit.'

'Please don't rile them.'

'Look at them, Dr Carter. Big men with guns. Then look at me. You think this is fair?'

'They know what you did in that house in Mayfair. So they're not over concerned with what you look like, just what you're capable of. And you showed that in spades down in the cell. You can't judge a book by its cover.'

'Well that's certainly true,' said Woody. 'But let's not forget that I didn't kill the two guys in the cell. I could have done, but I didn't.'

'You held yourself back.'

'Sort of.'

Dr Carter frowned and pushed his glasses further up his nose. 'Why?'

'What do you mean?'

'You didn't hold yourself back in the house in Mayfair.'

Woody smiled. 'The guys in Mayfair were trying to kill me. Your guard dogs are just trying to control me. That's why they didn't shoot

90

me as soon as they came into the room.' He twisted around and grinned at the two soldiers. 'Right, guys?'

They glared back at him, their eyes flint hard.

Woody turned back to look at Dr Carter. 'What is they call it? Reasonable force? I used just enough force to achieve my objective.'

'And what is your objective?'

'Ultimately? To get out of here.'

'The quickest way to achieve that objective is for you to answer all our questions.'

'Is it, though? I tell you everything and you take off this collar and send me on my way? I think we both know that's not going to happen.'

Dr Carter nodded for several seconds as he scrutinised Woody over the top of his glasses. 'How did you find your way here from the holding cell?' asked Dr Carter eventually. 'You were hooded.'

'You think I'm helpless without my eyes?' asked Woody. 'We're gifted with five senses, Dr Carter. Unlike most people, I use all five of mine.'

'And the two men you attacked in your cell? What happened?'

Woody shrugged. 'Mitch was going to taser me.'

'Mitch?'

'One of the guards. You don't know their names?' Woody smiled. 'I guess you don't.'

'Why was he going to taser you?'

'I wasn't letting them put the hood on me. As I've just shown, the hood is a waste of time. Other than as a way of demonstrating your power over me.'

'That's not what the hood's about,' said Dr Carter.

'It is. That's the whole point of it. And that's why you make me sleep in a cell and eat off a plastic tray. Then Sam offers me a nice steak dinner and I'm supposed to embrace her like a long lost friend.'

Dr Carter held up his hands. 'There's clearly no point in arguing with you,' he said.

'Well I'm glad we've established that,' said Woody.

Dr Carter smiled and shook his head. 'Would you like a coffee? Water?'

'Coffee would be good.'

Dr Carter looked over at the two men by the door. 'Could you bring us two coffees please. And a bottle of water for me.'

'Still or sparkling?' said one of the men, his voice loaded with sarcasm.

'Sparkling would be good,' said Dr Carter.

The man went out.

'You realise he was being sarcastic?' said Woody.

'So long as we get our coffees and water, I don't really care.'

'He was taking the piss.'

'He's a soldier. That's what they do.' He opened the file and peered at it. 'So, the results are out.'

'Did I pass?'

'It's not pass-fail,' said Dr Carter. 'It's a spectrum.' Dr Carter sat back in his chair and studied Woody over the top of his glasses. 'Tell me, had you seen any of these tests before?'

'Why do you ask?'

'You have tendency to answer an awkward question with another question, don't you?'

'Do I?'

They both laughed and Dr Carter shook his head. 'As I said, there's no pass or fail with the tests we gave you. They're just a means of us assessing your personality. And from what I can see, you're well balanced, fair minded, with no psychological issues. You're fine.'

'That's good to hear.'

'Except of course, you're not. You killed several men in cold blood, and I'm fairly sure that if you had been hooked up to monitors at the time we'd have found your pulse never went above ninety and your blood pressure stayed rock solid.'

'We'll never know, will we?'

'I suppose not. But being able to carry those sorts of actions without showing any physical signs of stress is very unusual. If anything it hints at sociopathic or psychopathic tendencies.'

'I've never understood the difference,' said Woody.

'Really?' said Dr Carter.

The door opened. It was the soldier with two mugs of coffee which he placed on the table in front of Dr Carter. He had a bottle of Evian water tucked under his arm and he gave it to Dr Carter with a sly grin. 'They didn't have sparkling.'

'That's a pity,' said Dr Carter.

The man went over to the door and stood next to his colleague.

Dr Carter unscrewed the top of his bottle of water and sipped it. 'So. Psychopath and sociopath. It's complicated. As a rule we don't use them as clinical definitions, we tend to use antisocial personality disorder.'

'I've never thought of myself as antisocial,' said Woody. 'I like people.'

'Well that's good to know,' said Dr Carter. 'Generally psychopaths and sociopaths have a poor sense of right and wrong, and have difficulty interpreting feelings. Their own feelings and the feelings of other. But so far as the differences between them are concerned, generally we would say that a psychopath doesn't have a conscience. He'll do whatever he has to do to achieve his objectives.' He smiled. 'Of course if we use that as a definition we'd be including pretty much every politician and successful businessman in the country.' He took another sip of water. 'Now a sociopath has a conscience, but is able to override it. He or she knows that they are doing something wrong, but they'll do it anyway. They both lack any real empathy for others, but

93

the psychopath has even less regard for other people. He, or she, will often see people as things to be used.'

'Like pieces on a chessboard?'

'Exactly,' said Dr Carter. 'Psychopaths are difficult to spot. They can mimic emotions. So they can be charming, intelligent, the life and soul of the party. Sociopaths are less able to do that. They usually make it clear that they're not interested in the people around them.'

'They don't know how to fake it?'

Dr Carter nodded. 'That's it. Sometimes they use "hot headed" and "cold hearted" to describe the difference. A sociopath is hot headed, they act without thinking about the consequences. A psychopath will be more calculating, planning their moves like a grand master. So one of the tests we gave you was to see if you have any psychopathic tendencies. The one where we showed you a whole lot of images. Photographs and videos. And we monitored your brain waves, your breathing and your pulse.'

'I remember.'

'Of course you do. You see, when most people see blood or violence, their hearts beat faster, their palms get sweaty and they breathe faster and deeper. But a psychopath shows the opposite reaction - they become more relaxed when they see violent images. That's what makes psychopaths so successful. They don't fear the consequences of their actions.'

'And how did I do?'

Dr Carter smiled. 'Well, you're not a psychopath, that's for sure.'

'That's a relief.'

Dr Carter chuckled. 'No, you showed the requisite revulsion at the violence, your pulse went up as did your respiration rate. Exactly as a regular person would.'

'I'm getting the feeling there's a "but" on the way...'

Dr Carter nodded. 'Everything was normal, but it was very different from the physical tests we ran you through, remember?'

'Of course I remember. It was only yesterday.'

'We put you through the heart stress test, and your pulse didn't budge. Neither did your blood pressure. Tip top physical condition. But when we showed you the images, your pulse rate rose sharply.'

'Maybe I'm a sensitive soul?'

'That would explain the rises, yes. But it doesn't explain why your base line was so much higher when we did the psychological tests.'

Woody frowned. 'What do you mean?'

'Well, before you were exercising, your resting heart rate was sixty beats per minute. And it went up to seventy-five when you were exercising. As I said yesterday, they're the sort of results we'd see with an Olympic athlete. But when we did the psychological tests, your resting heart rate was bang on eighty. And it went up to a hundred or so while you were watching the violent images.'

'So why is that a problem?'

Dr Carter shrugged. 'I'm not sure that it's a problem. Just an observation. It's as if you were two different people. One who took the psychological test and someone else who performed the physical tests.' He smiled. 'That's impossible, obviously.'

'Obviously,' said Woody. He sipped his coffee.

The door opened and Woody twisted around in his chair. It was Sam, wearing a dark blue fitted jacket over black jeans. She was holding a cup of coffee.

'You look good today, Sam,' said Woody. 'Did you change the colour of your lipstick?'

'You're very observant, Woody. Yes, I have, actually. Contrary Fuchsia, by Yves Saint Laurent. I gather we had a problem this morning.'

'No problem,' said Woody. 'I was just making my feelings clear about the hood.'

'Message received and understood,' said Sam. She walked into the room and turned to the two soldiers. 'You can leave us alone, gentlemen,' she said.

'Our orders are to stay with the subject, no matter what,' said the one with the moustache.

'Well, I'm countermanding that order,' said Sam. 'You can check with your commanding officer but as he follows my orders he'll only tell you to do as you're told.'

The two men looked at each other and the one with the moustache gave a small nod. They both left.

Sam sat down next to Dr Carter. 'You've talked about the results?'

'Apparently I'm not a psychopath,' said Woody.

'Well I'm very glad to hear that,' said Sam. She sipped her coffee.

'Does that mean you're ready to make me an offer?'

Sam frowned. 'An offer?'

Woody smiled and shook his head. 'You're not as good an actress as you think you are, Sam.'

'I have no idea what you're talking about.'

'You weren't just watching Morozov's house, were you?'

Sam's eyes narrowed. 'What do you mean?'

'I mean it wasn't just a surveillance operation, was it? For that you'd have made do with a couple of watchers. But you had a full team with cars and a helicopter. That's how you got me, remember? If you'd only been running surveillance, you'd never have caught me.'

'So what's your point?'

'Why were you there, Sam? What was Morozov to you?'

'That's not the issue.'

Woody smiled. 'Oh but it is. The answer to that question explains why we're here, why you're questioning me and why you're running all these tests on me. You've clearly no interest in charging me with any crime. There's something else going on, isn't there?'

'Why don't you tell me what you think that is?' said Sam.

Woody smiled. 'See now, here's the thing, Sam. You and Dr Carter expect me to open myself up to you but when I ask you a simple question, you point blank refuse to answer.' He sipped his coffee and watched her with unblinking eyes.

'We want to understand you. You're a bit of a mystery and we don't like mysteries.'

Woody put his cup down. 'You were there to kill Morozov, weren't you? Maybe not that night, but the ultimate aim was to bring about his demise and I spoiled your plans. Took the wind out of your sails, so to speak.'

Sam's lips tightened but she didn't say anything.

'So I guess the big question is, who pays your wages, Sam? Do you work for some shady government department that eliminates enemies of the state? Or are you in the private sector, killing for cold hard cash?'

Sam still didn't say anything.

'If I had to guess, I'd say that you were some sort of hybrid. Private sector but you do jobs that the Government needs doing at arm's length. What's the expression they use? Plausible deniability, that's it. That would explain why you would be able to taser me in public without any fear of repercussions. And it would explain why you have the run of Regent's Park barracks.' He smiled. 'Come on, Sam, give me something.'

'I'm not the one who's here to answer questions.'

'No, that's true. But if you want me to co-operate, there has to be some give and take. Look, at least you can tell me why you were outside Morozov's house.'

'That really is none of your business.'

Woody chuckled. 'I could just as well say that what I did is none of your business. You're not a cop, you're not with MI5 or MI6. You're just a member of the private sector, you've got no more authority over me than if you worked for Rentokil or Vodafone.' He leaned towards her. 'What is it you want from me, Sam?'

'I've told you already. I want to know what happened, why you did what you did.'

'Morozov tried to rape me. When I resisted, his goons pulled out guns. I defended myself. End of. You have to tell me what you want. I think I know but I want to hear it from you.'

'You think I want something?'

'I know you want something, Sam. That's why you haven't turned me over to the police. You're playing a different game.'

'This isn't a game.'

'It's an expression. This isn't about you building a case, you want something from me. I want you to spell out what your end game is.'

Sam looked over at Dr Carter. He forced a smile but didn't say anything. Sam looked back at Woody. 'Okay, fine.' She linked her fingers together and took a deep breath. 'You have a skill set, clearly, that might well prove useful to us. We were on a surveillance mission that night, but it was a prelude to action that we were hoping to take against Morozov. You're quite right, you did take the wind out of our sails. But you did achieve the objective we wanted, so swings and roundabouts.'

'And? Say it, Sam. Spell it out for me.'

Sam sighed. 'We think we can use you. We think you might be an asset to our organisation.'

'And what if I don't want to work for you?'

She flashed him a tight smile. 'You killed a lot of people. In cold blood. So your choices are limited.'

'You'd hand me over to the police?' He smiled and shook his head. 'No, I don't think that's going to happen. You wouldn't want me talking in open court, would you? You've got too much to lose.'

'If I were you I'd look at the carrot rather than worry about a hypothetical stick. Look, yes, I think you could work for us. Would you be interested?'

'Maybe,' said Woody. 'What's the carrot?'

'Why don't we continue this conversation in my office?'

'No hood?' said Woody.

Sam nodded. 'No hood.'

# CHAPTER 27

WOODY sat down on the single chair facing Sam's desk. She had referred to it as "her office" but there was nothing personal in it, just a large modern desk with a computer on it, a high-backed black leather executive chair for her to sit on, and a chrome and black leather chair for Woody. There was a window to Woody's left but the blinds were down and the lights were on.

'So Dr Carter won't be joining us?' said Woody.

'Dr Carter tends not to get involved in operational matters,' said Sam.

'Need to know?'

'It's not really his area of expertise.'

'But it is yours?'

Sam smiled but didn't answer the question. 'You were quite right about what you said about Morozov. We weren't there for surveillance purposes.'

Woody nodded but didn't say anything. She had obviously decided to tell him everything and questions would only slow things down.

'In the past, the British government has shied away from using assassination as a political tool. Other countries have done it with zeal, of course. Russia, Iraq, Iran, Libya. The Saudis. They see nothing wrong with killing in the interests of the State. But everything changed after 9-11. America began to target individuals, taking them out with drone strikes wherever possible. But where it wasn't possible, they would send in assassins. Navy SEALs or Delta Force. The most famous example, of course, being the assassination of Osama Bin Laden. Once the British Government saw that the Americans were able to kill their enemies with impunity, they drew up their own hit lists. Generally the SAS and the SBS were used, and the killings were mainly carried out in Afghanistan, Iraq and Syria. Initially it was enemy combatants who were targeted, ISIS warlords, Al Qaeda bombmakers, what you could easily describe as military targets. Some of the successful missions were publicised, and the Great British public was, in the main, enthusiastic. The authorities then started adding British citizens to the hit lists, Brits who had gone abroad to fight alongside the fundamentalists. That too seemed acceptable to the public.' She smiled thinly. 'What has happened in recent years is that the government has turned its attention to enemies of the State who are here, in the country, and elsewhere in the world. Enemies who cannot be combatted by conventional means.'

'So you assassinate them?'

'We do what the SAS and the SBS have been doing in war zones for years. The principal is the same.'

'Except that the government can't be seen to be in the assassination business, can it? At least not here in the UK.'

Sam nodded. 'Exactly. They want it done but it has to be at arms length.'

'So it is about plausible deniability?'

'Yes. We are not a government department, we have no official standing, but we have the full support- behind the scenes - of Number Ten.'

'But who pays you? Where does the money come from?'

'Our funding is routed through a dozen offshore centres, it's untraceable.'

'And who does the dirty work? Who pulls the trigger?'

'All our people are effectively freelance, and paid offshore,' said Sam. 'Mainly former special forces. But occasionally we come across people with exceptional talents from outside the military. Horses for courses.'

Woody smiled. 'And that's where I come in?'

Sam nodded. 'Your talents and abilities could be very useful to us. But it's your profile that makes you so unusual. Most of our operatives are male and in their thirties and forties. You are… well, you look in the mirror every day, you know what you are. Morozov underestimated you. I think most people do. We could use you to get close to people who are generally thought to be unreachable.'

'Tits and teeth?' Woody flashed her a smile.

'That dress you wore at the club, every man in there was looking at you.'

'Girls gotta do the best with what she's got,' said Woody.

'But you understand what I'm saying?'

'Of course.'

'And is that something you'd be prepared to do?'

Woody smiled. 'What if it isn't? Having told me that you run a team of off-the-books government assassins, you're not just going to let me go, are you?'

'Why not?'

'I could go to the papers. I could tell the world.'

'No journalist would listen to you. And no newspaper would print your story anyway.'

'So you wouldn't add my name to one of your hit lists?'

'We don't kill civilians. We kill enemies of the State.'

'And what's the stick? What happens if I turn you down?'

'I sincerely hope we don't get to that,' said Sam 'But if we have to go down that route, the video of you entering and leaving Morozov's mansion would be made available to the police. Along with your fingerprints and DNA. You could play the rape card, but a lot of people died at your hands. You'll be in prison for a long time.'

Woody nodded thoughtfully. 'And the carrot?'

'We look after our people well. You get to use your skills in a productive way, you help your country, and you earn a great deal of money.'

'Medals?'

'No medals. Sorry.'

'And if I get caught?'

'You'll be taken care of.'

'In a good way?'

Sam laughed. 'Yes, in a good way. In the very unlikely event that you are apprehended by the police during the course of an assignment, you would be released without charge within hours. You will be given a phone number to memorise and calling that number will effectively be your "get out of jail free" card.'

'And what happens to the Morozov investigation if I agree to work with you?'

'It'll go away. The killings will be blamed on a rogue bodyguard and the police won't be looking for anyone else.'

'You can do that?'

'We can do a lot of things.'

'And when would I start?'

Sam smiled and opened a drawer. She took out a manila file and opened it. 'We have a job that needs doing tomorrow night.' She opened the file and took out a photograph and slid it across the desk to Woody. It was a Chinese man in his fifties, with a square face, a dimple in the middle of his chin and thick-lensed spectacles. 'This is Kwok Chun-ying, a nasty piece of work who has been doing the Chinese government's dirty work here in the UK. He's behind the torture and killing of two Taiwanese independence advocates here, and also funnels funds to various terror groups here.'

'Can't you just arrest him?'

'He has diplomatic immunity. All we could do is throw him out, and if we do that he'll be replaced within days. The decision has been taken to liquidate him, as much as a warning to the Chinese as anything. Unfortunately Kwok is a very careful man. He has bodyguards and is always very well protected. We've had him under surveillance for three months and can see only one opportunity to get near him. But getting near him and getting the job done are two different things. You might be able to break the impasse.'

'I'm all ears.'

Sam took another photograph from the file and passed it to Woody. It was a pretty Chinese woman with a pixie haircut and a row of small pearls around her neck. 'This is Sally Lai, she runs an upmarket escort agency. Really high end, her girls cost £500 an hour and £5,000 overnight. Every few weeks, Kwok entertains visiting Chinese dignitaries at his estate. Sally Lai supplies the company. We have someone in the agency but she doesn't have the skill set to do the job. But she can get you in with the girls who visit the estate.'

Woody grinned. 'In case you haven't noticed, I'm not Asian.'

'Sally Lai is Chinese, but her girls aren't. They're all Caucasian. Catwalk model types.'

'So I go in with the escorts?'

'They take up to a dozen girls at a time. As I said, five grand a night, minus the agency commission.'

'And how much will I get paid for this?'

'I think we'll regard this as your final test,' said Sam. 'We can discuss payment after the job is finished.'

'That's not much of a carrot.' Woody shrugged. 'But, okay, we'll treat it like a test.'

'Excellent,' said Sam, taking back the photographs. 'Now, you'll need to be dressed appropriately, so we'll take you back to your house and pick up what you need.'

Woody shook his head. 'That's not going to happen.'

'Why not?'

'I'm a very private person. And I want to keep it that way. I don't want you knowing where I live. At least not until we know each other better.'

'Then we'll go on a shopping trip.'

'That'll work,' said Woody. He gestured at the collar around his neck. 'But this will have to come off. And no hoods.'

Sam nodded. 'Not a problem,' she said.

# CHAPTER 28

WOODY sat in the back of the Jaguar, next to Sam. He smiled as they drove out of Regent's Park Barracks and headed south, the park to their right.

Sam noticed the smile. 'Yes, well done, you worked out where you were,' she said.

'I've always had a good sense of direction,' said Woody.

There was a man sitting in the front seat next to the driver. He looked like a soldier but was wearing a blue pinstripe suit and a red tie. Sam hadn't introduced him but Woody was sure he was a minder.

'So, we'll be needing a dress,' said Sam. 'Something smart but sexy. The red dress you wore at the club was nice but perhaps a little too revealing. Plus stockings and high heels. They like their girls tall. You'll need a coat for the trip there. And a handbag. We'll pick up some casual clothes, too. There's no need to keep you in that tracksuit.'

'Will I be staying in the barracks, because that cell isn't great.'

'No, we won't be going back to the barracks. There's a safe house we use in Hampstead, not far from the heath.'

'Nice.'

'It's more comfortable than the barracks. And we'll have some privacy. So we'll be buying toiletries for you. And make up. You'll need make up. The Chinese like their girls made up.'

'*Jasmine*,' said Woody. '*You're up.*'

# CHAPTER 29

JASMINE looked out of the window as the Jaguar pulled up at the side of the road. 'Oh, Selfridges,' she said. 'I love Selfridges.'

'Who doesn't?' said Sam.

Sam opened the door and stepped out. Jasmine shuffled across and used the same door. The minder also got out and the three of them walked into the department store.

'I think we should get the dress first,' said Sam.

'What about a Chanel bag?' said Jasmine.

'A bag, yes,' said Sam. 'But I think a Chanel bag is out of our budget.'

'Louis Vuitton then? Escorts usually have designer handbags. And not fakes, either.'

'Let's get the dress and the coat first. And the heels.'

Jasmine sighed. 'Okay.'

They took the escalators to the second floor. The minder followed. Jasmine turned to look at him. 'What's your name, baby?' she asked.

He looked at her, stone faced, but didn't reply.

Jasmine smiled. 'You look a bit like Brad Pitt,' she said. 'So I'll call you Brad.'

'Please don't tease him,' said Sam.

They reached the fashion floor and Sam took Jasmine along rows of designer dresses. Sam took out two black dresses and showed them to Jasmine. Jasmine grinned. 'Perfect,' she said. 'For a funeral.' She pulled out a short yellow dress with a plunging neckline and thin straps across the back. 'I look good in yellow.'

'It might be too revealing, but sure, try it on.' Sam put the two black dresses back and took out a black and white striped dress. 'What about this?'

'Great if I want to look like a zebra,' said Jasmine. 'Look, I know you're trying to help, but I think I know what looks good on me. And to be honest, I could probably throw a little fashion advice your way if you wanted.'

'I'll pass, but thank you for the offer,' said Sam, putting the dress back. 'Why don't you choose a few and try them on.'

Jasmine held the yellow dress up against herself and smiled at the minder. 'What do you think, Brad? Will I look hot in this?'

The minder stared at her but didn't reply.

'Maybe I'll look hotter out of it, what do you think, Brad?'

'We haven't got all day,' said Sam.

Jasmine blew the minder a kiss, then walked along the racks pulling out dresses.

'There might be a limit on how many you can take into the changing room,' said Sam.

'You and Brad can hold them for me,' said Jasmine. 'I should try on underwear at the same time, right?'

'Okay, yes, I suppose so,' said Sam. She and the minder followed Jasmine through to the lingerie section.

'I love silk against my skin,' said Jasmine. 'What about you, Brad? Do you like silk against your skin?' She held up a red bra. 'What about this? Do like red or black?' She laughed at his discomfort, then gathered up a selection of lingerie items and gave them to him to hold, before heading to the changing rooms. She selected three of the dresses and gave the rest to Sam. 'Shall I come out and show you, or do you trust my judgement?'

'I'd prefer to see them,' said Sam.

'Okay, I won't be long,' said Jasmine. She blew the minder a kiss and flounced into the changing rooms. She pulled back the curtain of one of the rooms and went in. It was about five feet square with a mirror on one wall and a wooden chair. There were two hooks on the wall facing the mirror and she hung the dresses on them. She looked up at the ceiling. It was a suspended ceiling with large white tiles separated by grey metal rails.

'*Okay, Jim,*' said Woody. '*You're up.*'

# CHAPTER 30

JIM moved the chair closer to the wall. He stood on it and reached up to move the white tile above his head. There was a gap of about two feet between the false ceiling and a metal ventilation duct which ran left to right. The duct was rectangular and about two feet wide. It looked strong enough to bear his weight. He bent down and then sprang up, his fingers splayed. He grabbed the top of the duct and held fast, then drew up his legs and wrapped them around the metal. The metal groaned but didn't seem to be in danger of collapsing. He began to edge along the duct. Left hand. Right hand. Left foot. Right foot. Slowly but surely.

He moved away from the changing rooms. The further he went, the darker it became but his eyes quickly got used to the gloom. The metal was cold to the touch. Occasionally the duct would groan from his weight but it was holding steady as he continued to move. Left hand. Right hand. Left foot. Right foot. After he had travelled twenty feet or so he gripped the duct tightly with his feet and his left hand and used his right hand to reach down and remove one of the tiles. He was above a corridor. He replaced the tile and continued to make his way along the duct. Left hand. Right hand. Left foot. Right foot. His arms and legs were starting to burn from the effort of holding himself up but he could bear it.

He traversed another ten feet before reaching down and removing another tile. This time he was above a storage room. He gripped hard with both feet and lowered himself to get a better look. There were stacks of cardboard boxes and clothing on wheeled racks, a single door and no window.

He bent at the waist, held the duct with both hands, released his feet and lowered his legs through the hole. He took a breath and then let go, keeping his arms up. The ceiling flashed by and he relaxed his legs, tensing them as soon as his feet touched the floor. He bent his knees to absorb the shock, then straightened up. He hurried over to the door and pulled it open to reveal an empty corridor. He looked left and right. To the right was an emergency exit sign pointing to a fire door. There was a CCTV camera covering the door so he kept his head down as he hurried towards it and pushed it open.

Concrete stairs led up and down. There were no cameras. Jim hurried down to the ground floor. There was a sign on the door warning that it was alarmed but that didn't worry him and he pushed it open. As the alarm kicked into life he was already running down the alley to the main road.

'*It's okay, Jim,*' said Woody. '*I'm up.*'

# CHAPTER 31

WOODY slowed to a walk as he reached Oxford Street. Running attracted attention and it was important to blend. He figured the alarm would be confined to the door and to the store's security control room, it would be unlikely to sound throughout the building. And even if Sam and the minder did hear the alarm they would have to check the changing rooms before they realised that he had gone. He had more than enough time to reach Bond Street Tube station. There were cameras all over the Tube network so they would be able to track him, but it would be after the event and he would be long gone by then.

He didn't have any money but it was a simple matter to jump the turnstile. He received several angry looks but no one tried to stop him and there were no members of staff nearby. He walked to the down escalator and caught a train to Notting Hill Gate where he changed to the district line. He reached Earl's Court station and jumped the turnstiles again to get out onto the street. He walked slowly, doubling back from time to time and checking reflections in shop windows until he was sure that he wasn't being followed, then he headed for the flat.

'*Okay Marianne,*' said Woody. '*You're up.*'

# CHAPTER 32

MARIANNE smiled as she reached the door to her building. It was a white stucco house that in Victorian times had probably been home to a very wealthy family and their servants but which had at some point been converted into a dozen small flats.

Marianne's flat was on the top floor. She didn't have her key so she rang the bell of Mr McKillop, who lived on the ground floor. He had a bad leg and she would often run errands for him. 'Hello?' he said, over the intercom.

'Hello Mr McKillop, it's me, Marianne. I forgot my key again, can you buzz me in?'

'Silly girl,' he said. 'You'd forget your head if it wasn't screwed on.'

The door lock buzzed and she pushed the door open. 'Thank you, Mr Killop,' she said and headed up the stairs.

She kept a spare key under the carpet at the top of the stairs, and she used it to let herself in. She sighed with relief as she closed the door behind her. 'Home, sweet home,' she murmured.

It was a small flat with a sitting room with a small table, a sofa and an easy chair, and a bedroom that was just large enough to hold a double bed. There was a mirrored door on her built-in wardrobe which gave the room the illusion of space, but it was just that, an illusion. There was a small kitchen area off the main living room, a tiny workspace next to a sink, a small electric hob and a microwave oven on top of a fridge freezer. It was more than enough space for Marianne, she wasn't big on entertaining.

On the wall behind the table was a large whiteboard. Stuck in the middle was a head and shoulders shot of Boris Morozov. There were also photographs of his security team and the vehicles they used. There was a map of Mayfair and a set of plans of his mansion that had been lodged with Westminster City Council when the building had been renovated and expanded. Also on the board were copies of Morozov's mobile phone bills, bank statements, and a print out of his passport. Marianne made a gun with her right hand and pointed it at the photograph of the Russian. 'Bang, bang, you're dead,' she said. 'And you fucking deserved it.'

She went over to the kitchen area and took a bottle of Evian water from the fridge. She twisted off the cap and took a sip. She heard a scraping sound at the front door and she turned towards it, frowning.

The door crashed open with a loud bang that made her flinch. Two men in leather bomber jackets burst into the room with guns in their hands. They didn't say anything or announce who they were, they just moved towards her, their guns pointed at her face.

She backed up against the sink and the bottle fell from her fingers and smashed onto the floor, splattering water across her training shoes. 'No, p-p-please!' she stammered. She threw her hands up in front of her face.

A third man appeared, this one wearing a long leather coat, his eyes hidden behind dark glasses. He pointed his gun at her chest and pulled the trigger. Marianne screamed, certain that she was about to die, but a fraction of a second before she went into spasm she saw the two trailing wires from the gun ands realised that she had been shot with a taser.

# CHAPTER 33

MARIANNE woke up in the back of a van. The hood was back on her head and she was lying on her side. She didn't say anything. There was no point.

'She's awake,' said a voice. A man.

'Put her out.' Another man.

She felt someone grab her arm and then there was a brief pricking sensation and then her arm felt warm and then she closed her eyes.

When she opened them again the hood was gone and she was lying on a sofa. She sat up slowly. She was on a flower patterned sofa in front of a large cast iron Victorian fireplace. There was a large ornate gilt framed mirror above the fireplace and two dog figurines.

'How do you feel?' asked Sam.

Marianne flinched, she had thought she was alone in the room. Sam was sitting on an armchair, made from the same material as the sofa.

Marianne ran a hand through her hair. 'I'm okay.'

'You shouldn't have run,' said Sam.

Marianne shrugged but didn't reply.

'But at least we know where you live now. And we know who you are.'

Marianne sniffed and wiped her nose with the back of her hand.

'And of course it was fascinating to see what you had up on the wall. You'd been tracking Boris Morozov for a while?"

Marianne shrugged but didn't answer.

'You targeted him, didn't you? You knew who he was long before he walked into the club, didn't you? You were waiting for him?'

A tear ran down Marianne's cheek and she wiped it away.

'*It's okay, Marianne,*' said Woody. '*I'm up.*'

# CHAPTER 34

WOODY folded his arms and sat back on the sofa. 'Where are we?' he asked. 'This isn't the barracks.'

'It doesn't matter where we are,' said Sam.

'You didn't just taser me, did you? If it was only a taser I would have woken up on the way.'

'We learned our lesson,' said Sam. 'Even a hood over your head doesn't stop you tracking your position.'

Woody rubbed his left arm. 'So you injected me with something?'

'Just to put you out while you were in transit.'

Woody looked around the room. 'This is the safe house, isn't it? The one you told me about. Hampstead.'

'It's actually a different one,' said Sam. 'But its location isn't important. Where did that information come from? The information you have on your wall in your flat? The floor plan would be easy enough to get and anyone can take surveillance photographs, but you had his phone bill and his bank statement. And his travel documents.'

Woody shrugged. 'You've heard about that thing called the internet, right? It's all out there.'

'Well, it is but things like phone bills and bank statements aren't generally available. And how did you get a copy of his passport?'

'Basic intelligence gathering,' said Woody. 'It's not rocket science.'

'So you were tracking Morozov?'

'You know I was. So were you, remember? We were doing the same thing, it's just that I got there first.'

'So what happened wasn't you reacting to a rape attempt?'

'He couldn't keep his hands off me.'

'But you went to his home planning on killing him?'

Woody folded his arms again and smiled but didn't answer.

'What I don't understand is, why did you do it? Were you paid?'

Woody snorted. 'What, you think I'm some sort of professional assassin?'

'Well, I don't think there's any doubt about you being an assassin. The question is whether or not you were paid to assassinate Morozov.'

'I didn't do it for money,' said Woody quietly.

'So why did you do it?'

'Come on, Sam. That bastard deserved to die and the world is a better place without him.'

'Why do you say that?'

Woody laughed and shook his head. 'Are you serious? How can you sit there and ask me that? You had him under surveillance, you must have known what a shit he was. Bribery, corruption, he's been laundering money for the corrupt bastards in the Kremlin for years. He facilitates Russian agents who come over here to kill the enemies of the Kremlin. You know he was involved in the Salisbury poisonings, right?' He shook his head. 'Of course you do.'

'So you killed him because he was a threat to the State?' said Sam. 'That's very public spirited of you.' She shook her head and snorted softly. 'I don't understand why you won't be honest about this. We knew exactly what you did, we just need to know why.'

'Well let me ask you something, Sam? Why did you want him dead?'

'It was a decision taken right at the top, that Boris Morozov was a threat to the wellbeing of the State.'

'So why not just deport him?'

'Because none of the intel on him can be made public. And any way he has a British passport, courtesy of the Tony Blair Government. And he can't be tried for his crimes because he has diplomatic immunity.'

'Diplomatic immunity and British citizenship? That's unusual.'

'Boris was a very unusual man.'

'And what do you think he did wrong?'

Sam laughed. 'It's not a matter of thinking. We know exactly what he did. It just can't be proved, not in a court of law.'

'And the government, our government, gave you the go-ahead to kill him?'

Sam nodded. "They did, yes.'

Woody grinned. 'That being the case, shouldn't I get the fee? After all, I was the one who did the job.'

'I doubt that is going to happen,' said Sam. 'Why did you run?'

'Instinct, I suppose. I didn't plan to run, you just let me into the changing room on my own and I saw the tiles in the ceiling and I thought I'd just go for it.' He frowned. 'How did you find me?'

Sam smiled. 'Trade secret.'

'You had me tagged, obviously. There's no way you could have known where I lived.' He looked down at his feet, sighed and shook his head. 'My trainers,' he said. 'You put a tracker in my trainers. That means you didn't trust me.'

'Well, with hindsight, I was right, wasn't I?'

Woody laughed. 'I suppose so. I gave you a run for your money, though, didn't I?'

'You did. But the tracker meant we were never going to lose you. And at least we now know who you are. Marianne Donaldson.'

Woody flashed her a tight smile but didn't say anything.

'You are Marianne Donaldson, aren't you? The birth certificate is genuine and you have a passport and driving licence in that name. I'd hate to think that was another fake identity.'

Woody shrugged but didn't answer.

'What are we going to do with you, Marianne?'

'What are your options?'

'We could bring it all to an end, right now,' she said.

'That doesn't sound good.'

'Or we could move forward, as we planned.'

'Kwok Chun-ying?'

'Exactly. We would like to move against him tomorrow. But to do that, we need you.'

'So I have leverage?'

'You do have some leverage, yes. But it counts for nothing if we can't trust you.'

'We?'

'Our organisation.'

'Your boss, you mean. Who exactly is that? Who pulls your strings?'

'That's not really something you need to worry about. I'm the one that needs convincing.'

Woody shrugged. 'You know who I am now. Running has just got a lot harder.'

'It has, yes,' said Sam. 'Your bank accounts have been frozen and your driving licence and passport have been cancelled. You're very close to becoming a non-person. You can run, yes, but it's a tough old world without money.'

'The stick again. You do like your sticks.'

'I offered you the carrot, but you still ran.'

'I panicked. I'm sorry. I just thought that if I got away, if I was free, I could get back to my life.' Woody flashed an uncertain smile. Sam watched him, a slight frown on her face. Woody couldn't tell if she believed him or not, but he suspected not.

'And what about Morozov? You did target him, didn't you?'

Woody nodded. 'Yes.' That was the truth.

'Why? Why did you want to kill him?'

'He hurt a friend of mine.' A lie. But close enough to the truth that there shouldn't be any micro expressions to give him away.

'Who?'

'Just a friend. A girlfriend. He raped her and she wasn't like me, she couldn't fight back.' Almost the truth.

'So you did it for revenge?'

'Yes.' The truth.

'You got the singing job at the club you knew he visited. You waited for him to invite you back to his place and you killed him?'

'He attacked me. If I hadn't defended myself he would have raped me.'

'Okay. I understand that. But I don't understand how you acquired the skills you have. According to the MoD, you were never in the armed forces.'

Woody shrugged. 'YouTube.'

'No, I don't think so. You don't get weapons skills like you have by watching videos.'

'I've always had good coordination,' said Woody.

Sam stared at him for several seconds. 'Well I suppose what matters is that you have the skills, not how you acquired them.' She looked at her watch. 'Right, we need to get you ready.'

'Why the rush? You said the job is tomorrow.'

'It is. But it's in Hong Kong.'

# CHAPTER 35

MARIANNE woke up as the wheels of the Gulfstream jet touched down on the runway. She sat up and rubbed her eyes. It was light outside but she had no idea what time it was. It had been dark when the plane had lifted off from an airfield outside London. The van she had been in had blacked out windows so she wasn't sure exactly where the airfield was.

Sam was sitting on the other side of the plane, bent over an iPad in a dark brown leather case. They were the only occupants in the cabin. There were two pilots in the cockpit, but no flight attendant. Sam had brought Marks and Spencer sandwiches and salads with her and had twice made coffee for herself. Marianne drank only water and she wasn't hungry. 'What time is it?' asked Marianne as she rubbed her eyes.

'Four o'clock in the afternoon,' said Sam. 'Did you sleep?

'I was tired,' said Marianne. She peered through the window. The main terminal was some distance away and most of the planes she saw were in the Cathay Pacific livery.

The Gulfstream came to a halt and the engines powered down.

Marianne undid her seatbelt but Sam waved a hand at her. 'Stay seated until they've checked our passports.'

'The Customs people come to us?'

Sam smiled. 'That's one of the perks of flying on a private jet,' she said. She reached into her jacket pocket, took out a passport and passed it to Marianne. Marianne frowned and opened it. The photograph was hers but the name and all the other details were fake. 'Is this a real passport?'

Sam nodded. 'It's genuine, in the sense that it will be accepted at all UK borders. But as you can see, it's in a different name?'

Marianne smiled. 'You think I look like a Lucy?'

'Actually, I do. But I didn't choose your name. That would have been somebody in our documents department.'

'So you do this a lot? Giving people false identities?'

'If it's necessary, yes.'

'So who are you today?'

Sam took another passport from her pocket and opened it. She flicked through it and smiled. 'I'm Laura Reynolds.'

'You don't look like a Laura.'

'I suppose not.'

The pilots appeared from the cockpit and one of them opened the door and unfolded the steps. Two uniformed Chinese immigration officers walked up the steps. 'Good afternoon,' said the older of the two. 'Your passports please.' He sat down at one of the tables and took a stamp and pad from a leather pouch, scrutinised the passports of the pilots and stamped them. Then he smiled over at Marianne. 'Passport please.' He was in his fifties with steel grey hair and a gold tooth that glinted as he smiled.

Marianne went over to him and held out her passport. He took it and flicked through the empty pages. 'First time in Hong Kong?'

Marianne nodded. 'Yes.'

'And the purpose of your visit?'

'Business,' said Sam. 'We have several meetings scheduled.'

'According to your flight plan, you are departing for the UK tomorrow morning,' said the man. He compared the picture in the passport to Marianne's face.

'We have a very busy evening,' said Sam.

The man grunted, then stamped Marianne's passport and gave it back to her. He held out his hand for Sam's passport. She gave it to him. Unlike Marianne's passport, Sam's was filled with stamps and visas. 'I see you have been to Hong Kong before,' he said.

'Several times,' she said. 'It's a fascinating city.'

'And Beijing?'

'An equally fascinating city.'

'What is your business?'

'Property mainly. Shopping centres, hotels, industrial units.'

'Enjoy your stay, short as it is.' He stamped her passport. He stood up and went to the front of the plane and left with his colleague.

'That's it?' asked Marianne.

'That's it,' said Sam. 'That's the beauty of flying on a private jet. No queues, no waiting for bags, no hassle.'

'How the other half lives.'

Sam laughed. 'I think it's how the top half of one per cent lives,' she said.

They collected their bags and headed down the steps where a green Rolls Royce was waiting for them. The uniformed driver put their bags in the boot while they climbed into the back of the car. 'This is a Rolls Royce,' said Marianne, in awe.

'It is, yes,' said Sam. 'We're staying at the Peninsular Hotel and they use Rolls Royces for their airport pick-ups.'

They drove out of the airport and headed for the tower blocks of Hong Kong. Half an hour later they were pulling up in front of the Peninsular Hotel, a colonial style white building dwarfed by two more recent towers in the centre. A liveried bellboy took their bags inside.

Check-in was quick and efficient and within a few minutes they were in one of the tower blocks looking out over the bustling harbour. Directly opposite them on the other side of the harbour was a large white ferris wheel, and next to it the Star Ferry terminal, where a green and white ferry was preparing to depart. Both were dwarfed by the glass and steel towers around them,

'So, we're in Kowloon, on the mainland,' said Sam. 'The party tonight is on Hong Kong Island, at a private house.' She pointed at the island ahead of them. 'It's on the other side of the Peak. Our contact will be here in an hour or so and she'll brief you on what you can expect.' She sat down on a sofa, opened her briefcase and took out her laptop. She powered it up and showed the screen to Marianne. It was a photograph of Kwok Chun-ying. Sam showed her a number of photographs of the man, on his own and in group settings.

'Okay? You'll recognise him?'

'Sure. Yes. Of course.'

Sam showed Marianne photographs of a sprawling single-storey house, the rooms filled with Chinese furniture and works of art. The exterior shots showed a swimming pool and a patio area, and a large hot tub. 'This is where you'll be going,' said Sam. 'A van will collect the girls from the Mandarin Oriental hotel on the island and drive them to the house. The same van brings the girls back the following day, they usually have breakfast at the house and depart just before noon. Obviously the schedule will be changing on this occassion.'

'You'll give me a gun, right?'

Sam shook her head. 'The girls are searched before they get on the van, and again as soon as they arrive at the house. They're mainly looking for drugs but it means that any weapons will be seen.'

'This Kwok is anti-drugs?'

'Very much so. He's involved in the drugs trade and profits from it, but he never uses illegal drugs and insists that no one uses any drugs around him. Alcohol is his drug of choice, and he smokes like a chimney. But that's it.'

'So if I don't have a gun, what am I supposed to do?'

'You didn't have a gun when you went inside Morozov's mansion. It's a similar situation. You'll have to improvise.'

'Kwok's bodyguards are armed?'

'Yes. But if you have trouble getting a gun, you might consider this.' She showed Marianne a photograph of a collection of Japanese samurai swords displayed in racks. 'Kwok is a big collector of samurai swords, and he has one of the best collections outside Japan. Sharp as hell, I'm told.'

Marianne nodded. 'Okay. But then what? I'll be trapped in the house.'

Sam pressed a key on the laptop and a satellite image of the area filled the screen. Sam pointed at the swimming pool. 'On the far side of the pool is a gazebo with loungers in it, facing the pool. It's sturdy and about twelve feet high. The gazebo is about ten feet from the wall, so you can jump it. Beyond the wall is a road that cuts across the Peak. There'll be a car waiting for you about a hundred yards down the road to the left, close to this intersection.' She tapped the screen. 'They'll drive you back here and then we'll head to the airport.'

'They're your people?'

'Of course.'

'Why weren't they on the plane with us?'

'They're Chinese. Locals.'

'And what's my fallback position? What if something goes wrong?'

'Marianne, if something goes wrong when you're in the house, you're on your own. There's no back up, there's no one going to come to your rescue.' She tapped the screen again. 'You need to get here, come what may.' Sam looked at her watch. 'Do you need to shower? Or eat something? You've got time.'

'I'm fine.'

That was a lie. Marianne wasn't fine at all.

# CHAPTER 36

MARIANNE was staring out of the window at the harbour traffic when the phone rang. Sam answered it. Down below, two green and white Star Ferry vessels were passing each other, carrying passengers between the island and the mainland. Off to the right a red and white hydrofoil craft was slicing through the water and dozens of cargo ships were making their way to and from the container port. Interspersed between them were hundreds of small pleasure craft, weaving to and fro to avoid colliding with the larger vessels.

Sam put down the phone. 'Emma is here,' she said.

'She works for you?'

Sam wrinkled her nose. 'She supplies intel. She's an escort, working out of London, Paris, New York and Hong Kong mainly. She picks up a lot of useful intel which she passes on to me - for a price.'

'But how can she get me close to Kwok?'

'One of the agencies she works for is based here in Hong Kong. It's run by Sally Lai and she's looking for new girls. They're short for tonight so Emma put your name forward. Sally wants to see you but assuming you pass muster you'll be on the team tonight.'

'But what happens to Emma afterwards? They'll know that I killed this guy, and if she vouches for me, won't they suspect her?'

'If necessary she'll say that you're just a friend of a friend, that you worked for the same modelling agency in London. It'll be fine.'

There was a knock on the door and Sam went over to open it.

'*Okay, Jasmine,*' said Woody. '*You're up.*'

# CHAPTER 37

JASMINE smiled as Sam showed Emma into the room. Emma was in her mid twenties, a tall willowy blonde with shapely legs and breasts that were so perfect that they had to be the work of a surgeon. Emma was model pretty with razor sharp cheekbones, pale blue eyes and perfect teeth. She air-kissed Jasmine, then held her hands and took a step back. 'Beautiful,' she said.

'Thank you,' said Jasmine.

'Mr Kwok will love you,' said Emma. 'Great legs, tits he can bury his face in, and you have a very sexy mouth.'

Jasmine laughed. 'I love it when you talk dirty.'

Emma grinned and turned to Sam. 'She'll be fine,' she said. She let go of Jasmine's hands and dropped down on to a sofa.

'Where time will the pick up be?' asked Sam.

'Eight o'clock at the Mandarin Oriental. Sally will vet the new girls and then the van will take them to Kwok's house.'

'You're not going?' asked Sam.

'I've told her I'm on my period so I can't work,' said Emma. 'I'm introducing her to three new girls, including Lucy here. Once Sally gives them the okay, I'll be flying to Singapore.'

'What have you told them about me?' asked Jasmine.

'You're a model, you work through an agency in London that I worked for, I don't know you personally but a friend recommended you. You've got a bit of a cocaine habit that you fund with escort work.'

'I thought Kwok is anti-drugs?' said Jasmine.

'He is, in that he doesn't want them in the house. But most escort girls are on one drug or another.'

'Will Sally have any questions for me?'

'She'll probably want to know what you will and won't do. Kwok is pretty vanilla but you never know what his guests are in to. I went with one guy who wanted me to suck his toes, and that wasn't pleasant.' She shuddered at the memory.

'The clients are all Chinese?' asked Jasmine.

Emma nodded. 'Sometimes triad gangsters, local high rollers, and there's usually officials from the Chinese government there.'

'Does Sally Lai go with you?'

'No, she arranges everything but we get taken there by a driver and a minder. The minder is a former Hong Kong cop, Ricky Yu. He's a nasty piece of work and is always trying it on with the girls when Sally isn't around.'

'And what happens when we get to the house?' asked Jasmine.

'The van drives into the compound. There'll be lots of bodyguards and they're armed. You'll be searched as you leave the van and then you'll be taken inside the house. Any coats and bags will be taken off you, and then you have the run of the house and the grounds. Basically you follow any instructions you're given. If one of the men wants to take you into a bedroom, you go. If they want you to strip off and play in the pool, you do that. It's like a party, generally, and you're there for their amusement. Sally will pay you the following day but you can pick up lots of tips, especially from the triads. The triads are serious tippers. The Chinese bureaucrats, not so much.

'What about Kwok? Does he join in?'

'Big time,' said Emma. 'Pops Viagra like they were M&Ms. But he's got a tiny dick so you barely notice that he's there.'

'Minimum wear and tear?' said Jasmine.

Emma grinned. 'Exactly.'

'Is there CCTV inside the house?' asked Jasmine.

'No, there are no cameras, and no burglar alarm. There are always armed guards inside and no one would be stupid enough to steal from Kwok.' She looked at her watch. A rose gold Rolex. 'We've got a couple of hours before we leave. You should get the hotel to fix up someone to do your hair,' she said. 'And your make up.'

'I can do my own make up,' said Jasmine.

'I know what Kwok likes,' said Emma. 'Let me call a girl I know, she'll take care of you.'

Jasmine looked over at Sam. Sam nodded. 'Okay, sounds like a plan,' said Jasmine.

# CHAPTER 38

JASMINE took a deep breath as the taxi pulled up outside the Mandarin Oriental Hotel. It was a featureless twenty six storey block overlooking the harbour, but Emma had already explained that it was one of the city's top hotels with suites costing thousands of pounds a night. Jasmine was wearing one of the dresses from Selfridges, and her hair had a slight wave in it, courtesy of a young Chinese girl supplied by the hotel. Jasmine wasn't taken with the make up that another Chinese girl had applied, there was more eyeliner and lipstick than she would usually use, but Emma had insisted that it was what Kwok liked. Another girl had applied bright red nail varnish to Jasmine's fingernails and toenails.

Emma paid the taxi driver and they walked into the reception area. Two pretty girls were sitting on a sofa, a blonde and a redhead. There were brightly coloured cocktails on the table in front of them. The blonde waved at Emma and Emma waved back. 'There they are,' she said to Jasmine. 'You'll like them. Claire is a glamour model in the UK and Nicola is an up and coming porn star from New Zealand. She's just started an OnlyFans page but she's escorting until that takes off.' They went over to the two girls and Emma introduced them. Claire was the blonde, tall and busty wearing a tight silver dress that showed off her very impressive cleavage. Nicola was shorter and slimmer and was wearing a very short pale blue dress and Christian Louboutin high heels. Her red hair was cut short and she had a sprinkle of freckles across a snub nose. They were both wearing heavy eyeliner and had bright red lipstick and red fingernails.

'And here is Sally,' said Emma, looking over at the main door. A small dumpy Chinese lady was walking towards them, dressed in a lilac Chanel suit with white edging, and carrying a glossy black Chanel handbag. To complete the effect she had Chanel diamond earrings and the Chanel logo was on her belt. Jasmine had to force herself not to grin - she looked like a walking advert for the fashion house.

'Miss Lai, wonderful to see you,' gushed Emma. She bent down and air kissed the woman on both cheeks, then introduced Jasmine, Nicola and Claire. Sally Lai looked at the girls like a farmer weighing up cattle. She motioned with a ring encrusted hand. 'Walk,' she said.

Claire and Nicola stood up, and together with Jasmine they walked the length of the reception area, performed graceful model turns, and walked back to her. Jasmine put a swing in her hips and smiled as she made eye contact with the woman.

Sally Lai nodded her approval. 'Good, Emma. Yes. Very nice. Mr Kwok will be pleased. They know the arrangements, and the fee?'

'They do, yes.'

'Perfect. The van will be outside in about fifteen minutes. And you're sure that you can not go?'

'I'm afraid not, Miss Lai.'

'You could always leave your knickers on.'

Emma laughed and blushed. 'I actually don't feel good, Miss Lai,' she said. 'Cramps.'

'Menopause can be a blessing,' said Sally Lai. She looked at her diamond-studded wristwatch and grunted, then turned and headed for the door.

'Well, you have Sally's seal of approval,' said Emma. She grinned at Jasmine. 'Let's have a cocktail while we wait, shall we?'

# CHAPTER 39

JASMINE's heart began to pound as the Toyota van slowed. There was a set of ornate metal gates ahead of them and it was clearly their destination. She was sitting on the back row of the van, with Claire and Nicola next to her. There were another six girls in the van and the minder, Ricky Yu, was sitting in the front passenger seat next to the driver. Emma was right, Ricky Yu was a nasty piece of work and he had patted Jasmine on the backside as she'd followed Claire and Nicola into the van. Jasmine hadn't reacted, her job was to get into Kwok's house, not to pick fights with dirty old men.

Emma had stood outside the hotel and waved goodbye, mouthing 'Good Luck' as the van pulled away.

Sam had made it clear that the van wouldn't be followed, and that there would be no back-up in the vicinity of the house, other than the car waiting for her at the intersection to pick her up. She took several slow, deep breaths to calm herself down.

'Are you okay, baby?' asked Claire, patting her on the leg.

Jasmine forced a smile. 'Sorry, I was miles away.'

'You've done this before, right?'

'Escorting? Sure? But this is my first time in Hong Kong.'

Claire laughed. 'You won't have any problems, baby.' She held up her right hand and wiggled her little finger. 'Chinese men have small dicks, you won't even feel it.'

'That's a blessing.' She grimaced. 'Emma said that sometimes there were triads in Kwok's house. They're gangsters, right?'

'A guy is a guy,' said Claire. 'They're all the same. Treat them nice and suck their dicks and they'll open their wallets.'

'I thought you were a glamour model?' said Jasmine.

Claire leaned towards her. 'Glamour model slash escort,' she whispered. 'And escorting pays better.'

Nicola nodded in agreement. 'Escorting pays better than porn movies, too. I get two grand for two scenes in a movie, but I get double that for an overnighter as an escort. Plus tips. No one ever tipped me for screwing in a porn movie, but like Claire says, treat them right and money falls like rain.'

'Emma said you were a model,' said Claire.

Jasmine smiled. 'Model slash escort.'

Claire and Nicola giggled. The gate opened. It was made of wrought iron with various Chinese symbols forming part of the metalwork. The van edged forward and Jasmine got her first sight of the house. It was just one storey but with a green pagoda-style roof that made up half the height of the building. There was a grey Maserati, a red Ferrari and four white SUVs parked in front of the house. There were two well built Chinese men standing by the cars, and another two at the entrance to the house.

The van pulled up next to the Maserati. Ricky Yu climbed out and opened the side door of the van. 'Right, out you get, ladies, and line up over there.' He pointed at the Ferrari. The girls climbed out and Ricky Yu took the opportunity to slide his hand along their bodies as they stepped down. When Jasmine got to the door she fixed him with a steely glare. 'If you touch me, motherfucker, I'll break your fingers off and shove them up your smelly arse.' It wasn't what she said that made the man's jaw drop and his eyes widen, but the fact that she had said it in fluent Chinese.

'What the fuck?' he said.

'You heard me, cocksucker. Keep the fuck away from me!' Again her Chinese was faultless.

The men in black suits started laughing and Ricky Yu gritted his teeth and took a step back. Jasmine stepped out of the van and walked over to the line. Claire and Nicola hurried to join her, their high heels clicking on the driveway. 'You speak Chinese?' asked Claire.

'Mandarin,' said Jasmine. 'His first language is probably Cantonese, but I think he got the drift.'

Nicola laughed. 'I think you're right.'

Ricky Yu started patting the girls down and taking their handbags off them. He gave the bags to the men in black suits, and after each girl had been searched they headed for the entrance.

When Ricky Yu got to Jasmine, he put his face close to hers. She could see the hairs sprouting from his nose and smell something bitter on his breath. 'I have to search you,' he hissed.

'Search me with your eyes, you can see I'm not carrying anything,' she said, in fluent Mandarin. 'But you lay a finger on me and I'll break it.'

'You think you can hurt me, whore?'

'Maybe not. But I bet Mr Kwok will hurt you when I tell him that you've been touching up all the girls you deliver to him. We're his property to fondle, not yours.' She raised her hands in the air and did a slow turn so that he could see every inch of her, then she stood with her hands on her hips. 'Happy now?'

The men in black suits were laughing again and Ricky Yu turned and swore at them. He was still cursing as Jasmine walked away.

'Your Chinese is good,' said one of the men at the door as he pushed it open for her.

'So is yours,' said Jasmine.

She walked into a large hallway with marble floors and oak panelled walls. There were two doors to the left, both closed, and a pair of open double doors to the right that led to a large sitting room with half a dozen modern sofas and gold and glass coffee tables. There was a grand piano at the far end of the room and a pretty Chinese girl was playing something classical. Chopin, maybe.

There was a young girl with waist length hair wearing a black and white maid's uniform standing inside the door, holding a tray with filled champagne flutes. Jasmine took one and sipped as she surveyed the room. A Chinese man was sitting on one of the sofas and a blonde girl was kneeling in front of him, her head bobbing up and down. The man was staring out of the floor to ceiling windows, a brandy glass in one hand, a cigar in the other as the girl continued to pleasure him. 'You go, girl,' whispered Jasmine.

Two of the girls from the van, both brunettes, had gone outside to the swimming pool with a small Chinese man. He walked in between them and had his arms around their waists. They were both wearing towering heels and were almost a foot taller than him.

'Well this looks like fun,' said Claire, appearing at Jasmine's shoulder. She took a glass of champagne from the tray and sipped it. She spotted the girl on her knees and laughed. 'Well she got off to an early start.'

Two brutish men in expensive suits were talking to a tall brunette in a tight-fitting gold dress and she threw her head back and laughed. 'I know her,' said Jasmine. 'I mean, I've seen her somewhere.'

'From the Gucci adverts,' said Nicola, coming up behind them. She took a glass of champagne.

'Why would she be here?' asked Jasmine.

'Why are any of us here?' said Nicola. 'Cold hard cash.'

The woman walked with the two men past the piano and through a door. 'I guess that's where the bedrooms are,' said Claire. 'Oh, I think I've pulled.' She raised her glass at a Chinese man who was sitting on a sofa by the window. He was in his forties wearing a dark green Mao jacket. He grinned and waved her over. 'Oh well, here we go,' she said. 'Wish me luck.'

'Good luck,' chorused Jasmine and Nicola.

Claire walked over to the man, swinging her hips a bit more than necessary, and sat down next to him. He immediately put his arm around her, pulled her close, and kissed her on the lips. Jasmine shuddered and sipped her champagne. She looked around the room. There were about a dozen Chinese men there, but there was no sign of Kwok.

A man with slicked-back hair in a dark blue suit and a thin blue tie walked up to Jasmine and smiled. 'You're pretty,' he said.

136

'Thank you,' she said. She handed him her champagne glass. 'Hold this for me, will you?'

He took the glass and frowned as she walked over to the piano. The girl was still playing Chopin, her face a blank mask. She looked up at Jasmine as her fingers continued to move across the keys. 'Good evening,' said Jasmine. 'Do you know The Moon Represents My Heart.'

If the pianist was surprised to hear Jasmine speak fluent Chinese, she didn't show it. 'By Teresa Teng? Of course.'

'Can you play it?'

For the first time her face registered surprise. 'You can sing it?'

'I can try,' said Jasmine.

'Okay.' The pianist transitioned from the Chopin tune into The Moon Represents My Heart, a slow ballad about a girl trying to explain to her boyfriend how much she loves him. Jasmine put her back against the piano and started to sing. Almost immediately heads turned to see who was singing, and the inquisitive looks turned to surprise when they saw it was Jasmine.

She had just finished the second verse when Kwok appeared at the doorway, holding a brandy glass. He stopped and listened, and then walked over just as she was finishing.

'You sing in Chinese?' he said.

'I love Chinese songs,' said Jasmine. 'The Moon Represents My Heart is one of my favourites.'

He nodded and smiled. 'I am Kwok Chun-ying.'

'You have a beautiful house, Mr Kwok.' She spoke in Chinese.

'Thank you,' he said, switching to Chinese. 'And your name is..?'

She was going to lie, but realised there was no need to. He wouldn't be around to tell anyone later. 'Jasmine,' she said.

'Now that is a beautiful name. Do you know the song Mo Li Hua? Jasmine Flower?'

'Of course,' said Jasmine. It was a famous Chinese folk song from the 18th century and had been used during the 2008 Summer Olympics in Beijing.

'My mother used to sing Jasmine Flower to me when I was a baby.'

Jasmine turned to look at the pianist, who nodded and immediately started to play.

Jasmine looked into Kwok's eyes as she sang the song, and midway through she actually saw tears welling up. He blinked them away and drank from his glass. When she finally finished he patted her on the shoulder 'That was lovely,' he said. 'This is your first time here, isn't it? I would have remembered if you had been here before.'

'Yes, my first time,' she said.

'Let me get you a drink.' He waved a waitress over, took a glass of champagne off her tray, and gave it to Jasmine. She thanked him in Chinese and sipped it.

'Why is your Chinese so good?' he asked.

Jasmine shrugged. 'I enjoy singing Chinese songs,' she said. 'I learned from watching YouTube videos and that got me interested in the language.'

'But you have been to China?'

'Never. This is my first trip.'

'I'm impressed,' he said. 'And how did you meet Miss Lai? You are one of her girls?'

'A friend introduced me.' She shrugged. 'I needed money.'

'Everybody needs money.'

'That is certainly true, Mr Kwok.'

'You can call me Chun-ying.'

'I will, Chun-ying. Can I ask you a question?'

'Of course.'

'I heard you had an amazing collection of samurai swords.'

Kwok frowned. 'Who told you that?'

'One of the girls who had been here before. She said you had a superb collection.'

Kwok beamed. 'I do.'

'So where are they?'

He smiled. 'My bedroom.'

'Seriously?'

'Seriously. Would you like to see them?'

She laughed. 'Is that just a way of getting me into your bedroom?'

He reached over and stroked her cheek. 'Whatever it takes,' he said. 'You are very, very pretty.'

'Thank you.'

'I'm going to enjoy fucking you, Jasmine.'

'Well, that's why I'm here, Mr Kwok.' She grimaced and corrected herself. 'Chun-ying.'

'This way,' he said, holding her arm, just above the elbow.

Jasmine allowed herself to be guided through the doorway that led to the bedrooms. Kwok's room was at the far end of a long corridor. It was a huge room with a massive four poster bed against one wall, two sofas in one corner and double doors that led to a dressing area and presumably the bathroom. There was a ten foot tall mirror in a gilt frame leaning against the wall by the bed.

Jasmine gestured at the mirror with her glass. 'You like to watch yourself?' she asked.

Kwok grinned. 'Who doesn't?' He pulled her towards him and kissed her on the lips. She fought her revulsion and kissed him back, but almost gagged when he thrust his tongue into her mouth. She pulled away and went over to a display of samurai swords on the wall facing the bed. There were more than two dozen, lined up in racks.

'Oh my God, these are amazing!' she said. 'You really are a collector.'

'I like beautiful things,' he said. 'I like to touch them and hold them - and use them.' As she looked at the swords, Kwok came up behind her and slipped his hands around her breasts. He squeezed them, hard. 'Take off your dress,' he said. 'I want to fuck you.'

'*Okay, Sofia,*' said Woody. '*You're up.*'

# CHAPTER 40

SOFIA pushed back against Kwok. She could feel how hard he was and she smiled. 'You like that?' she asked.

He grunted and said something to her in Chinese.

'I only speak English when I fuck,' said Sofia.

'That's fine by me,' growled Kwok.

'Which is your favourite sword?' she asked.

'What?'

'Of all the swords you have, which is your favourite. I want to see it?'

'You don't want to fuck?'

Sofia laughed. 'Swords make me horny,' she said,

'Really?'

'Really. They make me wet.'

'You are a very strange lady.'

'You don't know the half of it, honey.' She twisted out of his grip. 'Come on, show me your favourite sword.'

'The word is katana. Not sword.'

'So show me your favourite katana.'

'My favourite? That is like asking me to choose my favourite child. I love them all.'

'But there must be one that is special.'

Kwok grinned and pointed to a sword in the middle rack. 'That one was made by the legendary craftsman Sengou Muramasa. I am told it took longer to create that blade than it took Michelangelo to paint the

Sistine Chapel. The saya alone took a year to make and the tsuba is a work of art in itself.'

Sofia nodded. The saya was the scabbard, the tsuba was the hand guard piece, and Kwok was right, both were exquisite.

'Is it valuable?'

Kwok laughed. 'It is priceless. That katana is almost five hundred years old.'

Sofia stepped forward to get a better look. 'Is it sharp?'

'Of course it's sharp.'

'I heard that if you took a samurai sword from its saya, there had to be blood on it before you put it back. Even if it meant that you had to use your own blood.'

Kwok laughed. 'That is an old wives story.'

'That's good to know,' said Jasmine. She lifted the sword from the rack and slowly pulled the blade from its saya. The metal whispered against the lacquered wood. She held the blade up and it glistened in the overhead lights. 'Wow,' she said.

'It's beautiful, isn't it?'

'Oh yes.'

'Is it making you wet?'

She smiled at him. 'Honey, you have no idea.'

'Do you want to hold it while I fuck you?'

'Oh, you are a naughty man.'

'Take off your dress,' he said.

'One more question,' she said. She turned the blade from side to side. 'Do you think you could cut off someone's head with this?'

'Of course. Easily.'

'With just one blow?'

'That's what it's designed to do.'

'Do you want to bet?'

'Bet?' He frowned. 'What do you mean?'

'I mean, do you want to bet that I could take your head off with one blow?' She smiled. 'Never mind.' She swung the blade up, then chopped down at the side of his neck. The finely honed steel sliced through skin and muscle and barely slowed as it cut through his spine and out of the other side of his neck. For a second the head stayed where it was, a look of surprise fixed on Kwok's face, then it fell back as blood spurted from what remained of the neck. The arterial spray was so fierce that it hit the ceiling and Jasmine had to take several steps back to avoid the shower of blood.

Kwok's body actually stayed upright for several seconds, then it fell to the floor.

Sofia put the sword back in its scabbard, then put the weapon on the display stand. She walked over to the mirror and checked that there was no blood on her, then she left the bedroom, closing the door behind her.

She walked back to the sitting room, taking a glass of champagne from a waitress as she went over to Nicola. 'That was quick,' said Nicola.

'Yes, I thought so.'

'Happy ending?'

'For me, sure.' Sofia sipped her champagne. 'Where's Claire?'

'In one of the bedrooms.'

'What about you? No one propositioned you, yet?'

Nicola laughed. 'I need a few more drinks before I'm ready to dive in. There's plenty of time. We're here all night.'

'I guess so.' Sofia waved her glass at the swimming pool. 'I'm going to have a walk around.'

'Go for it.'

Sofia headed for the door that led to the patio. She walked through a barbecue area where a man in a chef's whites and hat was preparing thick steaks. She walked by the pool, her high heels clicking on the flagstones. A blonde girl was in the shallow end, holding the side of the pool as a young man covered in tattoos took her from behind. The woman was making encouraging sounds but her face looked bored and she flashed Sofia a thin smile as she walked by.

Sofia turned and looked back at the house. So far, so good, it looked as if Kwok's body hadn't been found. She turned and headed for the gazebo. She was about twenty metres away when she heard shouts from the house. She looked over her shoulder and men in black suits were running around inside. The man in the pool had turned around to see what was happening. There were more shouts from the house, then the tattooed man pointed at Sofia and shouted back at them.

Sofia dropped her champagne glass, kicked off her shoes and ran across the grass towards the gazebo.

'*Okay Jim*,' said Woody. '*You're up.*'

# CHAPTER 41

JIM sprinted towards the gazebo. It was about twenty feet across with trellises either side of the entrance. The perimeter wall was about twelve feet tall and jumpable from the gazebo roof, but Sam had neglected to mention that there was razor wire running along the top of the wall. There was a man and a girl in the gazebo. The man was sitting on a wicker sofa, the girl was kneeling down in front of him, her head bobbing up and down. The man frowned as he saw Jim but he had no time to react before Jim had launched himself at the trellis.

He scrambled up. As he reached the roof, bullets thudded into the trellis below him. The woman below him screamed and the man roared in pain. Either he'd taken a bullet or the woman had been shocked into biting him.

Jim looked over at the wall, considering his options at lightning speed. The roof sloped but the highest point was way too far from the wall to have any chance of him making it. In a perfect world he'd be able to land on the top of the wall but the razor wire and bare feet made that an impossibility. More rounds smacked into the roof. He took a look over his shoulder. Three men in black suits were running towards the gazebo, guns in the air. He looked back at the wall. It was doable. He ran up to the peak of the roof, bending double to make himself a smaller target. There were more shots but the men were firing as they ran so all the rounds went high.

He reached the top of the roof, took a deep breath and ran down the slope, his bare feet slapping against the wood. He reached the edge and jumped, throwing his arms forward and keeping his legs high. As his feet left the roof he tucked his knees into his chest and went into a roll. As he inverted he kicked out with his feet and arched his back. He sailed over the wall, missing the razor wire by a hair's breadth. He tucked in again and the second his feet touched the ground he went into a forward roll down the slope, keeping his chin against his chest

145

so that his shoulders took the pounding. As he came up he put his arms out for balance but he was moving too fast to stay upright so he went into another forward roll. The contact with the ground slowed his momentum and this time he was able to stand on his feet. He ran down the slope to the road, turned left and sprinted towards the intersection.

A taxi went by, the driver beeping the horn to see if Jim wanted a lift. Jim continued to run as fast as he could.The intersection was ahead of him but he frowned as he realised there was no car waiting for him.

He looked over his shoulder. The road was empty. He reached the intersection. Traffic was moving along the main road but there were no parked cars. He frowned. Something had gone wrong, but what? Had he been too quick, had he carried out the job much faster than they'd expected?

A horn sounded but it was another taxi touting for trade. He shook his head and the taxi went by. A taxi wasn't an option because he didn't have any money on him.

He looked left and right. Nothing. Then as he looked back to the right he saw two white SUVs heading towards him from the direction of Kwok's front gate. Jim's mind raced. He needed to go down the Peak towards the harbour but there was no way he could outrun the SUVs.

He turned and ran back the way he'd come. To his left was a wall around another house. It was about ten feet tall and there was no razor wire on the top so he sprinted towards it. He heard the squeal of tyres behind him but he didn't look back. He jumped, placed his right foot against the wall and pushed himself up so that he could grab the top of the wall. As he pulled himself up, he heard car doors open followed by rapid gunshots. Bullets thwacked into the wall by his knees and he swung his right leg over the top of the wall. There were more shots as he rolled over and fell onto a bush. He scrambled to his feet and ran around the side of the house. There were no lights on inside but as he ran across the grass a security light came on, illuminating him with a dazzling white beam. He kept his head down as he sprinted towards the front of the house.

There was a large gate ahead of him, but as he ran towards it another security light came on, sending a huge shadow across the lawn. He heard the squeal of brakes and one of the white SUVs drew up outside. The front passenger door opened and a man pointed a gun over the top of the roof and pulled the trigger. Shots whizzed by Jim and a window shattered. Almost immediately a burglar alarm sounded.

Jim turned to the right, running parallel to the road, as more bullets thudded into the grass at his feet. There was a wall ahead of him. He ran at it, jumped, and rolled over the top.

There were lights on in the house to his right and he saw two figures in the front room. One of them pointed at him. Jim waved, trying to show that he wasn't a threat, but he was dazzled by a brilliant white security light that suddenly illuminated the whole front lawn.

He turned right again and ran around the side of the house and by a swimming pool. He headed for the far corner of the garden, planted his left foot against one wall and pushed himself to the right, vaulting over and dropping down into a crouch by the side of the road.

There were no cars in sight but further down the road he saw a food delivery driver pulling two pizza boxes from the Food Panda box on the back of his bike. Jim stayed in a crouch until the driver walked through the gate with his pizzas, then he ran towards the motorbike.

'*Liz, you're up,*' said Woody.

# CHAPTER 42

Liz reached the bike. The engine was running. She slid on, kicked it into gear and twisted the throttle. It wasn't especially high powered but it accelerated down the road. The slipstream whipped at her hair and she bent down low over the handlebars as she gave it full throttle.

She sped down the road. She took a quick look in her right hand mirror and saw a white SUV behind her. She was going flat out but it was gaining on her.

She passed the wall around Kwok's house and reached the intersection. Another white SUV was pulling out of the driveway. The passenger was talking into his phone and he pointed at the bike. Jim accelerated and headed down the hill.

The road twisted and turned so she had to keep her speed down, and as she checked her mirrors she realised that the SUV was gaining on her.

As she turned a corner her way was blocked by a minivan that was braking. She swerved around it but there was large truck heading towards her and she only just missed clipping it. She heard the SUV's horn blare as she accelerated away.

The road straightened and she took the bike up to its full revs. She roared past two minivans but had to brake hard when a bus pulled out in front of her. She checked her mirrors. The white SUV was still there.

She tried to overtake the bus but there was a minivan coming towards her so she had to tuck the bike in. As the minivan flashed by she tried again and this time managed to get by the bus though the driver of the car heading her way flashed his headlights angrily and pounded on his horn.

She was driving along a road flanked by gleaming tower blocks now, weaving through the traffic and ignoring any red lights that threatened to slow her down.

In the distance she saw the huge white ferris wheel that overlooked the harbour. She headed towards it, undertaking and overtaking whenever she could.

She cut in front of a tram, her wheels juddering on the metal tracks, and the driver sounded his horn angrily.

A taxi's brake lights came on ahead of her and she had to swerve to avoid it.

She was closer to the ferris wheel now. To the left of it was the Star Ferry terminal. A green and white ferry was getting ready to leave. Liz's eyes flicked to her right hand mirror. There were two white SUVs behind her now. She accelerated, zig-zagged between two taxis, and pulled up in front of the ferry terminal with a squeal of brakes.

'*Jim*,' said Woody. '*You're up.*'

# CHAPTER 43

JIM leaped of the bike and let if fall to the ground. He sprinted towards the Star Ferry terminal, his bare feet slapping on the tarmac. There was a line of turnstiles ahead of him but he didn't break stride, he ran towards them and vaulted over. He hit the ground running and sped down the pier at full pelt. The pier was deserted and at the far end a green barred gate had been closed, blocking the way to the ramp that led to the departing ferry.

The ferry's horn sounded as its propellors thrashed the water into white foam. Jim scrambled up the gate, rolled over the top and dropped to the ground.

The ferry was about ten feet away from the ramp now, its bow pointing towards Kowloon. Jim started running, his arms pumping like pistons. The lower deck was about level with the ramp so he wouldn't need much height as he jumped, it was all about the horizontal distance. Olympic athletes could manage about thirty feet for a long jump. Jim would never be a contender for the Olympics, but on a good day he could get close to that, though it helped if there was a vertical component.

His eyes took in the gap between the ramp and the ferry. Twenty feet and growing. He took a breath, gritted his teeth and jumped. He knew that if he fell short he would be falling into the propellors which would churn him into bloody chunks in less than a second but he blotted out the gruesome thought and concentrated on the ferry, now more than twenty five feet from the ramp. He reached out his hands, fingers splayed. Gravity was bringing him down but if he had calculated properly the bottom of the arc would intersect with the railing at the rear of the ferry.

The wind whipped at his hair and the spray peppered his face so he narrowed his eyes as he focussed on the railing. He was aware of the growl of the engine and the thrashing of the propellors but all he cared about was the landing. He was falling short, he realised. He was going to miss the rail. Not by much, just an inch or two, but an inch was as good as a mile. His mind ran through all his options at lightning speed. There was no way of gaining height and on his current trajectory he would hit the ferry just below the deck. His only hope was to grab the deck with his hands and haul himself up but the metal would be slippery and he had no idea how well he'd be able to grip it.

The last few feet rushed by in a blur and he hit the metal hard, his hands slapped onto the deck and almost immediately he felt himself slide backwards. He pushed up with both hands and then grabbed for the bottom railing. He caught it, held it tight for a second, then hauled himself up. He swung his right foot up and used that as leverage, pushing himself up and over the railings.

He straightened up and realised that one of the Star Ferry workers was watching him open mouthed, a thick length of rope in his hands. For a moment Jim thought that the man was going to give him a hard time but he just grinned and flashed him a thumbs up. Jim smiled, gave him a mock bow, and walked towards the bow. Ahead of him were the skyscrapers of Kowloon and behind them the darkness of the mountains.

The crossing wouldn't take more than a few minutes, which was a lot longer than it would take Kwok's men to drive through one of the cross-harbour tunnels. He was safe. For the time being, anyway.

'*Okay Marianne,*' said Woody. '*You can take it from here.*'

# CHAPTER 44

MARIANNE walked into the hotel. Several people stared at her bare feet as she crossed the reception area but she ignored their disdainful looks. She reached the lift and went up to Sam's floor. Her mind was in a whirl. If Sam had checked out, what then? She had no money, she had no way of getting to the airport and even if she did, Sam could have already left Hong Kong. And if she had flown out, what then? She would be stranded in a unfamiliar city with no money and no way of getting home, and if the police weren't after her, Kwok's men certainly were.

She walked down the hallway to Sam's room, her feet padding on the carpet. A maid pushing a trolley smiled at her and Marianne smiled back. She reached the door to Sam's room and knocked, her heart pounding as if it wanted to burst out of her chest. There was no reply and tears sprang to Marianne's eyes. She'd been abandoned. Thrown to the wolves. She'd done everything Sam had wanted and Sam had betrayed her. Tears ran down her face as she knocked on the door again.

'Can I help you, Miss?' called the maid, who had stopped pushing her trolley and had turned to look at Marianne.

Marianne shook her head and forced a smile. 'I'm okay.'

'Are you a guest here?' asked the maid.

Marianne opened her mouth to reply but stopped when the door opened. It was Sam. 'Hello, Marianne,' she said. 'What kept you?' She was wearing a white bathrobe and her hair was damp. She stepped to the side. 'Come in, come in.'

Marianne hurried into the room. There was a room service cart in front of the television with the remains of a salad on it, along with a half drunk bottle of wine. Sam closed the door and gestured at the wine. 'Would you like a drink? I'll get you a glass from the bathroom.'

Marianne stared at Sam in disgust. 'You abandoned me!' she said. 'I could have been killed.'

'But you weren't, so that's good.' She walked over to the bed and sat down.

'You think this is funny? I could have died.'

'But you didn't. So you passed the test.'

Marianne frowned and ran a hand through her hair. 'Test? That wasn't a test. You betrayed me.' She went over to the window and looked out over the harbour. She brushed away her tears with the back of her hand, determined that Sam wouldn't see her cry.

'Sometimes missions go wrong, Marianne. Not everything goes to plan. We needed to know how you perform under pressure.'

Marianne turned around to face her. 'And if the police had caught me?'

Sam shrugged. 'Then you would have gone to prison. Or at least Lucy Jenner would have.'

'And if I'd told them about you?'

'Told them what?'

'Everything. Who you are, what you do, what you wanted me to do.'

'No one would believe you. And once they'd checked with Interpol, they wouldn't believe a word you said.'

'What do you mean?'

'Lucy Jenner has a history of mental illness and has been in and out of prison.'

'What?'

'We didn't just prepare a passport, there's a whole backstory to go with it. The sort of backstory that means the Hong Kong cops wouldn't believe anything you told them. And Lucy has been violent in the past, bless her.'

'Why would you do this to me? I thought you trusted me?'

'You ran in London, remember?'

'So this was payback?'

Sam shook her head. 'No, as I said, we wanted to test you. We wanted to see how you would react under pressure. Would you keep your head or would you fall apart?'

'And if I'd been caught, you would have abandoned me?'

'Marianne, if you had been caught, you'd have been no use to me. There are no second chances in this business. No resets. If you can't do the job, better we know up front.'

Marianne shook her head. 'You're crazy.'

'If you were able to look at it from my point of view, you'd realise that what I did makes perfect sense. It was a stress test. You were put under stress to see how you would react, and you performed even better than we expected.' She smiled. 'Well done.'

'How can I ever trust you again?' Marianne whispered.

'You have no choice.'

Marianne frowned. 'What do you mean?'

'Think about it, Marianne. You killed Kwok Chun-ying. And you were seen doing it. Kwok Chun-ying has some very powerful friends in the Chinese government, friends who will want his death avenged. So long as you work for me you have my protection, they won't get anywhere near you. But if you should ever run away again, you'll be on your own. And how long do you think you'd last without any protection?'

Marianne folded her arms and stared at the floor. 'This is not fair.'

'Life's not fair,' said Sam. 'But at least when you're working for me you're on the side of the angels.'

'That's supposed to make me feel better?'

'Actually, yes. It should.'

'Well it doesn't.'

'I can see you're angry. I understand. I empathise. But one day you'll look back at this and realise that it was all for the best.'

'I don't think so.'

'We're your family now, Marianne. We'll protect you.'

'So long as I do what you want?'

'There's a quid pro quo, yes. We help each other.'

'By help, you mean I have to kill for you.'

Sam smiled. 'That's what you're good at. We're just making the best use of your talents.'

Marianne dropped down onto a sofa and shook her head. 'So what happens now?'

Sam looked at her watch. 'You can shower and change into something more comfortable and then we'll head to the airport. Are you hungry?'

'Am I hungry? Are you crazy? After what just happened, you think I can eat?'

Sam held up her hands. 'I was just asking. If you like, I could order a club sandwich and a salad from room service and you could eat it on the plane.'

Marianne shook her head in disgust and headed for the bathroom.

# CHAPTER 45

MARIANNE looked out of the window as the Gulfstream's engines began to wind down. They had parked next to a large hangar at an airport with a single runway. There were more than a dozen private jets lines up and several limousines parked nearby. She looked over at Sam who was studying her iPad. 'Do we wait here?' she asked.

Sam nodded but didn't look up from her tablet. 'Yes, they'll come and check our passports but it's a formality. Our names and passport details are on the flight plan that was filed before we left Hong Kong.'

'What about our luggage? Do they check that?'

Sam shrugged. 'Sometimes. But generally not.'

'But that means we could bring anything in with us.'

'We could, yes. But this plane is flagged as being for VIPs and to be left alone.'

'It's a different world,' said Marianne.

'You don't know the half of it.'

After twenty minutes, one of the pilots opened the door and two black uniformed Border Force officers came on board. One spoke to the pilots while the other went over to Sam, gave her passport a cursory glance and then did the same with Marianne. 'Welcome home,' the man said to her, then he and his colleague left.

Sam and Marianne collected their bags and headed down the steps where a black Mercedes was waiting with its engine running. A driver in a dark suit and sunglasses took their bags from them and put them in the boot. Sam and Marianne climbed in the back. The windows weren't tinted and there was no suggestion that she should be hooded - probably the result of having proved herself in Hong Kong.

The driver got back into the car and they drove out of the airport. Marianne saw a sign - Biggin Hill. 'Do you always fly by private jet?' Marianne asked.

'On business, yes,' said Sam. 'It's quicker and, as you saw, there are fewer checks.'

'I didn't realise we'd be working outside the UK.'

'Sometimes we do,' said Sam. 'It depends on where our targets are.'

They rode the rest of the way in silence. Sam busied herself on her iPad and Marianne stared out of the window. It was a strange feeling, riding in the back of a luxury car, knowing that she was still very much a prisoner. There were no handcuffs, no hood, no shock collar, but she knew that she was now totally in Sam's power. Tears sprang to her eyes but she blinked them away, determined not to show Sam how upset she was.

They drove through Croydon and Mitcham and reached Wimbledon. Almost an hour after they had left the airport, they arrived at a large Victorian house surrounded by a high brick wall. A black metal gate swung open and the Mercedes drove through. There were three other vehicles already there, a Mercedes van and two SUVs. 'Home, sweet home,' said Sam as the gate closed behind them.

'This is where you live?' asked Marianne.

'No, but it's where you'll be staying, for a while anyway.'

'But my things are in my flat?'

Sam shook her head. 'Your lease was terminated while you were away and all your belongings were moved here.'

They climbed out of the Mercedes and Marianne looked up at the house. There were CCTV cameras up near the roof and bars on the ground floor windows. 'It's like a prison,' she said.

'Think of it as a fortress,' said Sam.

The boot opened and Sam took out Marianne's bag and gave it to her. Her own suitcase stayed in the boot. As they walked to the front door it was opened by a man wearing black trousers and a black long-sleeved shirt. He was in his thirties with close-cropped dark brown hair and a goatee.

'This is Jason,' said Sam. 'He'll take care of you while you're here.'

'He's my guard?'

Sam laughed. 'Good gracious, no. Think of him as a housekeeper come butler. He makes sure that the house runs smoothly, and that any guests are looked after.'

'So there will be other people staying here?'

'Not right now. But people do come and go.' She nodded at the man. 'Jason, this is Marianne.'

'Pleased to meet you, Marianne,' said Jason. He had a soft Scottish accent. He reached for her bag. 'Let me take that for you.'

He took the bag and they followed him inside. 'Jason is also an excellent cook,' said Sam. 'If you want to cook for yourself, that's fine, but trust me, you'll be missing out.'

The hallway was lined with dark wood and the furniture was sturdy and darkened with age as if it had been here for decades. There was a coat stand by the door, and a large oak table with a bowl of wax fruit in the middle. The carpet was clean but well worn, and there were brass rods holding it in place up the stairs.

'I'll leave you here with Jason,' said Sam. 'I've got work to catch up on and I'll be back tomorrow. You can rest. Jason will show you around.'

'Can I leave the house?'

'You're not a prisoner, Marianne. But I'd prefer you stay indoors for the next few days. If you need anything, Jason can arrange for it to be delivered.' She pointed up the stairs. 'We brought everything from your flat, it's in your room. But you have the run of the house. And the garden, of course.'

'Okay. Thank you.'

'And I'll see you tomorrow. Okay?'

Marianne nodded. 'Okay.'

# CHAPTER 46

MARIANNE woke up to the sound of birds singing and for a few seconds wondered where she was before she remembered that she was in the safe house in Wimbledon. She sat up and rubbed her eyes. The bed had been so comfortable that she had fallen asleep almost as soon as her head had touched the pillows. The room was at the back of the house, overlooking the back garden. There were several trees and a small vegetable patch, and a bird table with a thatched roof.

Opposite the bed was a large Victorian wardrobe and a matching chest of drawers, which now contained all her clothes. All the information she had on Boris Morozov was in a cardboard box on top of an oak dressing table, along with the few personal belongings that she'd kept in the flat.

Jason had cooked dinner for her the previous night. Sam had been right, he was one hell of a cook. He had prepared a braised sea bass with spinach and new potatoes which she had eaten at the kitchen table, and followed it with possibly the best chocolate mousse she had ever eaten.

She had spent the rest of the evening in the living room, lying on the sofa and watching television. From time to time she had heard Jason moving around the house, but he had left her alone and there was no sign of him when she eventually went to bed.

She got up and padded across the carpet to the bathroom. There was an old roll top bath, a large washbasin and a Victorian toilet with an old cistern up on the wall with a chain to pull to flush. It looked like something from an old movie.

She ran a bath, added in some bubble bath that Jason had thoughtfully provided, and spent half an hour in the tub. There was a hair dryer in the dressing table and she used it to dry her hair, then she pulled on a pair of Diesel jeans and her favourite comfy sweatshirt.

She'd had it for almost five years and it was her go-to garment when she felt down in the dumps. It was grey and several sizes too large, but when she slipped it on it was like wearing a cloud. She tied her hair back with a scrunchie and headed downstairs to the kitchen where Jason was wiping down the sink with a cloth. 'Sleep well?' he asked.

'I did, yes,' said Marianne as she sat down at the table.

'Do you want tea? Coffee? Juice?'

'Just a bottle of water, please.'

'I have a really nice Welsh water, drawn from a spring in the valleys, I'm told.'

Marianne laughed. 'Sounds perfect.'

Jason went to a large fridge that looked as if it was more than fifty years old. It hissed as he opened the door. 'And eggs? I have some delicious duck eggs,' he said. 'I could scramble them or make you an omelette? I have some very sharp cheddar, I could put that in with some tomatoes.'

'That sounds amazing,' said Marianne.

'Toast?'

'Just an omelette, thank you.'

'Give carbs a miss? Good idea, darling. We have to keep our figures, don't we?'

Jason gave her a blue bottle of water and took a box of eggs over to the stove, which was as antiquated as the fridge. They chatted as Jason cooked her breakfast. He was good company and made her laugh several times. For a while she forgot that she was in a safe house belonging to an organisation that thought nothing of flying assassins around the world in private jets.

She was just finishing her cheese and tomato omelette when the front door opened. She heard voices and then Sam appeared at the kitchen door. She was wearing a dark blue blazer over a pale blue dress. 'Good morning, Marianne,' she said. 'How did you sleep?'

'Good,' said Marianne.

'And Jason has been looking after you?'

'He has.'

'He's a dream, isn't he? I always think of him as the perfect husband.'

'I wish Giles thought the same,' said Jason. 'I tell him how lucky he is to have me, but he says I'm the lucky one.'

Sam laughed. 'Well, to be fair, Giles is a catch,' she said.

Marianne heard a scuffling sound in the hallway and then Dr Carter appeared behind Sam. He was carrying a scuffed leather briefcase and wearing another Hugo Boss suit.

'Good morning, Marianne,' he said. He nodded at Jason. 'Jason.'

'Simon. Do either of you want breakfast?'

'We're good,' said Sam. 'We dropped into Starbucks on the way.' She looked at Marianne and smiled. 'We'd like a chat if that's all right with you, Marianne.'

'Is something wrong?'

'No, no. We just need a chat.'

'Actually, I thought I could perhaps have a one-to-one with Marianne,' said Dr Carter.

Sam frowned in confusion. 'Really?'

'It might be beneficial to have one point of contact on this,' he said.

Sam shrugged. 'Okay, if you want, sure. Why don't the two of you use the library?'

'That works for me,' said Dr Carter. He smiled and nodded at Marianne. 'Shall we go through?'

Marianne looked over at Sam. 'Is there something wrong?'

'Nothing's wrong, Dr Carter just has some questions, that's all.'

'I'm not in trouble, am I?'

'Have you done something wrong?'

162

Marianne shook her head. 'Of course not.'

Sam smiled brightly. 'There you are, then. Just have a chat with Dr Carter, you'll be fine.'

Marianne stood up, grabbed her bottle of water, and followed Dr Carter out of the room. He took her across the hall and opened a door. The room was quite small and lined with bookshelves. There were two winged leather chairs either side of a mahogany coffee table. The curtains were drawn and Dr Carter pulled them back to allow light into the room. He sniffed and frowned. 'Does it smell musty?'

Marianne sniffed and shook her head. 'It smells fine to me.'

Dr Carter shrugged. 'My sense of smell has never been the same since I had covid,' he said. He sat down in one of the chairs and gestured for her to take the other. He swung his briefcase onto his lap, opened it and took out a laptop. He put the briefcase next to his chair and powered up the computer. 'I gather that you did very well in Hong Kong,' he said.

'You heard what happened?'

'I was told you carried out your task very efficiently.'

'And did Sam tell you that she abandoned me?'

'Abandoned you?'

'I was supposed to be picked up after I'd done what they wanted, but they never turned up. I was left to my own devices. I could have been caught by the cops. Or killed.'

Dr Carter frowned. 'I didn't know that, no.'

'Sam said it was a test. To see how I'd perform.'

'And you performed well, I was told.'

'You're not listening to me.'

'Actually I am. That's what I do. I listen to people. And I can hear your anger at what you believe was a betrayal. But it had nothing to do with me.' He smiled and pushed his glasses further up his nose. 'Tell me, are you right handed or left handed?'

Marianne frowned. 'Why would that matter?'

'I'm just curious.'

'No, you're not. You've got a reason for asking.'

'Well, yes, I do, obviously. So can you answer my question?'

'I don't like you talking to me like this,' said Marianne. She brushed a tear from her eyes. 'It's like you're bullying me.'

'I'm just asking you a few questions, that's hardly bullying.'

*'It's okay, Marianne,'* said Woody. *'I'm up.'*

# CHAPTER 47

WOODY smiled at Dr Carter. 'Why does it matter if I'm left handed or right handed? That's a simple question, isn't it? You expect me to answer your questions, so you should at least answer one of mine. This was supposed to be a chat, not an interrogation.'

Dr Carter smiled. 'I'm just trying to build a picture of who you are.'

Woody sat back in his chair and folded his arms.

Dr Carter's smile widened. 'See now, that's a very defensive posture. Almost as if you're trying to hide your hands from me.'

'Or I could be folding my arms to resist the urge to smack you in the face.'

'Well I hope you won't do that, I saw what you did to those men in the training hall, remember?'

Woody frowned. 'You weren't there.'

'It was videoed. Pretty much everything you did was videoed. For your safety.'

Woody chuckled. 'For my safety? Seriously?'

'Let me make it easier for you, Marianne. On the night you were first questioned, you were clearly right handed. You were offered water and you took the bottle with your right hand and drank it using your right hand. Sometime later you asked for coffee and you drank coffee with your left hand. You also scratched yourself with your left hand, brushed the hair from your eyes with your left hand.'

Woody shrugged.

'But when you were on the firing range, you were clearly able to shoot with both hands. You were equally accurate, left or right.'

'So I'm ambidextrous. Plenty of people are.'

'Well, yes, that's what I thought. But there was no sign of that during your first interview.' He leaned over to open his briefcase and took out a yellow pad and a pen and placed them on the coffee table in front of Woody. 'Would you humour me and write something with your right hand.'

'I'm not playing that game, Dr Carter.'

'What game?'

'Whatever game it is that you're playing. It makes no difference what hand I use. It's irrelevant.'

'So humour me. It doesn't cost you anything.'

'No.'

'Okay, well let me show you something,' said Dr Carter. He opened his laptop, tapped on the keyboard and then turned it so that they could both see it. It was showing a video of the Mayfair mansion. As they watched, Marianne appeared at the upstairs window and made her way down the side of the building.

'See how you came down from the top floor? That is some expert parkour. You must have done gymnastics at school, right? You are fearless.'

Woody shrugged but didn't answer.

'You took care of the two bodyguards and then you took the Lamborghini keys from the pocket of one of the Russian heavies.' He froze the picture on the tablet. 'And you used your right hand to do that.'

Woody looked at the screen. 'So?'

'Well, when I interviewed you that first time, you only used your left hand. But when it came to getting the keys, you used your right hand.'

Dr Carter started the video again. 'Then you walked to the Lamborghini and used your right hand to unlock it and start the engine.' He stopped the video and nodded at the yellow pad. 'So you're obviously comfortable using your right hand. So please, humour me, and just write something with your right hand. Show me

166

that you are ambidextrous. You clearly are when it comes to firearms. Your performance on the firing range was very impressive.'

Woody shook his head. 'I don't want to.'

'Okay. Fine. So let me show you something else that intrigues me.' He went to the start of the video, when Marianne first appeared at the upstairs window. 'Like I said, you're fearless. I mean, there's no way I could come down a building like that. I'd be scared to death of falling.' He froze the picture and zoomed in to Marianne's face, 'But you were scared when you first looked out of the window. Really scared. As scared as I would have been.' He let the video play for a few seconds and then froze it again. 'But then something changed. You weren't scared any more. You were fearless. Look at you now. Totally confident, almost happy. You had the same smile on your face in the training hall. You knew you were going to kick the shit out of those men. Something changed up there. One moment you were scared, apprehensive, the next you were totally confident. What happened?'

'I did what I had to do. Courage is just the ability to overcome fear.'

Dr Carter played the video up to the point where Marianne was sitting in the Lamborghini and stopped it again. 'And something similar happened in the car. You got in, using your right hand to open the door, and then you hit the steering wheel. Banged it with your hands. And you sat there as if you'd lost control. And then suddenly you smiled and were in control again. It's as if you were a different person.'

Woody shrugged. 'So what do you think that all means?'

Dr Carter smiled. 'You know what I think.'

'So say it.'

Dr Carter sighed. 'Fine. I think you have what we used to call Multiple Personality Disorder. These days they call it Dissociative Identity Disorder.'

'A rose by any other name.'

Dr Carter smiled. 'I suppose so. Basically people with DID have two or more separate identities. At any one time any of the personalities can be in control of the host. Each personality has its own traits, its own likes and dislikes, and even physical characteristics, such as which is the dominant hand.'

'And you think I have that?'

'Yes,' said Dr Carter. 'I do. So can I ask you, is the personality I am talking to the original personality?'

Woody smiled and sat back. 'What do you think?'

'I think you're the dominant personality, but not the original identity. You seem to be very much in control. And - if you don't mind me saying - I get the feeling that you're quite masculine.'

'I'm not sure you're in any position to be defining my gender,' said Woody.

Dr Carter put up his hands. 'Absolutely, there's no way I would define your gender for you.' He leaned forward. 'But let me ask you, how do you identify your gender?'

'I don't have to define anything, Dr Carter. Look at Jason out there. Would you ask him what gender he is, or do you just accept him for what he is? And if his gender differed from the way you saw him, would you treat him any differently?'

'This isn't about Jason, though,' said Dr Carter. 'Jason doesn't have your skill set.'

'He is an amazing cook, though.' Woody watched Dr Carter for several seconds without speaking, then he smiled. 'You're quite clever aren't you?'

'I do my best.'

'Masters? PhD?'

'Yes and yes.'

'You've dealt with people like me before?'

'Actually I haven't, no. Genuine cases of DID are extremely rare. I notice you're avoiding my question.'

168

Woody looked at him again without speaking. 'My name's Woody,' he said. 'Pleased to meet you.'

'Pleased to meet you, too,' said Dr Carter.

Woody held out his hand. Dr Carter eyed it suspiciously. 'I won't hurt you,' Woody said.

Dr Carter shook Woody's hand. 'You've got a good, firm grip,' he said.

Woody took back his hand.

'So I'm correct in saying that you weren't the original personality?'

Woody shrugged but didn't answer.

'So who is the original personality? Is it Marianne?'

Woody shrugged but again he didn't answer.

'Can I talk to Marianne?'

'Maybe. Once I'm sure you mean her no harm.'

'You protect Marianne?'

'That's what I do.'

'And the others?'

'The others?'

'How many personalities are there?'

Woody shook his head. 'One step at a time, Dr Carter.'

'The reason I ask is that it wasn't you who killed the Russians and knocked out all those guys in the gym. And I don't think it was Marianne. So that means there are at least three identities. You, Marianne, and somebody who is very good with a gun and their fists. And I get the impression that whoever drove the car that night is another personality. So at least four. And maybe the parkour expert. So that would be five.'

'My job is to protect Marianne, not to act as a spokesman for whoever might or might not be here,' he said.

'So can I speak to Marianne?'

Woody stared at Dr Carter for several seconds. 'Okay,' he said eventually. 'But go easy on her.'

*'Marianne, you're up.'*

# CHAPTER 48

MARIANNE sighed. She sat back in her chair and folded her arms. 'You're a bully,' she said.

'Really, I'm not.'

'I said I didn't want to talk to you and I don't. I've done everything Sam asked me to do but it's still not enough, is it?'

'You heard everything that I said to Woody?'

'I'm not deaf.'

Dr Carter smiled. 'I'm just trying to understand what's happening here. When I talk to Woody, you can hear everything?'

'Of course.'

'And Woody can hear what we're saying?'

'Woody is here with me, yes.'

'But you are the principal personality?'

Marianne frowned. 'What do you mean?'

'You were there first. It's your body.'

'I suppose so.'

'So you created Woody?'

Marianne grimaced. She picked up the bottle of water, unscrewed the cap and drank.

'You didn't like that question?' asked Dr Carter.

'I don't get what you mean,' she said. 'I didn't create Woody. That makes it sound like I made him up. I needed help and he came to help me.'

'Why did you need help, Marianne?'

'I don't want to say.' She held the bottle of water against her chest.

'Okay, I understand. Was it because something bad happened to you when you were little?'

'I don't want to talk about that.'

'I understand, but if you talk to me, maybe I can help you? Wouldn't that be a good thing, if I was able to help you?'

Marianne's eyes widened and her nostrils flared. 'I don't want to talk about it!' she screamed.

Dr Carter jerked as if he had been slapped across the face.

'*It's okay, Marianne,*' said Woody. '*I've got this.*'

# CHAPTER 49

WOODY pointed a finger at Dr Carter. 'Don't upset her like that,' he snarled.

'Woody?'

'I don't want you upsetting her, do you understand?'

Dr Carter nodded. 'Yes, I understand. But believe me, I didn't intend to upset her, I'm only trying to help.'

Woody waved the bottle of water in the air. 'This isn't about helping her. We both know that.' He unscrewed the top and drank.

'Woody, really, you've got me all wrong. I'm a psychiatrist, I simply want to find out what's troubling her so that we can put together a treatment plan.'

Woody stared at Dr Carter with cold eyes as he put the bottle back on the table. 'This isn't about treatment, Dr Carter. If it was we'd be in a hospital and you'd be scanning our brain to see what's going on. And what did that business in the gym have to do with treatment? And does part of that treatment involve firing Glocks? I don't think so.'

'I need to assess your capabilities before we decide how to move forward.'

'And that assessment required us to sleep on a concrete bed wearing a shock collar, did it?' Woody narrowed his eyes. 'You really don't want to lie to me, Dr Carter. I might send Sofia to talk to you, and she really doesn't like liars.'

'Sofia is the killer, is she? The one who killed the Russians and who did the job in Hong Kong?'

Woody took a deep breath and exhaled slowly as he stared at Dr Carter. 'Tread very carefully, Dr Carter,' he said.

'Woody, really, I'm not the enemy here. I just want to talk to you. And to Marianne. And to anyone else with you.'

'Just talk, huh?'

'Just talk.'

'Why?'

'Why? Because if I'm right, Marianne suffered immense trauma when she was little. Trauma that somehow fractured her personality. I might be able to help.'

'Maybe she doesn't want your help?'

'Maybe you're right. But shouldn't that be her choice?'

Woody shrugged but didn't answer.

'Woody, I need to know how you got to this point in your life.'

'Me?'

'You. Marianne. Whoever else is in there. Something happened to you, didn't it? Something turned you into the person you are. The people you are.'

Woody shrugged. 'Nature versus nurture? You don't think I was born this way?'

'Just tell me what happened, Woody.'

'I can't.'

Dr Carter frowned. 'Why not?'

'Because it's not my story.'

'Whose story is it, then? Marianne's, right? So what happened to Marianne?'

'I can't speak on her behalf.'

'Then can I talk to her? Can she explain what happened?'

Woody took a deep breath and exhaled slowly. 'You have to tread carefully.'

'I will.'

'She's still very raw. Even after all these years.'

'I'll be careful.'

'If at any point it looks as if you're upsetting her, I'll step in.'

'Understood,' said Dr Carter. 'So do we have a deal?'

Woody nodded.

'*Marianne,*' said Woody. '*You're up.*'

# CHAPTER 50

MARIANNE sniffed and blinked away tears. She wiped her eyes with the back of her hands. Dr Carter took a handkerchief from his pocket and gave it to her. 'It's clean,' he said. 'I haven't used it.'

'Thank you,' she said, and dabbed at her eyes.

'Marianne, I need you to understand that I only want to help you.'

She shook her head. 'That's not true.'

Dr Carter frowned. 'Why do you say that?'

She stared down at his laptop with unseeing eyes and bit down on her lower lip.

'You can talk to me, Marianne. Really. I mean it when I say I'm here to help.'

She looked at him, blinking away tears. 'You want me to work for you. You want me to kill for you. That's what this is about.'

He shook his head. 'Sam wants you to work for her. I want to help you. I'm not operational.'

'What does that mean?'

'It means that Sam runs the operations, but my role is to make sure that the people who carry out those operations are in the best of health, physically and mentally. We checked out the physical side and yes, you're fit. Super fit. But I worry that mentally…'

'You think I'm mad?'

Dr Carter laughed. 'We don't use words like "mad", Marianne. You're not mad, not by any standards. But you're troubled. And Woody is a symptom of that trouble.'

'Woody helps me.'

'Yes, I know he does. But you created Woody, didn't you?'

Marianne shook her head but didn't answer.

'Woody said it was okay to talk to me,' said Dr Carter.

'Yes, I know.'

'So can you tell me what happened? When you were little?'

'I don't want to.'

'It might help you.'

'I don't want to!' shouted Marianne, so loudly that Dr Carter flinched.

'Okay, okay, I'm sorry,' he said, hurriedly, holding out his hands to placate her. 'I don't want to upset you.'

She dabbed at her eyes and sniffed.

'Would you you like a cup of coffee? Or tea?'

'I don't drink tea or coffee,' she whispered.

'But Woody does, right? He likes his coffee.'

Marianne forced a smile. 'He does. He drinks it a lot.'

'But you don't?'

Marianne shook her head.

'But you can see how that's a little strange, can't you? Woody drinks a lot of coffee, and you never drink coffee.'

'Why's that strange? We're different people.'

'Right. Yes. Of course.' He pushed his glasses further up his nose. 'Is that how it feels to you? You're not the same person?'

Marianne frowned. 'That's a stupid question. Woody is Woody. I'm Marianne. Why would you even think we were the same person?'

'Because…' He waved his hand at her. 'There are two of you in the same body. Your body doesn't change.' He wrinkled his nose 'Actually, that's not right, is it? Your body does change. The Marianne who did the heart stress test was very different from the Marianne who completed the psychological tests.'

She nodded. 'Yes. Woody did the psychological tests but it was Jim who was on the treadmill. Jim is super fit.'

'Yes, he is,' said Dr Carter. 'And Woody mentioned Sofia. Sofia is the one who is good with guns, right?'

Marianne nodded again. 'Sofia is dangerous,' she said. 'You don't want Sofia angry at you.'

Dr Carter smiled. 'Well I'll try not to make her angry,' he said. 'So is that everybody? You and Woody and Sofia and Jim?'

Marianne shook her head. 'There are more.'

'How many more?'

Marianne shrugged but didn't answer.

'Okay, so maybe you can tell me how long Woody and Sofia and Jim have been with you.'

Marianne frowned. 'What do you mean? They've always been with me.'

'Are you sure? Wasn't there a time when there was just Marianne?'

Marianne took the top off her bottle of water and took a sip.

'When you were very young, there was just you, wasn't there?'

'I don't remember.'

'What's the first thing you can remember? From when you were very small?'

Marianne closed her eyes and shuddered. The door handle turning. The smell of lager and sweat. And the words. 'Get dressed'. She shook her head and tried to block out the memories. 'I don't remember when I was small,' she whispered.

'You don't remember or you don't want to remember?'

Tears welled up in her eyes again and she dabbed at them with the handkerchief. 'I don't want to talk about it,' she whispered.

'That's okay, that's fine,' said Dr Carter. 'We won't talk about it. Let's talk about something else. Tell me about when you were a teenager. When you were fifteen or sixteen. What was your life like then?'

'Better,' she said.

'Where were you living?'

'In London.'

'With your parents?'

Marianne snorted. 'No.'

'Who were you living with? Relatives?'

'Friends.'

'Whereabouts?'

Marianne shrugged. 'All over. Kilburn. Stoke Newington. Notting Hill. Camden.'

'You moved around a lot?'

'All the time.'

'Why?'

'Why?' She frowned. 'That was just the way I lived.'

'Did you go to school?'

'No. I hated school.'

'Why?'

'I just did.' She took another sip of water.

'So, you were staying in foster homes?'

'No.'

'So who took care of you?'

'I took care of myself.'

Dr Carter tilted his head on one side. 'I'm not sure I understand. This was when you were fifteen?'

'Fourteen, fifteen, yes.'

'But you're not allowed to live on your own at that age.'

'No one cared,' she said.

'Really? The council didn't talk to you? The police?'

'So long as you don't break the law, nobody cares what you do.'

'Okay, but who did you live with?'

'Different people, different places. Squats mainly. People in squats are usually happy to share.'

'You just turned up and they let you live with them?'

'Pretty much, yes. I stayed in a tent camp in Brighton for a while. That was fun.'

'And what did you do for money? You couldn't sign on for Universal Credit at that age.'

'I worked. I did jobs.'

'At fifteen?'

'There's always jobs if you want to work.'

'Well, yes, but employers can get in to trouble employing fifteen year olds.'

She shrugged. 'If I was desperate, Billy and Karl could always get money.'

'Billy and Karl?' Dr Carter said. 'Who are they?'

'Billy is a computer whizz. A hacker, really. And Karl...' She smiled. 'Karl is a naughty boy, there's no getting away from that. He could always get food if I was hungry.'

'How? How did he do that?'

She smiled. 'Let's just say that he's a bit light fingered.'

'Are they with you and Woody?'

'I suppose so. Yes.'

'Can I talk to Karl?'

Marianne frowned. 'Why do you want to talk to Karl?' she asked.

'*It's okay, Marianne,*' said Woody. '*I'm up.*'

# CHAPTER 51

WOODY leaned forward and pointed a finger at Dr Carter. 'What do you think you're doing?' he said.

Dr Carter frowned. 'Woody?'

'What are you playing at? You said you wanted to speak to Marianne.'

'She mentioned Karl. I thought it might be helpful if I spoke to him.'

Woody wagged his finger at Dr Carter. 'That's not what we said. We said you'd speak with Marianne. Just Marianne. I didn't say you could go rooting through our mind and take a roll call of whoever you find there.'

'Our mind? Not Marianne's mind?'

'You're playing with words.'

'No, I'm trying to understand what's going on here. It's Marianne's mind. It's her body. If she wants to give me access to Karl, that's her decision.'

'She doesn't want to give you access to him, or to anyone else.'

'Then she can tell me that, for herself.' Dr Carter picked up his laptop and closed it.

'Marianne doesn't do conflict, Dr Carter. That's why she needs me to protect her. And that's what I'm doing.'

'Woody, if I'm to help Marianne, I need to know what makes her tick. Otherwise I'm just working in the dark.' He put the laptop back into his briefcase.

'We're done for the day, Dr Carter.' Woody folded his arms.

'Okay, that's fine,' said Dr Carter. 'We can take it up again another day. But please believe me, Woody, I only want to help.'

'We'll see about that,' said Woody.

Dr Carter looked at his watch. 'Our time is just about up, anyway.'

'I didn't realise we had an allotted time.'

'I have another meeting.' He stood up, smiled and nodded. 'I'm sorry if I offended you, Woody. Or Marianne. That wasn't my intention.'

'We're good,' said Woody. 'You just need to be aware of the ground rules, that's all.'

'I am, and I will be more careful in future.'

He smiled and left the room. After a few minutes, Sam popped her head around the door. 'Is everything okay?' she asked.

Woody flashed her a smile. 'All good,' he said.

Sam stepped into the room and closed the door. 'How did it go with Dr Carter?' She was carrying her iPad.

'Fine.' He frowned. 'So you weren't watching on CCTV?'

'There's no CCTV inside the house.'

Woody pointed up at a smoke detector in the ceiling. 'I just assumed that there was a camera in there.'

'Then you assumed wrong.'

'Good to know,' said Woody.

'Is everything all right?'

'Why do you ask?'

Sam looked pained. 'Dr Carter seemed a bit perturbed, that's all.'

'He was asking some very personal questions.'

'That's his job. He's a psychiatrist.'

'I don't need psychiatric help, Sam. I'm fine.'

Sam smiled. 'I'm glad to hear that.' She looked at her watch. 'We've got a job for you.'

'We're only just back from Hong Kong.'

'This one has come up at short notice and we need your particular skill set. Come in to the sitting room, I'll run through the details with you.'

# CHAPTER 52

WOODY took the mug of coffee from Jason and thanked him. He sniffed it. 'This smells good.'

'Nespresso,' said Jason. He gave Sam her coffee, then let himself out of the sitting room. The room was dominated by a sofa and two armchairs in a flowery pattern, arranged around a white cast iron Victorian fireplace with what appeared to be a working grate and a full set of brass tools, any one of which could be used as a lethal weapon under the right circumstances. Above the fireplace was a gilt-framed oil painting of a farming scene, and either side of it were porcelain cats with marbles for eyes. There was a table in one corner with a chess set on it, and a matching table by the window with a large crystal bowl full of sweet-smelling potpourri. The carpet was a mish-mash of red, blues and greens that had faded over the years, and there was a thick rusty-coloured rug under a wooden coffee table with carved feet. Woody suspected that whoever had done the interior design might well have been colour blind.

Woody was sitting on the sofa. Sam had dropped into one of the armchairs. She opened the leather case that protected her iPad and switched it on as Woody sipped his coffee. 'Okay, so the target is one Janco Van Niekerk,' said Sam. She placed the iPad on the coffee table so that Woody could see it. 'Originally from South Africa but like most of the ultra rich he has passports from several countries, including the US and Ireland. He now spends most of his time on his yacht - the Safe Haven. It's a true superyacht, going on for a hundred metres long. On the yacht he's pretty much untouchable as it's usually in international waters. We've tried getting our people on board but his head of security is former CIA and their background checks are second to none.'

She pointed at a head and shoulders picture of a bald man in his fifties, with hooded eyes and thin lips. 'Van Niekerk made his money by helping the Chinese buy up large parts of Africa. Property, natural resources, farms, he's channeled billions of Chinese dollars into the continent.' She tapped on a photograph of a huge sleek yacht with four decks above the waterline. 'And he has reaped the benefits.'

'So now you can get killed for being a capitalist?'

'Hear me out,' said Sam. She called up several photographs of Van Niekerk meeting with several African government officials. 'Van Niekerk knows exactly who to bribe in pretty much every country in Africa. And he takes a cut from every bribe. A big cut. And if money doesn't get the Chinese what they want, he's perfectly capable of removing any opposition. He's been responsible for dozens of deaths and disappearances across the continent. If an activist looks like they might come close to blocking a Chinese investment, there's every chance that said activist will turn up dead. Or vanish, never to be seen again.' She clicked on half a dozen photographs of corpses, all young black men and women, most of whom had been shot in the head.

'So he's a nasty piece of work?'

'Exactly,' said Sam, sitting back in her chair. 'And in recent years he's been operating in the UK. He uses his hedge fund to cause mayhem on the financial markets, and spreads disinformation through various websites he controls. We know he was behind at least three recent attacks on the pound. Each time the pound drops, the Chinese have swooped in and bought up assets on the cheap. And we believe that he's started to import the skills he learned in Africa - bribery and targeted killings. Either way, the Chinese are rewarding him handsomely.'

'So the Government has put him on their hit list?'

'It's a bit more complicated than that, but basically, yes, we have been tasked with taking him out.'

'A date?' said Woody.

Sam smiled. 'Not on a date, obviously. The Safe Haven has just docked in Puerto Banús tonight. We're going out to meet it.'

'And then what?'

'Then you do what you do.'

Woody nodded thoughtfully. 'Have you tried before?'

'This will be the first opportunity that we have had since we started looking at him. The Safe Haven spends most of its time in international waters.'

'Hence the name,' said Woody.

'Exactly.'

'So just me?'

'We'll take a team.'

Woody smiled. 'So this time I'll have back up?'

'Hong Kong was a test,' said Sam. 'You passed with flying colours. From now on you have our full support. You're family.'

'I'm not a big one for families,' said Woody.

# CHAPTER 53

MARIANNE looked out of the window of the Gulfstream jet as its wheels kissed the tarmac at Malaga Airport. The sky was a cloudless blue and the sun glinted off the pristine private jets lined up at the general aviation terminal.

'Have you been to Malaga before?' asked Sam, who was sitting on the other side of the plane.

'Never,' said Marianne. 'This is my first time in Spain.'

'Playground of the rich,' said Sam. 'Or least Marbella and Puerto Banús are.'

'And more London villains then you can shake a stick at,' said Murray, who was sitting with another SAS man at a table at the front of the plane. Murray had swapped his camouflage fatigues for a vibrant blue Ted Baker shirt and Versace jeans, and was wearing Oakley sunglasses. His colleague was younger, in his late twenties, with curly black hair and a square jaw, wearing a red Ralph Lauren Polo shirt and blue jeans. His name was Davie and from the few times he'd spoken Marianne figured he was from the Midlands. Birmingham, maybe, or Wolverhampton. 'Plenty of North African bad guys too,' added Murray. 'You need to watch yourself when you're out at night.'

'I'll bear that in mind, Murray,' said Sam.

The Gulfstream came to a stop and the engines powered down. Immigration officials arrived within a few minutes to give their passports a cursory inspection. Marianne hadn't seen the passports and assumed that someone within Sam's organisation had prepared a fake one for her. Fake or not, it passed muster.

After the officials had left, Sam and Marianne went down the steps where a grey Mercedes with tinted windows was waiting for them, along with a blue Mercedes van. Two men wearing bomber jackets and jeans climbed out of the van. Murray and Billy came down the steps each carrying two large black kitbags. They greeted the two men in bomber jackets and together they loaded the bags into the van.

Sam and Marianne carried their cases to the car and put them into the boot.

'Who are those guys?' asked Marianne as she joined Sam in the back of the car.

'They're with us, they flew over last night.'

'So this is all a rush?'

'It's an opportunity that has occurred at very short notice, yes.' She nodded her head at the driver and Marianne took the hint. Business wasn't to be discussed in the car. She settled back in her seat.

They followed the coastline, the Mediterranean off to their left, and forty-five minutes later pulled up in front of a large brown U-shaped hotel overlooking the beach.

'Well, this looks nice,' said Marianne. 'Five star?' She saw a sign - Gran Hotel Guadalpin Banus.

'It is, yes, but I was more concerned with the view than than the quality of the rooms,' said Sam.

They climbed out of the car and took their bags into the hotel. Check in was smooth and efficient. Sam turned down the offer of a welcome cocktail and they were escorted up to their suite by a pretty Spanish girl who spoke perfect English.

The room had two double beds, a dining table that seated six and a sitting area by large picture windows overlooking the beach and the port off to the left. Sam tipped the girl and waited for her to go before walking over to the window. 'There's the Safe Haven,' she said, pointing to the left.

Marianne joined her at the window. Sam slid it open and they went out onto the balcony. There were three superyachts moored next to each other in the port, dwarfing the other vessels. The Safe Haven was in the middle, and it was the largest of the three with four decks and a helicopter pad at the bow. There were three grey spheres on top of the ship, presumably for radar and communication. 'It's pretty,' said Marianne.

'Beautiful, isn't it? I can't imagine how much it cost. Hundreds of millions of dollars, I'm sure. He travels all around the world on it.'

'Is he married?'

'He was. She died soon after announcing she was divorcing him. Heart attack, they said. But she was only twenty-eight and super fit.'

'He killed her?'

'He probably had her killed. A man like Van Niekerk wouldn't do the dirty deed himself. He was on the ship when it happened, she was in Paris.'

'Kids?'

Sam shook her head. 'No. This is a man who is married to his work. That's his life. Wheeling, dealing and acquiring as much cash as he can. A family would get in the way.'

'Not much of a life,' said Marianne. 'What does he do for fun?'

'He buys art, and that's about it. Spends millions every year on paintings. Some are on the Safe Haven but most are in storage. He doesn't even look at them. That's why it's been so hard to get to him. He's rarely off the ship. That's why we're so keen to take advantage of the fact that he's docked here. We don't know when it'll happen again.'

'Strike while the iron's hot,' said Marianne.

'Exactly. He's meeting one of his Chinese contacts, a high-ranking Government official by the name of Zhang Shi. Zhang is the conduit between the Chinese Government and Van Niekerk and has already left Beijing in a private jet that has filed a flight plan to Malaga.'

There was a knock on the door. Sam went to open it. It was Murray, carrying a North Face backpack. As she closed the door, Murray walked over to the sofa, sat down, and opened his backpack. He took out two radios, then he took out a pair of Nikon binoculars and an envelope containing half a dozen printouts showing floor plans of the Safe Haven.

'Right, all our ducks are in a row,' said Murray. 'Let's start the briefing.' He looked over at Sam and she nodded her agreement.

'*It's okay, Marianne,*' said Woody. '*I'll take it from here.*'

# CHAPTER 54

WOODY sat down on the sofa next to Murray. Sam pulled up a chair. Murray spread the printouts across the dining table. 'Van Niekerk is definitely on board, we've had eyes on him,' said Murray. 'No sign of Zhang Shi yet but we're expecting his plane to land at Malaga within the hour. We're working on getting you on to the Safe Haven between one and two o'clock in the morning.'

'You've got me an invite, have you?' said Woody.

'I wish,' said Murray. 'We can get you on board with an MCS - a magnetic climbing system. Basically hand held units and shoes that stick magnetically to the hull. They're easy enough to use. I'll drop you at the bottom by jet ski. You can go all the way up to the terrace on the fourth deck and from there to the bedrooms.'

Woody frowned. 'I don't understand. Anyone could do that, right? And if I'm climbing up the side, I can take a gun with me.'

Murray nodded. 'I've brought a Glock and an HK45 and suppressors for them both.'

'The point I'm making is that anyone could do this.' He smiled. 'Even you, Murray.'

'Murray isn't operational in that way,' said Sam. 'He trains and handles logistics.'

'He doesn't actually pull the trigger, then?'

'Horses for courses,' said Sam. 'And there are advantages to having you on site. If someone sees Murray on board, they'll know right away that there's a problem. But if a pretty girl appears - well, there'll be hesitation, won't there? It might only be for a fraction of a second, but…'

'Every little helps?'

Sam smiled. 'Exactly.'

Murray tapped on one of the print outs. 'This is the fourth deck,' he said. There was one large cabin on the port side and two starboard, with a wide corridor running between them. There was a stairway at the end of the corridor. Murray tapped the larger cabin. 'This is Van Niekerk's bedroom. There is a dressing room, a large bathroom, and an office area. And he has a private balcony. Two, actually. Zhang Shi will probably be in one of the VIP cabins on the same deck. If not, he'll be in one of the cabins on the third deck.'

'This Zhang Shi, is he also a target?'

'Definitely not,' said Sam. 'And his bodyguards are also untouchable. Your target is Van Niekerk and Van Niekerk's security team would be regarded as acceptable as collateral damage. But the Chinese mustn't be harmed.'

'It's going to be difficult if Zhang's cabin is next to Van Niekerk's.'

'We have the boat from under observation so we might be able to tell which cabin he is in,' said Sam.

'Ship,' said Woody.

'I'm sorry, what?'

'It's a ship. Not a boat.'

Sam frowned. 'I thought they meant the same.'

'Then you thought wrong.'

'So what's the difference?'

Woody laughed. 'It's complicated. The simple answer is that a ship can carry a boat, but a boat can't carry a ship. Having said that, ferries carry lifeboats and they're not considered as ships. The best answer I always think is that a ship's captain gets annoyed if you refer to his vessel as a boat, but a boat's captain is okay if you refer to his vessel as a ship. Oh, and submarines are always boats, no matter how big they are.'

'I'm none the wiser,' said Sam, shaking her head.

'I get that, but trust me, Safe Haven is a ship, not a boat.'

'I shall remember that in future,' said Sam. 'So, we will have the *ship* under observation and hopefully we'll ascertain where Zhang Shi is sleeping.'

'The issue isn't which cabin he's sleeping in, it's how many bodyguards he has with him,' said Murray.

Woody frowned. 'This is starting to get complicated.'

'Not really,' said Murray. 'Zhang Shi hasn't boarded yet. The Safe Haven is literally that so it would be showing disrespect to take on too many bodyguards. It would suggest a lack of trust. The bodyguards might well remain on shore, but if not I doubt that more than one or two will go on board with him.'

'And what's the story with Van Niekerk's security team?' asked Sam.

'At any one time he has a team of six, plus a supervisor,' said Murray. 'All are former Delta Force. Two stay close to him, two are within a hundred feet or so, and two are off duty but in the vicinity, sleeping or resting. The supervisor is wherever he needs to be, but is usually close by. When the boat - sorry, ship - docks, two stand guard at the rear gangplank, twenty-four seven and check everyone who boards.'

'Will they be armed?' asked Woody.

'Zhang Shi's team almost certainly not,' said Murray. 'But Van Niekerk's team will definitely have access to arms. So far as we can see, the two at the gangplank aren't carrying concealed weapons. But they'll certainly have them on board. There are pirates everywhere these days, and not the Johnny Depp kind.'

Woody picked up the binoculars and went over to the window. He focussed on the two men standing at the gangplank at the stern. They were young, in their late twenties, with crew cuts and impenetrable sunglasses, wearing grey suits. They couldn't have looked more like bodyguards if they'd tried.

'Where are your guys?' asked Woody, scanning the dockside with the binoculars.

'Close by,' said Murray.

Woody trained the binoculars on the superyacht. 'Okay, so I board at the side in a blind spot,' he said. 'But that means I'll be climbing up from the water.'

'We've fixed up a jet ski and we're muffling the engine as we speak. One of our guys will take you from the beach, around the port, and get up next to the Safe Haven. You climb up, do what you have to do, then you can climb down and you'll be picked up.'

'Assuming this isn't a test,' said Woody.

Murray frowned. 'What?'

'Just a joke,' said Woody. 'This MCS thing, do I get to practise with it?'

'No need,' said Murray. 'It's idiot-proof. No offence. There are four units, one for each hand and one for each foot. You maintain three points of contact while you move the fourth. The SAS and SBS use them for ship boarding, but commercial operators use them too. They are pretty much fail safe. Once we're ready we'll take you to the lock up we're using and get you set up with the MCS and a gun.'

'Until then, you can relax,' said Sam. She held out a room service menu. 'Are you hungry?'

Woody took the menu. 'I can always eat,' he said. 'I hope they've got steak.' He looked over at Murray. 'Fancy a steak, Murray? I'm guessing you're a medium rare kind of guy.'

# CHAPTER 55

WOODY was just finishing a delicious sirloin steak with red wine sauce when Sam's radio crackled. She was listening through her earpiece so he could only hear her side of the conversation, consisting mainly of the word 'yes' repeated in different tones, some enthusiastic, some hesitant. She stood up and went over to the windows and looked over at the Safe Haven as she continued to talk.

Murray inserted his earpiece so that he could listen in.

When Sam finished her conversation she removed her earpiece and looked over at Woody. 'Van Niekerk is getting ready to leave the Safe Haven. We're not sure where he's headed.'

'What about Zhang Shi?' asked Woody.

'His plane has just landed,' said Sam.

'Maybe he's going to collect him from the airport?'

Sam shook her head. 'If he was he'd have been there to meet him. They must be planning to meet somewhere else.' She frowned and looked over at Murray. 'What's going on, Murray? What are they up to?'

'No idea, but we have the ship and the airport under surveillance so we'll know sooner or later.'

'Hopefully sooner,' said Sam.

'Maybe Zhang Shi isn't sleeping on the ship tonight,' said Woody.

'No,' said Murray. 'We've been monitoring phone traffic to and fro. All Van Niekerk's communications are encrypted, but the chef has been telling his girlfriend about the Chinese breakfast he has to cook tomorrow.' He shrugged. 'Maybe they're having a night on the town.'

'I thought Van Niekerk hardly ever left the Safe Haven,' said Woody.

'That's true. But Zhang Shi is a special case. He's the source of much of Van Niekerk's money, so what he wants, he gets. Zhang Shi spends most of his time in Beijing where he can't afford to put a foot wrong. Plus his wife is the daughter of a top Chinese general.' She sighed. 'Anyway, there's no point in trying to guess, as Murray says, we've got them under surveillance. We'll find out what they're up to eventually.'

'My guess is that Zhang Shi wants a bit of fun before they get down to business?'

'It's possible,' said Sam. 'But it doesn't change anything. They'll head back to the boat - the ship - eventually.'

Woody rubbed his chin. 'There might be a better way.'

'I'm listening.'

'If they do go out to a bar or a restaurant, why don't I try to meet them? Chinese men seem to like me. If I play my cards right, Zhang Shi might offer to take me on board.'

'But you won't be armed,' said Sam.

Woody grinned. 'That's not been a problem in the past. As Murray says, there'll be plenty of guns on board.'

Sam looked over at Murray. 'What do you think?'

Murray shrugged. 'An invite would make our life easier. And if it falls through, we still have the MCS option.' He nodded. 'I say we go for it.'

'We?' said Woody. 'That would be the royal "we", would it?'

Sam smiled. 'You're part of a team now,' she said. 'Okay, we still need to know where they're going, but yes, why don't you get ready?'

'*Jasmine*,' said Woody. '*You're up.*'

# CHAPTER 56

JASMINE looked over at the entrance to the club. Two doormen in black suits were standing guard and more than two dozen hopefuls were lined up hoping to get in, their way barred by a velvet rope.

Sam was sitting next to her in the rear of a white Hyundai SUV. Murray was in the front passenger seat. He had his hand up to his radio earpiece and he was frowning as he listened.

The venue was La Terrazza, one of the top upmarket clubs in Marbella. There were two sections, a large 16th century villa that had been converted into a nightclub that featured top DJs from around the world, and a sprawling terrace that overlooked the sea.

'Okay, our man inside says that Van Niekerk and Zhang Shi are in the VIP section on the terrace,' said Murray, twisting around in his seat. 'There are four bodyguards with them. Two of Van Niekerk's guys and two Chinese. The bodyguards are sitting separately.'

'Do they have female company?' asked Sam.

'Not yet, but hookers are circling them like sharks around an Aussie swimmer.'

'I better get in there,' said Jasmine. She was wearing a tight fitting red dress that barely covered her thighs, with thin straps across her back, and had a small Louis Vuitton bag with a gold chain. 'How do I look?'

'Hot,' said Murray.

Jasmine grinned at him. 'Why Murray, I didn't know you cared.' She looked at Sam. 'I'll need some cash. Usually I get into clubs on my looks but money always helps smooth the way.' Sam looked at Murray and he took out his wallet. He handed Jasmine half a dozen twenty Euro notes and she laughed. 'When was the last time you tipped a doorman, baby?'

He forced a smile and gave her a hundred Euro note.

'Be careful in there,' said Sam. 'We have one guy inside but he's only there for surveillance purposes.'

'I'll be fine.'

'Assuming you can get yourself invited on board, we'll follow you back to the ship, but at a safe distance. And we'll keep it under observation with a view to picking you up when it's done.'

'I'll use the gangplank,' said Jasmine. 'Assuming that there's no fuss I'll just tell the bodyguards I'm done for the night.'

'And if there is a fuss?' asked Sam.

Jasmine grinned. 'I'll improvise.' She blew Murray a kiss and climbed out of the SUV.

'Tits and teeth,' she whispered to herself as she walked over to the entrance. One of the doormen spotted her and she put an extra swing into her step. She walked confidently, knowing from experience that it was confidence as much as the tip that persuaded a doorman to lift the velvet rope.

The doorman was clearly weighing her up, his face impassive. The dress showed off her arms as much as her legs. her skin was tanned and unblemished, her eyes bright and clear, so he could see that she wasn't a drug user. She might be a hooker but he'd have her pegged as a high class one and that would be no bar to entry.

She had the hundred Euro note in her right hand and she opened it enough for him to get a glimpse. 'How are you tonight, baby?' She purred, leaning forward to kiss him on both cheeks as she pressed the banknote into his hand. He had an earpiece in his right ear with a spiral wire tucked into his collar, presumably leading to a hidden transceiver.

'Always a pleasure,' he said, unclipping the velvet rope and ushering her in. 'You have a wonderful night.'

'Oh baby, I intend to,' she said. She walked up a short flight of wide steps and on to a sweeping terrace dotted with towering palms.

To the left was the main villa with two more black suited doormen standing guard at the entrance.

To her right was a bar, manned by three young men in matching white shirts and tight black trousers. They could have been triplets, with slicked-back glistening black hair and piercing blue eyes. One was mixing a cocktail, throwing a silver shaker high in the air every few seconds, occasionally twirling around in a full 360.

One of the bartenders saw her and flashed her a gleaming smile as she walked over. He had tanned skin and designer stubble and had left enough buttons undone to give her a clear view of a hairless glistening chest. 'What can I get you?' he asked in accented English.

'I'd like a dirty martini,' said Jasmine. 'The dirtier the better.'

The bartender grinned. 'Coming right up,' he said.

He opened a fridge and took out a chilled martini glass, then filled a mixing glass with ice, gin, vermouth and olive brine. He stirred, then used a straw to check it before straining the mix into the chilled glass and adding a skewed olive. 'I hope that's dirty enough,' he said with a sly smile.

She sipped it and nodded her appreciation. 'Perfect,' she said. She turned and looked over at the VIP area, plotting her route. Ideally she didn't want Zhang to see her coming, she needed the element of surprise. She headed towards the villa. There was a throbbing beat that she felt as much as heard, and several men tried to catch her eye as she walked by. She skirted around the villa's entrance, then went around the edge of the terrace. She stopped and looked over at the VIP section. Zhang and Van Niekerk were deep in conversation. The four bodyguards - two Chinese and two white - were sitting at a separate table, bottles of water in front of them. She sipped her martini. A Spanish man in a tight-fitting blue suit tried to catch her eye but she blanked him.

Zhang and Van Niekerk were sitting on adjacent sofas at right angles to each other, with a glass coffee table between them. The VIP area made up about a quarter of the terrace, bordered only by brass poles connected with thick red ropes. Some VIP areas were all about privacy but at the La Terrazza being a VIP meant flaunting your status.

There was a single doorman at the entrance to stop the non-VIPs entering but Jasmine knew from experience that access to most VIP areas could be gained by paying an extortionate bottle fee.

There were Arabs at several of the tables and a smattering of ornate hookah pipes. Most of the sofas were occupied by older men in designer suits accompanied by much younger women in tight-fitting dresses. A lot of selfies were being taken, with most of the women taking more interest in their phones than their companions.

Jasmine took another sip of her martini. Zhang was sitting on a sofa at the edge of the VIP area, his back to her. On the table between the two men was a bottle of champagne in an ice bucket. Van Niekerk was saying something and Zhang was nodding. They didn't seem interested in having any female company. She smiled and steadied herself. 'Tits and teeth,' she whispered.

She walked slowly towards the VIP area, then as she reached the brass poles she turned right and headed towards where Zhang was sitting. He was still nodding, all his attention focussed on Van Niekerk.

As she drew level with their table she slowed her walk, then faked a stumble, knocked into a brass pole and slopped her martini over Zhang Shi's shoulder. He yelped in surprise, then stood up and brushed his sleeve. The two Chinese bodyguards leapt to their feet but relaxed when they realised it was only a clumsy girl who had startled their boss.

'Oh my God, I'm so sorry, I'm so clumsy,' said Jasmine, reaching over the red rope to put a hand on his shoulder. He turned to glare at her, his nose wrinkled in disgust. She switched to Chinese. 'Please forgive me, Sir, I am so stupid. I will pay to have your suit cleaned, it is totally my fault.' She lowered her head in a submissive bow.

His glare softened. 'It's not a problem,' he said, in Mandarin. He smiled. 'You speak Chinese?' The two bodyguards were still standing watching them but Zhang gave them a dismissive wave and they sat down.

'A little,' she said. 'Please, I hope you will forgive my stupidity. I slipped on the catwalk last week and my ankle has been weak ever since. I shouldn't be wearing high heels, I know.'

He looked down at her legs. 'Oh no, I don't agree,' he said. 'You suit high heels.' He reached out and stroked her arm. 'The catwalk, you said. So you are a model?'

'I am. I am putting myself through university by wearing expensive clothes.' She smiled coyly. 'Someone has to do it.'

'And what are you studying?'

'Law.'

'Oh no,' he said, shaking his head. 'Surely the world has enough lawyers?'

'You never see a poor lawyer.'

'Ah, so you want to be rich?'

'Doesn't everybody,' she said.

He chuckled. 'What is your name, pretty lady?'

'Jasmine.'

'Now that is a lovely name.'

'May I ask your name, even though I ruined your suit.'

'I am Shi. Zhang Shi.' He held out his hand and they shook. He kept hold of her hand as if he was scared she would run off. 'Will you join me?'

'Really? After I threw my drink over you?'

'It would be my pleasure.'

'You are too kind, thank you.'

Zhang waved over at the bouncer, pointed at Jasmine, then pointed at his sofa. The bouncer nodded and Zhang finally released his grip on Jasmine's hand. She walked over to the bouncer who stepped aside to let her through. She went around to the sofas where Zhang and Van Niekerk were sitting.

Zhang was waiting for her, bobbing up and down with excitement. He grabbed her arm as soon as she was within range and sat her down. 'This is my friend, Mr Van Niekerk,' he said, in accented English as he sat down next to her.

'Pleased to meet you,' said Jasmine, extending her hand.

Van Niekerk smiled coldly. For a second she thought he was going to snub the offer, but then he looked up at Zhang, smiled, and shook her hand. 'Likewise,' he said, with zero enthusiasm.

'Please, Jasmine, sit,' said Zhang, switching back into Chinese. He waved at a waitress for a glass. 'Would you like champagne? We are drinking a very nice Dom Perignon.'

'That sounds lovely.' She smiled at Van Niekerk and he smiled back without warmth. 'Thank you so much for inviting me to sit with you,' she said.

'I didn't,' he said. 'It was Shi's idea. I have to say, if you'd thrown your drink over me I'd have sent you packing.'

'I'm so clumsy,' she said.

'Right,' said Van Niekerk. 'That would explain it.'

The waitress returned with a crystal flute. She filled it with champagne and handed it to Jasmine. Zhang picked up his glass and clinked it against hers. 'To chance meetings,' he said in Mandarin.

'They are always the best,' she replied, and sipped her champagne.

Van Niekerk folded his arms and sat back in his sofa. He obviously wasn't happy at her arrival, but clearly wasn't going to say anything.

Zhang slid across the sofa so that his leg was touching hers. 'Why is your Chinese so good?' he asked. 'I have never heard a foreigner speak Chinese as good as you.'

'Karaoke,' she said.

'Karaoke?' He laughed. 'I don't believe you.'

'It's true! I love karaoke and I went to a club in Chinatown in London and they had Chinese songs. They had the lyrics in Chinese characters but they also had the phonetic sounds so I was able to sing them. After a while I started to recognise the characters. I have a good memory and without even trying I soon had a vocabulary of a few hundred words. Then I got really interested in the language and started studying it properly, mainly on YouTube.' She realised that Van Niekerk was listening and switched back to English. 'Do you speak Chinese, Mr Van Niekerk?' she asked.

He shook his head.

'I was just explaining to Shi how I learned to speak it.'

'Her Chinese is perfect,' said Zhang, nodding enthusiastically.

'Good to know,' said Van Niekerk. He sipped his champagne and turned away, clearly unwilling to have any sort of conversation with her.

Jasmine turned her attention to Zhang, looking into his eyes as if he was the centre of her universe. He shuffled closer to her and put his hand on her knee. 'So is he your good friend?' she asked, switching back to Mandarin.

'More of a business associate,' he said. 'He is useful to the Chinese Government.'

'So you work for the government?' she asked.

He smiled. 'Jasmine, I am the government.'

'And you are doing business in Spain?'

'In Africa, mainly. Janco was born in Africa and he knows which wheels to grease. But better we meet here, on neutral territory.'

'I'm glad that you chose Marbella. If you had gone somewhere else, I wouldn't have bumped into you.'

He squeezed her thigh. 'Literally.'

She laughed. 'Yes, literally. Perhaps fate was guiding my hand.'

'Guiding your ankle, perhaps. To make you trip towards me.'

They chatted for half an hour, though it was mainly Zhang talking and Jasmine hanging on his every word. They finished the bottle of champagne and Zhang ordered another, then placed his glass on the table. 'Forgive me, I must visit the bathroom.'

'Hurry back,' she said.

'Wise men are never in a hurry,' said Zhang, patting her thigh. 'But in your case, I will make an exception.' He leaned over and kissed her on the cheek, then headed for the bathroom. Jasmine watched him go.

'Shi is obviously very taken with you,' said Van Niekerk.

'He's a nice man,' said Jasmine. 'Very interesting to talk to. He has many stories.'

'And what about you, Jasmine? What's your story?'

'Oh, I'm not sure that I have a story, Mr Van Niekerk.'

He smiled thinly. 'Everybody has a story,' he said. 'I look at you, and I can read your story as if it were a book.'

'Really?'

'You're a hooker on the make,' he said. 'You spotted Shi and thought he'd be a good earner. You spilled your drink on him and showed off your Mandarin language skills, which are obviously impressive. Do you have a lot of Chinese clients?'

'You've got me wrong, Mr Van Niekerk. I'm just here for a night out. My friends went home early and I decided to stay. Bumping into Shi was just a happy coincidence.'

Van Niekerk leaned towards her. 'Darling, you've got hooker written all over you. But I don't care. Provided you keep Shi sweet, I'm more than happy to pay for your champagne.' He grinned. 'And any other charges.'

Jasmine frowned. 'I don't think I understand.'

Van Niekerk laughed and patted her leg. 'It's not rocket science, sweetheart. You give Shi what he wants, and I'll pick up the tab. How much do you charge?'

Jasmine shrugged. 'It depends. If it's all night, five thousand.'

'Euros or dollars?'

'When in Spain....'

Van Niekerk smiled. 'Euros it is, then. I'll pay that, so don't ask him for any money.'

'No problem, Mr Van Niekerk.'

'Where do you normally take clients?'

'That's up to them. Dancing, eating, catch a show. Whatever they want.'

'I meant for the happy ending.'

Jasmine laughed. 'Usually their hotel. Or their home if they're local and there isn't a wife. There are hotels I can use if they don't have a place.'

'I don't want you taking him to a seedy hotel.'

Jasmine raised her eyebrows. 'What do you think I am? Nothing less than four stars.'

'I mean I don't want you taking him to any hotel, I don't care how many stars it has. Shi has a reputation to protect.'

Jasmine frowned. 'So what am I supposed to do?'

Van Niekerk held out his hand. Jasmine wasn't sure what he wanted, but then he clicked his fingers and pointed at her bag. She handed it over. He opened it and scrutinised the contents - the cash that Sam had given her, an unopened pack of condoms, a tube of KY jelly, a pen, comb, a lipstick and a hotel keycard. Van Niekerk wrinkled his nose and looked at her. 'No passport or ID card?'

'I don't carry either while I'm working.'

'No credit cards?'

'The client pays for everything.'

'Okay. But no cellphone? How do you work without a cellphone?'

'The client gets my undivided attention. There's no way I would answer my phone if I was with a client.'

'You could put it on silent.'

'Robbery is an ever present risk in this line of work. I had a phone stolen once. Never again.'

'That's why no jewellery or watch?'

Jasmine smiled and nodded. 'Exactly.'

Van Niekerk gave her back the bag. "Right, here's the deal. Shi is staying with me on my yacht. It's the Safe Haven, moored at Puerto Banús.'

Jasmine grimaced. 'I don't like yachts. I get seasick.'

'The Safe Haven isn't a regular yacht. It's big. Trust me, no one goes on board and complains about the size.'

'Size isn't everything, Mr Van Niekerk,' she said with a sly smile. 'Is it one of those superyachts?'

Van Niekerk chuckled. 'Yes, it is.'

She leaned towards him, giving him a glimpse of cleavage. 'So are you, mega rich?'

Van Niekerk grinned. 'I am, yes. But don't get any ideas, Jasmine. I have never paid for sex and I never intend to.'

'Oh Mr Van Niekerk, everybody pays,' she said with a sly smile. 'One way or another.'

'That might well be true,' he said. 'But Shi is your client, remember that. If he wants a happy ending tonight, that's fine. But don't charge him, I'll pay your bill in full. Just make sure that you do everything that he wants.'

'That's what the KY is for,' she said.

Van Niekerk laughed and slapped his knee. 'I like you, Jasmine.'

'I like you too, Mr Van Niekerk.'

'I think you should call me Janco.'

'Then I will, Janco.'

'The client always gets what he wants?'

She held his look and smiled. 'Definitely. One hundred per cent.'

He looked over her shoulder. 'Okay, he's coming back. Do what it is that you do, I'll settle up with you later.'

Jasmine sat back and crossed her legs slowly. 'I look forward to it,' she purred.

# CHAPTER 57

JASMINE looked up at the Safe Haven as the white stretch limo came to a halt. 'Now that is a big ship,' she said. 'It looks like the dictionary definition of a superyacht.' She was sitting next to Zhang at the back of the limo. His hand was massaging her thigh as if he was kneading dough, and he was openly leering at her breasts. He was drunk, sweating and blinking and breathing all over her.

Van Niekerk was sitting to the side, his legs stretched out as he puffed on a cigar. 'Have you been on one before?' he asked.

'No, I'm a superyacht virgin,' she said, and Van Niekerk chuckled and shook his head.

A red SUV pulled up behind them, containing the four bodyguards. The four men climbed out and looked around. One of the Chinese men walked over to the limo and opened the door. Zhang climbed out first and kept hold of Jasmine's hand so that she had no choice other than follow him out.

They had parked close to the yacht's rear gangplank. There were two more suited bodyguards standing on the dock, and two members of the crew on the yacht itself, a man in his thirties and a younger woman, both wearing white uniforms with logos of the yacht on their breast pockets.

Van Niekerk led the way. The two bodyguards greeted him with nods, the two crew members saluted and the man welcomed him back. Van Niekerk gestured at Jasmine. 'This is a guest of Mr Zhang, she will be with him on deck three. Let me know if she goes anywhere else.'

'Will do, Mr Van Neikerk.'

Van Neikerk strode towards an elevator. Zhang followed, still clutching Jasmine's hand.

'Welcome aboard, Mr Zhang,' said the man, saluting. He nodded at Jasmine. 'Miss.'

'Thank you so much, Captain,' said Jasmine.

'He's not the captain,' snapped Van Neikerk, without looking around. He jabbed at the button to call the lift. The four bodyguards headed for the stairs.

Zhang and Jasmine joined him as the lift doors opened. It was a large lift with brass rails and mirrored walls, and there was a chandelier hanging from the ceiling. There were six buttons and Van Neikerk prodded the ones for the third and fourth deck. 'Mr Zhang is staying on deck three,' said Van Neikerk.

'And you're in the penthouse?'

'The master cabin,' said Van Neikerk.

She held his look. 'Because you're the master?'

'Because it's my yacht.'

The lift doors closed and they rode upwards. Zhang was staring at Jasmine's cleavage and he squeezed her hand so tightly that she could feel her fingers grinding together.

'So, I will see you in the morning for breakfast, Shi,' said Van Neikerk.

Zhang nodded, his eyes fixed on Jasmine's breasts. 'Yes, breakfast. Good, good.'

The doors opened and Zhang stepped out, pulling Jasmine with him. Jasmine looked over her shoulder. Van Neikerk flashed her a cold smile and pointed upwards. Jasmine got the message. He wanted her to go to his cabin after she'd finished with Zhang. She grinned and winked. That had been her plan from the start.

The doors closed and Van Neikerk disappeared from view. The two Chinese bodyguards appeared at the stairs, gasping for breath. Van Niekerk's bodyguards continued up the stairs to the top deck.

'Do they follow you everywhere?' asked Jasmine.

'Yes, everywhere,' he said.

'You need protection from me?'

Zhang laughed. 'Not from you, but people in power are always at risk.'

'You have enemies?'

'Everyone has enemies,' said Zhang. 'Especially people like me. I am in Government and sometimes the Government does things that make people unhappy. Like when we had Covid. We had to force people to stay in their homes and they did not like that. So they blame those in power and sometimes they lash out.'

Jasmine smiled and squeezed his hand. 'Well at least you are safe with me.' She nodded at the bodyguards. 'They don't stay in the cabin with you, do they?'

'Of course not,' he said. 'They stay in the corridor.' He looked at his watch. 'They will be finishing their shift, soon.'

'What happens then?'

'Two more will take their place.'

'So you have security 24-7?'

'It is the price of power,' said Zhang. He opened the door. He went through first, pulling her after him like a dog that was about to be disciplined.

The cabin was enormous, with a seating area with two large sofas and a large television, a dining table with eight chairs, and a large balcony overlooking the superyacht in the neighbouring berth.

'This is amazing,' said Jasmine, playing the wide-eyed ingénue to the hilt. She put her bag on a side table.

'I've been in better,' said Zhang, looking around. He pulled her through sliding doors that led through to a bedroom that was almost as big as the sitting room. The bed was a super king-size with pristine white linen and half a dozen overstuffed pillows. The walls were panelled and dotted with works of art and two more sliding doors led to a marble-lined bathroom.

'I could give you a bath and a massage,' said Jasmine.

211

'I want to fuck you,' said Zhang, squeezing her hand.

'Baby, that's a given,' she said. 'But let's take it slowly, shall we?' She prised her hand from his grasp, kissed him softly on the cheek, then slowly undid his tie. 'Let me undress you,' she whispered. 'I am here to serve you.'

He was trembling and his face was bathed in sweat.

She pulled the tie from his collar and held it up. 'Close your eyes,' she whispered.

'What?'

'Trust me.' She leaned forward and kissed him softly on the cheek.

He closed his eyes and she looped the tie around his head, twice, blindfolding him. She fastened it with a bow. 'Perfect,' she said.

She took off his jacket and dropped it onto the floor, then undid his shirt and slipped it off his shoulders. He was shaking now, and his man breasts wobbled like dying fish gasping for breath. She tweaked a nipple and he gasped. 'Shhhh,' she whispered, and kissed him on the cheek again.

She undid his belt and trousers and let them fall around his feet. He was wearing Ralph Lauren boxers, which were fighting to restrain his penis. The material was already damp from pre-cum, the guy was obviously a sprinter rather than a marathon runner. She ran her hand along his erection and he gasped and began jabbering in Chinese.

'English,' she said.

'I want to come,' he gasped.

'Well I can see that baby, but let's take this step by step. Lie down on the bed.' She held his arm and guided him over, then helped him lie down in the middle of the bed. His socks were black, matching his boxers, and she decided to leave them on.

'Hurry, please hurry!' he said.

'Almost there, baby,' she whispered, and walked over to the bathroom. There were two fluffy white robes on the back of the bathroom door. Sofia pulled out the belts and took them into the bedroom. She tossed one onto the bed and tied one end of the other one around Zhang's right wrist.

'What are you doing?' he croaked.

'You are my prisoner, Mr Zhang,' she said. 'I am going to do whatever I want and you won't be able to stop me.'

He was panting now and his penis was twitching in time with his ragged breaths.

'Is that what you want, Mr Zhang?'

'Oh yes. Please. I want.'

'Good boy,' she said. She threaded the belt around the headboard and tied the other end around his left wrist.

'I want to see you,' he gasped.

'It's better you don't,' she said.

'Your body is perfect. You are a goddess.'

'Oh, baby, you have such a sweet mouth.'

She used the second robe belt to tie his feet together. His erection was twitching like a metronome now and there was a dark patch on the front of his boxer shorts.

'Nearly there, baby,' she said. She took off her panties and climbed onto the bed. She straddled his chest and he gasped. 'Yes, yes, I want it!' he shouted.

'Hush baby, we don't want to alarm your bodyguards,' she whispered. She rubbed her panties over his face and he groaned. 'Do you like that, baby?' she whispered.

'Yes,' he grunted. 'I do. You are so sexy. I've never been with anyone like you before.'

'Oh, I'm quite sure that's true, baby,' she said. 'Now be a good boy and open your mouth.'

He did as he was told and she pushed the panties between his teeth. He began to gag and thrash around. 'Easy, baby,' she said. 'Breathe through your nose.'

Zhang's nostrils flared and he stopped struggling.

'Good boy,' she whispered. She leaned over the bed and pulled his leather belt from his trousers and fastened it around his mouth.

He started breathing quickly again and she patted him on the cheek. 'Don't panic, baby. You can breathe though your nose just fine.' She bent down and planted a light kiss on his forehead. 'Somebody will come and release you in a few hours,' she whispered. 'Until then just try to relax.'

She rolled off the bed. She had been in the cabin for less than ten minutes so to leave now would look suspicious. She sat down on the sofa and swung her legs up. Forty-five minutes would be the minimum. An hour would be better. She lay back and stared up at the ceiling. Zhang continued to struggle at his bonds but they were secure and there was no way he was getting loose. Provided he didn't hyperventilate, he'd be okay.

The minutes ticked by.

'*Sofia, you're up,*' said Woody eventually. '*Time to go.*'

# CHAPTER 58

SOFIA picked up her bag, checked herself in the mirror, and opened the cabin door. One of the bodyguards was sitting on a chair, looking at his smartphone. The other was standing by the lift. 'Mr Zhang is sleeping now,' she said. 'He doesn't want to be disturbed.'

The bodyguard leered at her and said something to her in Chinese. 'English,' she said.

'How about give me a blow job before you go?' he said in heavily accented English.

'Sure, you got a thousand Euros, honey?'

'Your mouth made of gold is it?'

Sofia grinned. 'Platinum, dickhead,' she said. She walked by him to the lift and pressed the up button.

The bodyguard by the lift frowned at her. 'Where are you going?' he asked.

'Mr Van Niekerk said he wanted to see me before I left,' she said. 'Maybe he has a thousand Euros.' She licked her lips suggestively and laughed.

The bodyguard scowled at her and muttered something in Chinese to his colleague.

The lift arrived and Sofia walked in. She pressed the button for the fourth deck and checked herself in the mirrored wall as the doors closed. She looked fine, but she added a touch of lipstick.

The lift doors opened onto a corridor almost identical to the one on the deck below, albeit with a much higher ceiling. There were two bodyguards standing in front of double doors. Clean cut white guys wearing grey suits. The younger of the two pulled a Glock from an underarm holster as she stepped out of the lift, then he grinned. 'It's only the hooker,' he said to his colleague, and put the gun away. He had an American accent.

'I like to think of myself as a high class escort, actually,' said Sofia, as she walked towards them.

'Yeah, well I like to think of myself as Brad Pitt but I am what I am,' said the older of the two. He was also American. He was big, broad-chested and well over six feet tall. Like his colleague he was wearing a crisp white shirt and a blue tie.

'Mr Van Niekerk said I was to drop in before I went,' she said.

'Yeah,' said the older one. 'He said.'

Sofia flashed him a sly smile. 'Aren't you going to frisk me?'

'Do you want to be frisked?' the man growled.

Sofia laughed. She raised her hands above her head and did a slow turn. They both gave her body a good looking over.

'You are fit,' said the younger one.

'You're pretty fit yourself,' she said. Actually he was gawky with a receding chin and a rash of old acne scars across both cheeks.

He grinned.'Where do you normally work?' he asked.

'Honey you couldn't afford me,' she said. She nodded at the doors. 'Better not keep Mr Van Niekerk waiting.'

The older one knocked on the door and disappeared inside, reappearing a few seconds later. 'He'll see you,' he said, holding the door open for her.

Sofia blew him a kiss and walked through. The bodyguard closed the door behind her.

The master cabin was almost twice the size of the one that Zhang was in. The doors opened onto a small room with modern art on the wall, paintings that looked as if they had been created by a toddler throwing paint at random. Two doors opened onto the main cabin. There were two large balconies to the left, one with a large Jacuzzi, the other with four sun loungers. There were three large white leather sofas around a glass coffee table. Van Niekerk was sitting in the

216

middle sofa, holding a crystal tumbler. He had changed out of his suit and was wearing a white robe, loosely tied at the waist. His hair was damp from the shower. He raised the glass in salute 'How did it go?' he asked. There were more double doors behind him, open just enough to reveal a super king size bed.

'He came, I went.' Sofia shrugged. 'Job done.'

'It is just a job for you, right? No emotional attachments?'

'I don't fuck for free, if that's what you're asking,' said Sofia.

Van Niekerk gestured with his glass at an envelope on the coffee table in front of him. 'Speaking of which…"

She walked over and bent down to pick up the envelope. She looked up and smiled when she caught him leering at her breasts. She took her time straightening up, then ran her thumb along the Euro notes. She frowned. 'This is more than we agreed,' she said.

He shrugged. 'I thought you deserved a tip.'

She gave him a small curtsy. 'Thank you, kind sir,' she said.

He waved his glass in the air. 'Do you want a drink?'

'What are you having?'

He grinned. 'A single malt whisky that was laid down before I was born.'

'I'll try that.'

He waved at a sideboard. 'Help yourself.'

Sofia put the envelope in her bag and walked over to the sideboard, on which were a dozen or so bottles of spirits. Among them was a bottle of 72 year old Macallan. It was half full. Sofia smiled. Or half empty, depending on your point of view. She unscrewed the top and poured a large measure into a crystal tumbler, then used her fingers to drop in three cubes of ice from a silver ice bucket. She sipped it and smacked her lips appreciatively. 'Oh, honey, that hits the spot. I'm usually a vodka drinker, but this is good.'

She drained the glass and he laughed. 'You're supposed to savour it,' he said. 'Not down it in one.'

Sofia poured herself another large measure.

'That costs more than a hundred grand a bottle,' he said. 'Just so you know.'

She picked up the bottle. 'Worth every penny,' she said. She took the glass and the bottle over to him. 'Can I top you up?'

He held out his glass and she filled it almost to the brim. 'Steady!' he said.

Sofia grinned. 'You can afford it, honey,' she said. She put her own glass on the table and screwed the cap onto the bottle, then headed back to the sideboard.

Van Niekerk sipped his whisky, taking care not to spill any.

As Sofia walked behind his chair, she turned and smacked the bottle against the side of his head. It made a dull thudding sound and he fell across the sofa. His glass fell from his nerveless fingers. 'Oh honey, you've spilled your drink,' she said.

She took her Louis Vuitton bag off her shoulder, wrapped the chain twice around his neck, then pulled hard, lifting his head against the back of the sofa. For a few seconds he remained still, then he began to claw at the chain. Sofia put her right foot against the back of the sofa and pulled harder.

His legs kicked out and his head thrashed from side to side but his fingers couldn't get underneath the chain so his movements got progressively weaker. The only sound he made was a soft grunting noise. She could only see the back of his head but she was sure that his eyes would be wide and fearful, knowing what was happening but being unable to do anything about it.

He clawed at his neck for about thirty seconds and then his hands fell away. Sofia kept her foot on the back of the sofa and continued to pull on the chain. Strangulation produced unconsciousness in less than a minute but it took up to four minutes to be fatal. It was less to do with stopping air getting to the lungs and more to do with disrupting the blood flow to the brain - but either way anything less than four minutes did not guarantee a kill.

Sofia counted off the seconds as she kept the pressure on. Only when she had reached two hundred and forty did she release her grip on the chain. There was froth on Van Niekerk's lips and his lifeless eyes were specked with blood.

'Sorry you spilled your whisky, honey,' she said as she unwound the chain from his neck. 'Send me the dry cleaning bill if you want.'

She slung the bag over her shoulder, then went over to a mirror and checked her make up. She took out her lipstick and added a touch more colour to her lips, then headed for the door.

The two bodyguards were standing with their backs to the wall. She could clearly see the bulges made by their holstered weapons. She smiled brightly and took the envelope of cash from her bag. She waved it in front of them. 'It's been a good night's work, boys,' she said. She opened the envelope and gave a hundred Euro note to the older of the two.

He frowned as he stared at the money.

'I always believe in spreading the wealth,' she said. 'We've all got our jobs to do, right?'

'Right,' he said. He took the banknote and put it into his wallet.

She gave another hundred Euro note to the younger one. He held it and grinned. 'What would this get me?' he said hopefully.

Sofia laughed. 'With me? A five minute dirty phone call.'

She put the envelope back in her bag. 'And with that, boys, I shall call it a night. It's been a pleasure.' She headed for the lift, swinging her hips to give them something to look at.

She had taken half a dozen steps when she heard one of the men knock on Van Niekerk's door. She cursed silently. The man knocked again, and then opened the door.

She increased her pace. She reached the lift but she didn't stop and headed for the stairs instead. The further away she was from the bodyguards, the better.

She was about ten feet from the stairs when she heard the older bodyguard shout. 'Stop the bitch!'

'What happened?' called the younger one.

'Van Niekerk's dead! Stop her!'

Sofia reached the top of the stairs but as she moved towards them she heard the crack of a gun and a round whistled by her head and thwacked into the wall. 'Stay where you are!' shouted the bodyguard. He fired again but the shot went wide.

The stairs were no longer an option. The Chinese bodyguards on deck three would certainly have heard the shots and the armed guards on the gangplank would be waiting for her.

She ran down the corridor, zig-zagging from side to side. A second shot rang out and this time the round passed so close to her that she felt the wind as it passed her by. She turned right and grabbed at the handle of a cabin door. To her relief it opened and she ducked inside.

It was a small cabin and as she slammed the door shut she realised there was a naked man lying on the bed, a Glock on the table next to him. She locked the door and leapt towards the man as he fumbled for the gun. He got to it but she grabbed the barrel and twisted it out of his grasp.

'What the…' he began but she caught him short by smashing the gun against his temple. He fell back on the bed, out for the count. She looked at the gun. A Glock 19. He was probably one of the off-duty bodyguards.

A fist pounded against the door. 'Eric, you got her?' shouted the older bodyguard.

'Eric's not available at the moment!' Sofia shouted.

'Listen, bitch, you're not going anywhere. You come out with your hands up, and we won't have to do any damage to your pretty little body.'

'Yeah, I'll pass,' said Sofia.

A shot rang out and a round thudded against the door, but it was strong enough to take the hit.

The older bodyguard said something, presumably talking to his colleague.

Sofia looked around the cabin. It was about twenty feet square with a door leading to a small bathroom. Staff quarters, obviously. There was a sliding window that opened on to a balcony where there was a single white plastic chair. Fighting her way out wasn't an option. And there was the possibility that they would call the local cops.

There was a wooden chair in a corner of the cabin. She took it and jammed it under the door handle. That should hold them for a while if they did decide to break in.

'So, are you coming out, bitch, or are we coming in?' shouted the older bodyguard.

'You know I've got Eric's Glock 19, don't you?' she shouted.

'Yeah, but do you know how to use it?'

'You'll find out soon enough if you try to come in,' she said.

She slid the window open and a cool breeze blew in. Opposite was another superyacht, about fifty feet away. She stepped onto the balcony and shuddered when she saw how high up she was. 'I hate heights,' she whispered.

'*Okay, Jim,*' said Woody. '*You're up.*'

# CHAPTER 59

JIM looked down at the water far below. A hundred feet, maybe more. Perfectly doable. He put the gun on the plastic chair, then kicked off the high heels and dropped them off the balcony. Anyone who had read the story of Cinderella knew that you could be tracked by your shoes. And it wouldn't be a handsome prince who was looking this time. He would have happily dumped the Louis Vuitton bag, too, but it seemed a shame to throw away all that cash so he wrapped the strap around his left arm.

The door shuddered and he heard the splintering of wood. It wouldn't hold for much longer. The neighbouring yacht was about fifty feet away from the Safe Haven, with nothing but water between them. He wouldn't be able to swim to the stern because there were two bodyguards there. He could swim to the bow but that would take time and he'd be a sitting duck. He smiled to himself. A swimming duck. Either way, an easy target, even with handguns.

The door shuddered again. Swimming wasn't an option. He stood on the chair, then stepped up onto the balcony railing and launched himself into the air in a perfect swan dive, legs tight together, arms outstretched as if he was crucified. The wind pulled at the dress as he soared through the air.

His mind raced. Diving feet first into water was always the safest bet, but he was an experienced diver and had no qualms about going head first. He wasn't sure how deep the water was but the keel of the Safe Haven must have been dozens of feet so there would be more then enough water to slow his descent before he hit the bottom. All he had to do was to make sure that he entered the water as straight as possible and that his fists punched their way through first.

As always when he was airborne, time seemed to slow to a crawl. He had all the time in the world to take in his surroundings and to make the small but vital changes to his posture to keep himself on the correct arc.

He began to pick up speed and his head and arms dipped down. He kept his arms outstretched and his legs together. He accelerated as gravity worked its magic. He was looking at the Safe Haven now, still moving in slow motion so he was able to see each deck clearly as it went by.

As he reached the bottom of the superstructure, he brought his arms together and bunched his hands into fists. He kept looking at the waves below as the water rushed up towards him, then at the last second he tucked his chin against his chest and closed his eyes.

He took a deep breath just before his fists smacked through the water, punching a hole for his head and shoulders to go through. The world went suddenly silent and he opened his eyes. His momentum was carrying him down towards the seabed. He angled his arms and arched his back so that he was moving towards the black hull of the neighbouring superyacht.

As he slowed he began to swim, pulling himself through the water. Once he got to thirty feet down, negative buoyancy kicked in and it became noticeably easier to keep moving down. He used his arms and his legs as smoothly as possible, keeping his metabolism low. Jim was an experienced free diver and under perfect conditions he could hold his breath under water for up to seven minutes, but swimming under the hull of a superyacht was far from ideal. The bag was banging against his left arm which was annoying and slowing him a little, but he stayed focussed. There was barely any light but he couldn't miss the black hull ahead of him. He needed to go deeper so he bent at the waist and kicked harder.

Finally he saw the bottom of the hull and he rolled over onto his back, using his hands and feet to push himself along. He reached the midpoint of the hull just as the breath reflex kicked in with a vengeance. The urge to open his mouth was almost unbearable, as was the burning in his chest. If it hadn't been for his training and experience, he would have given in to the reflex and sucked in water, but he knew that if he simply ignored what his body was telling him to do, the urge would pass.

He concentrated on moving along the hull, finally starting to head upwards. The burning reached a crescendo, then began to fade, and the sense of panic went with it. He no longer felt the urge to breathe, even though his body was consuming oxygen at exactly the same rate as before.

He pushed himself away from the hull and kicked with his legs, fighting against the negative buoyancy. Every kick and pull of his arms used up precious oxygen, but without the effort he would sink to the seabed.

He looked up but there was only darkness. He moved his arms slowly and rhythmically, clawing his way up to the surface. He reached the thirty foot mark and finally he became buoyant again and he was able to put his arms by his side and just move his feet slowly to keep rising

Eventually he burst through the surface and he opened his mouth and sucked in air, treading water as he looked around. He heard shouts from the Safe Haven, presumably the bodyguards trying to work out where he'd gone. There was no way they would know that he had swum under the neighbouring superyacht, they would almost certainly assume that the fall had been fatal.

Jim began to swim slowly towards the dock, using a relaxed breast stroke and moving his head from side to side, listening intently. There was every possibility that there would be crew members manning the gangplank, so he wasn't safe yet.

He reached the stern. The shouts had died down now. He worked his way under the wooden dock. The water was slapping against the metal support posts, which would cover any sound he made as he began to swim under the dock by the Safe Haven.

The dock was a couple of hundred metres in length and he moved slowly, so it took him the best part of ten minutes to reach the end. He found a ladder and slowly climbed up. There was no sign of any police cars or ambulances, but there were now four bodyguards standing on the Safe Haven's gangplank.

The dock split into two legs, each with moorings for dozens of small yachts and motor vessels. It was late but people were still walking around, mainly couples arm in arm, gawping at how the other half lived. In the distance he saw the white SUV, parked with its lights off. He was fairly sure Murray and Sam hadn't seen him, their attention would be focussed on the stern of the Safe Haven.

The bodyguards weren't looking in his direction so he climbed onto the dock and began walking away. He unwound the Louis Vuitton bag from around his arm and slung it over his shoulder. Several faces frowned when they saw how wet he was but he kept his head up.

He walked off the dock and headed towards the car park. To his right he heard a siren and in the distance he saw a police car heading towards the port, its blue light flashing. He ran towards the SUV, bent low, his bare feet slapping on the ground. Sam yelped in surprise as he grabbed the handle of the rear passenger door and pulled it open,.

*'Okay Jim,'* said Woody. *'I'm up.'*

# CHAPTER 60

WOODY grinned at Murray as he twisted around in the driving seat. 'What the hell happened?' Murray asked.

'Change of plan,' said Woody, slamming the door. 'I had to think on my feet.'

'Why are you wet?' asked Sam. 'You're soaked through.'

'I went for a midnight swim,' said Woody. The police car stopped next to a dockside bar. The siren went off but the blue light continued to flash.

'You must be freezing,' said Sam. She slipped off her jacket and wrapped it around his shoulders. 'Is it done?'

'Done and dusted,' said Woody. 'Can we go to the hotel? I need to change.'

'Yes, of course,' said Sam. She nodded at Murray. He put the car in gear and headed towards the hotel. 'What about Zhang?'

'I left him tied to his bed in his boxer shorts,' said Woody. 'I'm guessing they'll be untying him about now.' He grinned. 'He's got some explaining to do. I gagged him with my panties.'

Sam laughed. 'That was naughty. What about collateral damage?'

'None,' said Woody. 'I had to knock out one of Van Niekerk's bodyguards but he'll just have a sore head. They fired a couple of potshots at me but I decided that discretion was the better part of valour and jumped over the side.'

Sam frowned. 'You did what?'

Woody shrugged. 'I figured there was no way I could make it to the gangplank so I jumped.'

'From the fourth deck?'

'Well that was where Van Niekerk's cabin was.'

'You could have killed yourself.'

'Only if I screwed up, and I didn't.'

Sam shook her head in amazement. 'That wasn't the plan.'

'No, but once they'd pulled out their guns, my options were limited.'

'And what about Van Niekerk?'

'Like I said, job done.'

'How?'

Woody smiled and held up the Louis Vuitton bag. 'Strangled him with the strap.'

'Nice.'

Woody opened the bag and showed her the wet wad of Euros. 'And I was paid for my trouble.'

Sam laughed. 'Well done you.'

'No problem me keeping the ill gotten gains?'

'None at all,' said Sam.

'I'm starting to like this job.'

# CHAPTER 61

MARIANNE sipped her water and looked out of the Gulfstream's window. Below the plane was only darkness, she had no idea if they were flying over clouds or the ocean.

Sam came over with a mug of coffee and dropped down onto the seat opposite her. 'Penny for your thoughts,' she said.

Marianne shrugged. 'I wasn't thinking of anything, really.'

'You had very deep frown lines,' said Sam. 'As if you were struggling with something.'

'I'm fine. Really.'

'Can you talk me through what happened on the ship?'

Marianne's eyes narrowed. 'Why?'

'Just so I know what the ramifications might be. And if there are lessons to be learned.'

'You do this after every kill?'

'We prefer to call them operations, but yes.'

Marianne chuckled. 'I'm not sure that operation is the right word at all. An operation is what a surgeon does to make you feel better. We do the opposite.'

'I suppose so. Semantics. But "kill" isn't a word we like to throw around. Obviously we saw you get on to the Safe Haven with Zhang and Van Niekerk but we've no idea what happened after that.'

Marianne sipped her water, then went through everything that had taken place on the yacht. Sam listened and alternated between nodding and sipping her coffee. Murray and two of his men were at the rear of the plane, sleeping. At times Marianne felt as if she was in a confessional, unburdening herself to a priest. Except there would be no absolution from Sam. Nobody could absolve her. She had taken a life for no other reason than she had been told to.

'That is amazing,' said Sam, once Marianne had finished. 'You just jumped?'

'I had no choice, they were breaking the cabin door down.'

'And then you swam under the other yacht?'

Marianne nodded.

'How long did that take?'

'A couple of minutes.'

'You held your breath for two minutes?'

'Obviously.'

Sam laughed. 'No, I mean that's not something I could do. I've heard of free divers being able to hold their breath for minutes at a time, but only after years of training.'

'I didn't really have a choice,' said Marianne.

'Where did you acquire skills like that?' asked Sam.

Marianne shrugged and stared out of the window.

'You can dive, you're an expert marksman, you can fight guys twice your size, you speak Chinese and Russian. How can you possibly do all that?'

Marianne didn't answer. She could feel her heart pounding in her chest and she was finding it difficult to breathe.

'And you had no problems despatching Van Niekcrk or Kwok in Hong Kong.'

'I did what you told me to do.' Her mouth had gone dry despite all the water she was drinking.

'Yes, you did. You were a trooper. But you did it brilliantly, and with no regrets. No conscience. You're a killing machine, Marianne.'

'Which is why you use me, right?'

'But I don't understand how you acquired all those skills. Or how you're able to kill so effortlessly.'

Marianne could barely breathe now. Her chest felt as if it had been wrapped in steel. And she was seeing lights flashing at the periphery of her vision.

'I need to use the bathroom,' she whispered. The bottle fell from her fingers and hit the floor. She opened her mouth but this time the words wouldn't come and then her whole body went into spasm and everything went black.

# CHAPTER 62

MARIANNE opened her eyes. She was lying on her back and there were fluorescent lights above her. Her eyes began to water and she blinked away the tears. There was a beeping sound off to her left and she twisted her head to see a rack of monitors.

'She's awake, nurse,' said a voice. A woman. Marianne turned to look at her and smiled when she realised it was Sam.

'What happened?' said Marianne. Her throat was so dry that the words came out as a croak. She coughed and tried again.

'Don't talk,' said Sam.

'I'm okay,' said Marianne.

'You're clearly not okay,' said Sam. 'Nurse, please. Elle s'est réveillée,'

Sam moved away and a black nurse took her place, shining a small torch into Marianne's eyes and then peering at the monitors.

'What happened?' Marianne asked Sam again.

'You had some sort of seizure,' said Sam. 'You keeled over on the plane and the pilots diverted to Bordeaux. You're in hospital now.'

The nurse hurried away.

Marianne tried to sit up but the effort was too much for her and she fell back.

'Don't move,' said Sam. 'Let the doctor have a look at you first.'

Marianne sighed. 'Can you get me some water?' she croaked.

'Of course,' said Sam. She picked up a water bottle with a plastic straw and lifted Marianne's head to help her drink.

Marianne sipped greedily. Sam waited until she had finished before taking the bottle away. 'Thank you,' whispered Marianne.

The nurse returned with a doctor, a small man with a receding hairline in a starched white coat, with a blue stethoscope hanging around his neck.

'This is Dr Janvier,' said Sam. 'He has been taking care of you.'

Marianne forced a smile. 'Thank you, doctor.'

'Has this ever happened to you before, mademoiselle?' asked Dr Janvier in heavily accented English.

'When I was younger,' said Marianne.

'And were you diagnosed with epilepsy?'

'No. Not really.'

Dr Janvier frowned. 'I do not understand, mademoiselle. What did the doctors say was the cause of your seizures?'

'I didn't see a doctor,' said Marianne. 'It only happened a few times and my parents didn't take me to hospital.'

'What sort of parents wouldn't take their child to a hospital after a seizure?' Dr Janvier asked Sam.

'She had a difficult childhood,' said Sam.

Dr Janvier shook his head. 'Well, obviously we need to work out what is causing the seizures. I will arrange an MRI scan.'

'Can't we get that done back in the UK?' said Sam.

'I would advise against her flying until we've done a scan,' said Dr Janvier. 'There might be a scar or lesion on the brain that caused the event, and there could well be damage caused by the seizure and her subsequent fall. We need to know what we are dealing with.'

'I just want to go home,' said Marianne.

'I understand, mademoiselle. But I must insist that we run some tests first. There is a chance that the seizure was caused by an issue with the heart. Your EKG looks fine but I will order a full body scan so that I can be sure.'

'So when can I go?'

'If the scan doesn't show us anything that we need to be concerned about than I would not be averse to you flying to the UK. But either way you need to see a specialist in the near future. Seizures can be controlled with the right medication, but if you don't do something they could get worse and occur more frequently.'

'I'll make sure that she's taken care of, doctor,' said Sam. She patted Marianne on the shoulder. 'You're in good hands.'

Marianne heard the rattle of a gurney. 'Do you think you can get out of bed and on to the gurney, mademoiselle?' asked Dr Janvier.

'I think so,' said Marianne. Sam helped her sit up. Marianne was wearing a pale green hospital gown and it rode up around her thighs as she swung her legs over the side of the bed. The nurse took one of her arms and Sam held the other and together they helped Marianne on to the gurney.

Dr Janvier nodded at the orderly, a large black man wearing pale blue scrubs, and spoke to him in French.

'Would you like to accompany her?' Dr Janvier asked Sam.

'That would be wonderful, thank you,' said Sam.

The orderly pushed the gurney out of the ward and along a corridor. Sam walked alongside. 'How do you feel now?' Sam asked.

'I feel fine. Really. This is all a fuss about nothing.'

'You scared me half to death,' said Sam. 'One moment you were telling me you were going to use the bathroom, then your eyes rolled back into your head and you went into a spasm. You crashed to the floor like a sack of potatoes.'

'A bit like when you used the shock collar on me, then?'

'Ha ha,' said Sam. 'But joking apart, yes, it was as if you had been tasered. Your whole body was tense and trembling like you were being electrocuted. I remembered enough first aid to know that I should make sure you hadn't swallowed your tongue, but other than that I had no idea what to do. One of the pilots came out and he insisted that we declare an emergency and divert to Bordeaux.' She patted Marianne on the shoulder. 'Please don't ever do this to me again,' she said.

'I'll try not to.'

The orderly stopped pushing the gurney and opened a door.

'Laisse-moi te faire ça,' said Sam, holding it open for him.

The orderly pushed Marianne into a large room where an Asian lady in a white coat was waiting for them, standing next to a huge white scanner. She went over and smiled down at Marianne. 'Bon jour,' she said. 'Do you speak French?'

'Not really,' said Marianne. 'Sorry.'

'Not a problem. I am Dr Patel, I'll be doing your scan today. Have you had one before?'

'No,' said Marianne.

'Well, it's nothing to worry about, and it's quite painless. We will move you onto a trolley that will pass into the machine. So you will actually be inside it while the scan is carried out. It's quite noisy, a bit like being in a train tunnel. Are you claustrophobic at all?'

'A bit.'

'I always advise my patients to keep their eyes closed,' said Dr Patel. 'Dr Janvier has ordered a head and torso scan which will take almost an hour to carry out. Please move as little as possible during that time.'

'Okay,' said Marianne.

Dr Patel flashed her a smile and patted her on the leg. 'You'll be fine,' she said. 'I've never lost a patient yet.'

# CHAPTER 63

MARIANNE smiled as the Mercedes pulled up in front of the Wimbledon safe house. 'Home, sweet home,' she said. The MRI scan had revealed no obvious issues and Dr Janvier had been happy enough to allow her to fly back to the UK, with the proviso that she see an epilepsy specialist at the first opportunity.

'It's good to be back, isn't it?' said Sam, as the black metal gate rattled shut behind them. 'Private jets are all well and good, and five star hotels can be fun, but nothing beats a cup of tea in front of your own fireplace.'

Marianne grinned and shook her head. 'I was being ironic,' she said. 'It's not my home. The bars on the windows and the security cameras are a clue.'

'I'm sorry, I thought you were being serious,' said Sam. 'Really, I'm trying to make you as comfortable as possible. And this won't be for ever.'

'When can I stay in my own place?'

'When I'm sure that you'll be safe. I don't want anything to happen to you. Men like Zhang Shi, they don't like to be made fools of. You embarrassed him in front of his men, word will have got back to Beijing and he'll be lucky not to get booted off the National People's Congress.'

'He'll have a lot of explaining to do,' said Marianne. 'Least of all why my knickers were in his mouth.'

Sam laughed. 'That was a nice touch,' she said.

They climbed out of the Mercedes, just as Jason opened the front door. 'I'll get the bags,' he said. 'I've made tea in the sitting room and there are Jaffa cakes.'

'You read my mind,' said Sam.

Jason went to the rear of the Mercedes and opened the boot as Sam took Marianne into the house. Dr Carter was in the sitting room, along with the promised tea and Jaffa Cakes. He was sitting in the armchair wearing a dark blue suit, and he poured tea for Sam and Marianne as they sat on the sofa. 'Welcome back,' he said. 'I hear you gave everyone a bit of a shock today.'

Marianne shrugged but didn't say anything. Dr Carter passed her a cup. 'I'll let you add your own milk and sugar,' he said.

'Just water for me,' said Marianne.

Dr Carter took back the cup. 'No problem,' he said. 'I'll get you a water.'

'I'll take it, Simon,' said Sam, holding out her hand.

Dr Carter gave her the cup, then went to the kitchen to fetch Marianne a bottle of water. She heard Jason carrying her bag upstairs.

Sam poured milk into her cup and took one of the Jaffa cakes. 'How are you feeling?' she asked.

'You don't have to keep asking,' said Marianne. 'Really, I'm fine. Dr Carter's here because I had a seizure, right?'

'He's responsible for your wellbeing,' said Sam. 'We need to work out what brought on this seizure. What if it happened while you were driving a car?'

'I don't drive.'

'I saw you drive, remember? Away from the Russian's house. You're a regular Lewis Hamilton behind the wheel.'

'Who is a regular Lewis Hamilton?' said Dr Carter as he returned with Marianne's bottle of Evian water.

'Marianne, she drives like a pro,' said Sam. 'I was just saying, if she had a seizure while she was driving at speed, it could end very badly.'

'What did the French doctors say?' asked Dr Carter as he sat back in the armchair. He took off his black-framed glasses and polished them with a white handkerchief.

'Blood tests were all fine, no problems with her EKG, and the scan showed nothing to worry about,' said Sam. 'They gave me a set of the test results and the MRI scan,' she added, taking a thumb drive from her pocket.

Dr Carter took it from her. 'I'll look them over,' he said. 'So, Marianne, has this happened before?'

'A few times. When I was younger.'

'But not recently?'

Marianne shook her head. 'No.'

'When was the last time?'

Marianne unscrewed the top off her water bottle and drank. 'I can't remember.'

'Really? Something as major as a seizure and you don't remember?'

Marianne shrugged. 'I blot out bad memories.'

'That's not good,' said Dr Carter.

'It works for me.'

'I mean that locking away bad memories doesn't get rid of them. It allows them to grow and fester in the dark. You need to get them out and deal with them. They'll shrivel in the light.'

Marianne shook her head. 'You don't know me,' she said.

'Exactly,' said Dr Carter. 'I don't know you. But I want to.' He put his glasses back on and leaned towards her. 'Marianne, have you ever been hypnotised?'

She shook her head. 'No.'

'If you have some missing memories, hypnosis under the right conditions might recover them.'

Marianne smiled thinly. 'It's not that I can't remember, it's that I don't want to.'

'I understand that. But if I can understand those memories that you are trying to blot out, perhaps I can help you deal with them.'

Sam put down her cup. 'We're only trying to help, Marianne,' she said. 'We really don't want this to happen again.'

'Because then I won't be useful to you? That's all you're worried about.'

'That's not true,' said Sam.

Marianne felt her chest tighten as if there was a steel band around it and she began to breathe quickly, trying to get more air into her lungs.

'Are you okay, Marianne?' asked Sam.

'I'm not sure.'

'Do you think you're going to pass out again?'

Marianne shook her head but didn't answer.

Dr Carter stood up and went over to her. He took off his glasses and put them in his jacket pocket. 'Breathe slowly and deeply,' he said, kneeling down in front of her and holding her hands.

'What's happening to me?' she whispered.

'Assuming the French doctors were right, there's nothing major wrong with you,' said Dr Carter. 'It might be as simple as a panic attack or an anxiety attack.'

'I don't feel anxious.'

'It can be in your subconscious,' said Dr Carter. 'That's why I really need to know about any seizures you have had before, Marianne. It might help explain what's happening to you now.'

'What do you want to do?'

'I want to try hypnosis on you. To see if we can unlock some of those memories you've blocked.'

Marianne sighed mournfully. 'I don't know.'

'We can stop anytime you feel uncomfortable,' he said. 'Please, just give it a go.' He turned to look at Sam. 'Can you leave us alone?'

'If you think that will help.'

'It will,' said Dr Carter. 'Immeasurably.'

'I do have some work to be getting on with,' said Sam. She finished her tea, picked up a couple of Jaffa Cakes, and left the room.

'Alone at last,' said Dr Carter, with a smile.

'I'm not sure if hypnosis is a good idea,' said Marianne.

'Let's just try,' said Dr Carter. 'It can't do any harm, and it might help.' He reached into his jacket pocket and brought out a small cloth pouch. Marianne frowned as he opened the pouch and took out a pale green crystal attached to a chrome chain. He smiled. 'You were expecting a watch?'

'Actually I wasn't expecting anything,' she said.

'Stage hypnotists sometimes use a watch, but really it's just about giving your mind something to focus on while you listen to my voice. Some people use a video to achieve the same effect but I'm old school.' He let the crystal hang on the chain and held it a couple of feet from Marianne's face. 'Just keep your eyes on the crystal.'

She did as she was told and Dr Carter began to slowly swing the crystal back and forth. He began speaking to her in a low, hushed voice, telling her that she was safe and that she could relax, she could let herself go, she could lose herself in the sound of his voice. At first she felt herself resisting but soon her eyelids started to close and she felt herself sinking into a deep state of relaxation that was surprisingly comforting.

# CHAPTER 64

WOODY blinked. Dr Carter was staring at him, talking in a low, hushed whisper. He was holding a crystal on a silver chain. 'What's going on?' said Woody.

'Woody?'

'What are you doing?'

'It's Woody?'

'Yes, it's Woody. Now what the hell is going on?'

Dr Carter lowered the crystal. 'It worked. That's good.'

'What worked?'

'I hypnotised Marianne. I put her in a trance. So she's asleep and you came forward. Now if I'm right, we can talk without her being aware of our conversation.'

Woody frowned. 'What are you playing at?'

'I'm not playing at anything, Woody. I'm trying to help.'

'How does putting Marianne in a hypnotic trance help?'

Dr Carter placed the crystal on the coffee table. 'I need to know about the seizures she's had in the past. But every time I ask her about them, she clams up. It clearly makes her uncomfortable.'

'That's hardly surprising, is it?'

'No, it isn't. But I don't want to upset her and it occurred to me that you'd be able to tell me exactly what happened before.'

'Behind her back, you mean?'

Dr Carter looked pained. 'Woody. I'm trying to help.'

'Help who, exactly?'

'Marianne, of course. I need to know if the seizures are an ongoing problem.'

'Because it will interfere with Sam's plans?'

'Because if she's at the wheel of a car or operating dangerous equipment, a seizure could be fatal. I have Marianne's best interests at heart here.'

Woody nodded. 'You need efficiency, and seizures don't fit in with that, do they?'

Dr Carter ignored the question. 'How often do the seizures occur?' he asked.

'Not often,' said Woody.

'Once a year? Once a month?'

'These days, a couple of times a year.'

'And when she was younger?'

Woody nodded. 'It was part of her defence mechanism, when she was very small. She thought that if she pretended to have a fit that her father would leave her alone.' He grimaced. 'That didn't work. Awake or unconscious, he'd abuse her either way.'

'So initially she faked the seizures?'

Woody nodded. 'Yes, but then they began to happen spontaneously, usually when she was under stress. These days I do what I can to protect her. By keeping her out of stressful situations, the seizures don't happen.'

'So what happened on the plane?'

Woody shrugged. 'I guess I wasn't concentrating. I didn't realise how stressed she was until it was too late. I'll try to make sure that it doesn't happen again.'

'And the seizures only happen when her personality is in charge? They don't happen when it's you or Sofia or anyone else?'

'Exactly,' said Woody. 'If I sense that she's under stress, I or one of the others will step up.'

'And that works?'

'Usually.' He smiled. 'I see what you're thinking. We have to keep Marianne out of the way whenever we're on a job for Sam.'

'Actually that wasn't what I was thinking. I was thinking that if the cause is stress and that only Marianne is affected, then there's a good chance I can fix this. I haven't seen the scans myself yet, but the doctors in France seem sure that there is no physiological cause for the seizures which suggests that it is psychological and if it is there's a very good chance that I can cure her.' He smiled. 'That's what I do.'

'So what do we do next?' asked Woody.

'I'll talk to her. I'll put together a treatment plan and hopefully put a stop to the seizures.' He smiled. 'It's going to be okay, Believe me, I have her best interests at heart.'

'We'll see,' said Woody. 'Just don't forget that I'll do whatever is necessary to protect her.'

'I won't forget that,' said Dr Carter. 'I know how hard you've worked to keep her safe over the years. I can help you. And I will.'

# CHAPTER 65

MARIANNE blinked. Dr Carter was still talking to her and swinging the crystal. Her eyes felt heavy. In fact her whole body was tired, as if she had been exercising. 'Are you all right, Marianne?" he asked.

She nodded. 'It's not working, is it?'

Dr Carter lowered the crystal. 'What do you mean?'

'You can't hypnotise me. I'm not in a trance.'

'Actually it worked just fine,' he said.

'But I was never in trance. I just watched the crystal but I could hear everything.'

'It was fine for a first session,' said Dr Carter. 'How do you feel?'

'Tired.' She picked up her bottle of water and took a sip.

'That's to be expected.' He put the crystal back into its pouch. 'Why don't you take a nap and we'll talk later this evening?'

'Okay,' said Marianne. She stood up and felt suddenly dizzy.

Dr Carter leapt to his feet and put a hand on her shoulder. 'Are you okay?'

She smiled and nodded. 'I think I stood up too fast,' she said.

'Do you need help up the stairs?'

'Dr Carter, I'm not an invalid. I'm just tired. The last twenty four hours has been hectic, to say the least. I'll be fine after I've had a lie down.'

Dr Carter took her over to the door and opened it, then watched her as she climbed the stairs.

Marianne went to her bedroom and rolled onto the bed. She stared up at the ceiling but was asleep within seconds.

When she woke up the sky was darkening outside and somebody was knocking on her door. It was Jason. He opened the door slightly. 'Hi, sleepyhead,' he said. 'I've put together some cakes and sandwiches,' he said. 'In the living room.'

'Is Sam back?'

'No, but Dr Carter is down there demolishing my salmon and cucumber sandwiches, so you should get your skates on.'

'I will do,' she said. She sat up and ran her hands through her hair. She took a quick shower and changed into a clean sweatshirt and jeans, then went down barefoot to the sitting room.

Dr Carter had placed the chessboard on the coffee table and appeared to be in the middle of a game with himself, peering at the board though his black-framed spectacles. On the other side of the table was a pot of tea, two bottles of Evian water, a plate of triangular sandwiches and a plate of muffins and small cakes.

Jason popped his head around the door. 'I've done salmon and cucumber - though I think Dr Carver has eaten most of them already - cheese and tomato, tune and mayonnaise and pate and cornichons.'

'What are cornichons?' asked Marianne as she sat on the sofa and helped herself to a bottle of water.

'Little French gherkins,' said Jason. 'You'll love them.' He closed the door and Marianne picked up one of the sandwiches. Cheese and tomato.

'Feeling better?' Dr Carver asked.

'Much better.'

'Did you sleep?'

'I did, yes.' She nodded at the board. 'Are you playing yourself?'

He laughed. 'Yes, I am. I was just passing the time. Do you play?'

'Sometimes.'

'Would you like a game?'

244

'Sure. Okay. But I'm not very good.'

Dr Carter began replacing the pieces. 'That's okay, we won't play for money.'

'*Okay, Billy,*' said Woody. '*You're up.*'

# CHAPTER 66

BILLY waved at the board. 'You're set up for white, so why don't you go first,' he said.

'Are you sure?' Dr Carter pushed his glasses further up his nose.

'Of course.' Billy smiled to himself as Dr Carter moved his king's pawn two spaces forward. The king's pawn opening was the most common opening in chess and was the favourite move of many of the world's top players. The late, great, Bobby Fischer referred to it as the 'best by test', and often used it himself. It was also used by amateurs and beginners and was zero indication of what was to come. Billy briefly considered the Sicilian Defence and the Scandinavian Defence, but then moved his own king's pawn forward. It was the move most often taught to beginners, and while it was also used at World Championship level, it would probably convince Dr Carter that he was facing someone he could easily beat.

Dr Carter's next moves came quickly, bringing his bishops and knights into play. Billy matched him move for move. They exchanged a couple of pawns, then Dr Carter gave up a bishop in exchange for one of Billy's knights. Even-stevens. Eight moves later, Billy offered up his queen.

Dr Carter frowned and rubbed his chin. 'You're sure about that?' he said.

'Oh, bugger,' said Billy, pretending to only have noticed what he'd done.

'You can take it back,' said Dr Carter.

'No, no, never do that,' said Billy. 'No takebacks.'

'I feel bad.'

Billy shrugged. 'Everyone makes mistakes, Dr Carter. We live and learn.'

'I suppose we do,' said Dr Carter. He took the queen with his knight and placed the piece on the table next to the board.

Billy's next move was innocuous enough, but while he was a queen up, Dr Carter was unable to press his advantage and three moves later his jaw dropped when Billy claimed checkmate. 'I did not see that coming,' he said, sitting back in his chair.

'I was just lucky,' said Billy trying not to smile too much.

Dr Carter studied him with unblinking eyes. 'Are you Billy?' he asked.

Billy looked up. 'Why do you ask that?'

Dr Carter smiled. 'I'll take that as a yes,' he said. 'Woody likes to win, and I've no doubt he's a good player, but I bet he prefers winning to playing so it would make sense for him to let you take his place. Most hackers are good chess players.'

Billy chuckled. 'He does like to win. And you're a good player, Dr Carter.'

'That's nice of you to say so, but you beat me soundly.'

Billy grinned. 'Yeah, but you made me work for it. Usually I only think two or three moves ahead against opponents but I was up to four or five with you.'

'Who do you usually play with, Billy?'

'Myself, most of the time. Online when I can get to a computer.'

'You could probably be a grandmaster.'

Billy shook his head. 'I don't have the discipline.'

'Marianne says you're a computer whizz.'

Billy's grin widened. 'That's nice of her.'

'You're the one who set up her online identity, right? Her passport, her official records such as they are.'

'It's not difficult if you know what you're doing. And if I need help, I can ask for it from various hacker groups that I'm a member of.'

'Like Anonymous?'

Billy nodded. 'Among others.'

'And you got all the intel on Boris Morozov?'

'That was easy.'

'There have been more difficult ones?'

'Hell yeah.'

'How many did you track down for her?'

Billy frowned. 'Why do you want to know?'

'*It's okay, Billy*,' said Woody. '*I'm up.*'

# CHAPTER 67

WOODY picked up a muffin with his left hand and bit into it. He smiled as Dr Carter looked at his hand and drew the obvious conclusion. 'Yes, it's me, Dr Carter,' he said.

'You're upset, because I spoke to Billy? You shouldn't be. You sent him to play me.'

'I'm guessing you suggested a game of chess precisely because you wanted to talk to him.'

'And yet you still let him play.'

Woody shrugged. 'I wanted to see how good you were at chess. Now I know. You're good, but Billy is better.'

'He is very good. And an excellent hacker, too, obviously.'

'One of the best.'

'I can see how his hacking skills would be useful. He helped track down the men who hurt Marianne, didn't he?'

Woody smiled. 'Why do you want to know, Dr Carter?'

'I want to help you. And if I am to help you, I need to understand you.'

'Help me? Or help Marianne?'

'That's the same thing, isn't it?'

Woody's eyes narrowed. 'Is it? Have you thought that through, Dr Carter?'

'Have I thought what through?'

Woody waved the question away. 'Who is it who wants to help me? Is this Sam speaking, or are you doing this off your own bat?'

'I'm the one responsible for your wellbeing,' said Carter. 'Your mental health and your physical state. Sam is concerned with the operational side.'

'So these attempts to find out what makes me tick, they're solely to satisfy your curiosity?'

'It's not about satisfying my curiosity, it's about helping you.'

'But what if by helping us you destroy our usefulness to Sam? Have you considered that?'

'What do you mean?'

'I mean that by getting inside our head and moving things around, you might well destroy those talents and abilities that make us so good at what we do. Have you discussed this with Sam?'

'I will once I understand what it is I'm dealing with. At the moment I'm - as I said - trying to work out what makes you tick.'

'So these chats we're having, they're without her knowledge? Behind her back?'

'I wouldn't say that.' He flinched as the door opened and Woody smiled at the man's discomfort as Sam walked into the room.

'Speak of the devil,' said Woody.

'Excuse me?' said Sam. She was holding her iPad in one hand and a coffee mug in the other.

Woody looked over at Dr Carter, whose cheeks were reddening. There was a look of panic in Dr Carter's eyes, so Woody gave him a reassuring wink. Now wasn't the time to drop the psychiatrist in it. 'I was just asking where you were,' said Woody.

Sam looked at the chessboard. 'Oh, you're playing chess. Who's winning?'

'I won,' said Woody. 'But it was a close game. Can you play?'

'I can play, but not very well,' she said. She smiled at Dr Carter. 'Are you just about done? I need to brief Marianne on a job.'

'Yes, right, of course,' said Dr Carter, obviously still flustered. 'Done for now, yes. Though I would like another chat later.'

'I'll put it in my diary,' said Woody.

Dr Carter stood up, nodded, and headed out of the room. Sam sat down and looked quizzically at the chessboard. 'You were playing black?' she asked.

'I was.'

'And you won?'

'I did.'

Sam frowned as she looked at the pieces. 'But you lost your queen?'

Woody grinned. 'I did, yes. About halfway through.'

'And you still won?'

Woody shrugged. 'It was a deliberate sacrifice.'

'That's bold.'

'No, not really. Most people will grab at a quick victory if you offer it to them. He just didn't see what was coming.'

'What about you?'

'Me? I guess I always take the view that if something is too good to be true, it probably is.' He shrugged. 'Having said that, people do make stupid mistakes and you should always take advantage of that.'

Sam carefully pushed the chessboard to the side. Woody looked at the file. 'Another job so quickly?'

'I'm afraid so.'

Woody smiled at her. 'It's never ending, isn't it?' he said. 'Don't you sometimes think you're fighting a losing battle?'

'There are a lot of bad guys out there,' she said. 'And for every one we take out, there are two more ready to take their place. But what's the alternative? To allow the bad guys to prosper? To allow evil to win?'

'Maybe you should think about treating the disease rather than the symptoms.'

'Those sort of decisions are taken at a pay grade way above mine,' said Sam. 'In this case, the disease is called Hellbanianz and the symptom is one Aron Sako. The Hellbanianz are the new wave of Albanian mobsters and they already control the cocaine market in every English city other than Liverpool.'

Woody grinned. 'You've got to admire the Scousers,' he said. 'They really don't take shit from anyone, do they?'

Sam ignored his interjection. 'They started in London but were so successful there that they spread across the country,' said Sam. 'A number of them were sent down in 2020 but Sako then took control and they've been growing exponentially ever since.'

Sam set up her iPad so that Woody could see it, then showed him half a dozen photographs. One was a head and shoulders mug shot of a dead-eyed thug with a shaved head and a spiderweb tattoo across his neck, the rest had been taken from social media and showed Sako surrounded by scantily clad young girls, leaning against a Ferrari, drinking Cristal champagne and sporting expensive wristwatches.

'He likes to flaunt his wealth, obviously,' said Woody.

'He does, yes.'

'So can't you do an Al Capone on him, get him on tax evasion?'

'He pays his taxes,' said Sam. 'His cars are all taxed and insured, he takes dividends from a number of companies, all totally legitimate. He uses a big City accountancy firm and all the money he takes is legit and above board.'

'How old is he?'

'Twenty six.'

'That's young to be running a criminal organisation, isn't it?'

'Basically he kills anyone who gets in his way,' said Sam. 'He truly doesn't care. He suspected his own uncle of stealing from him and he hacked his head off with a machete. He's almost certainly a psychopath, he truly doesn't care how he treats others. Cocaine is the backbone of his organisation but he's also behind protection rackets and people trafficking. He has a group based in Calais who bring in

Albanian footsoldiers on rubber dinghies. They are met by Border Force and taken to hotels but almost immediately they're whisked off to London to join Hellbanianz and then to wherever in the country that Sako needs them.'

Woody pointed at the screen, at a photograph of Sako standing next to a Cessna jet, holding a bottle of champagne and a glass. 'I can see that he's an annoying little shit who is clearly giving two fingers to law enforcement, but that hardly merits a death sentence, does it?'

'As I said, the decision was taken above my pay grade.'

'Yes but Sam, this is a slippery slope, isn't it? It's one thing to kill in the interests of national security. That I get, it's war, just on a different battlefield. But killing criminals for being criminals without even a trial, well where does that end? Breaking legs if you speed, taking out the eyes of peeping toms, castrating rapists?'

'Sako is something of a special case,' said Sam.

'Well that makes more sense,' said Woody. 'Now are you going to tell me, or not?'

Sam sighed. 'I hope we're not going to have to do this every time I give you an assignment,' she said.

Woody didn't answer as he continued to stare at her with unblinking eyes.

'Over the past year, Sako has killed two NCA officers who were tasked with penetrating his organisation. Both were brutally tortured before being killed and dumped next to the NCA's headquarters in London.'

'Well that's not good.'

'It gets worse,' said Sam. 'The men weren't just tortured for fun, Sako wanted the name of their NCA handler. The first man died without giving him the name, but the second one broke and told him who his handler was. A couple of weeks later the handler and his family were murdered in their home. The wife was raped before she was beaten to death, as were their two daughters.'

Woody grimaced.

'The daughters were aged ten and eight,' said Sam. 'It looks as if the father was made to watch everything before they slit his throat.'

'I don't remember seeing any of this in the media?'

'It was hushed up,' said Sam. 'The wife was the daughter of a leading member of the government, and no, I'm not going to tell you who she is. The deaths were repackaged as a car accident.'

'So this is revenge?'

'Partly revenge, partly getting rid of a true enemy of the state. Is that good enough for you?'

'I'm perfectly happy with revenge as a motive,' said Woody. 'But there's something I want to know before we go much further. Who do you work for? Who is your boss?'

'Why do you need to know that?'

'Because the things you're asking me to do, I could get in big trouble if anyone found out. Let's say I kill this Sako, but the cops find out and I get arrested. I'm facing years in prison, and I'm damn sure the Albanians would have no trouble getting to me behind bars.'

'I've already told you that I'll protect you,' said Sam. 'You have a get-out-of-jail-free card. Nothing bad will happen to you while you are under my protection.'

'Yes, you said that. But I know nothing about you, Sam. No offence. For all I know you might have dozens of people like me doing your dirty work and one day you might just decide to throw me to the wolves.'

'That won't happen.'

'Well, that's easy for you to say, isn't it?' He leaned forward. 'I need the reassurance of someone with weight, Sam. Someone I can believe in. Someone in the public eye. The head of MI5, for instance. Or the head of MI6.'

'I don't report to either of them,' said Sam. 'And even if I did, I doubt that they would agree to meet you.'

'So who do you report to? Who does the buck stop with?'

Sam sighed and sat back in her chair. 'I doubt you'd know him,' she said. 'He's a former Chief of the Defence Staff, but he retired five years ago.'

'And he's the one who issues the hit lists?'

'We don't call them hit lists, and no, he doesn't have the authority to do that. The target notices are issued by Number 10, on the advice of the Defence Council, though more recently there has been input from the National Crime Agency.'

'So I could meet with the Prime Minister?'

Sam laughed. 'That's not going to happen. The PM doesn't know who you are. In fact he doesn't know who I am, or anyone else on our team. General Quintrell is the only point of contact the PM has. And they would never meet at Number 10 or in any Government office. Any meetings would take place well away from Number 10, behind closed doors. No minutes are ever taken, nothing is ever recorded.'

'So you can introduce me to this General Quintrell.'

'To what end?'

'So that he can reassure me that my interests are being looked after.'

'I've already told you, they are.' She closed the iPad.

Woody smiled thinly. 'Yes, but with all due respect, I don't know you from Adam. Or Eve. I'm not even sure that Sam is your real name. You still feel like a Charlie to me. But this General Quintrell is obviously a real person. He's probably even got his own Wikipedia page.'

Sam laughed. 'That's your mark of trust, is it? A Wikipedia page? You know that most of what's on Wikipedia is just plain wrong. The world's intelligence agencies have been manipulating it for years, you wouldn't want to depend on it for anything.'

'Maybe not, but I'd feel a lot happier if General Quintrell told me that he had my back.'

'But if there was ever a problem, it isn't him who would be pulling your irons out of the fire. That would be me.'

'Yes, and if ever I was thrown to the wolves, that would be you too. Remember Hong Kong?'

'That was a test,' said Sam. 'I've already made that clear.'

'It was only a test because I passed,' said Woody. 'If I'd failed, I'd be be dead now or behind bars. And if I had been caught and if I did spill my guts, what evidence did I have? Just your name. That's it. You have to prove that I can trust you. I figure it's the least you can do.'

'So you're saying that you don't trust me, but that you will trust General Quintrell, a man who you've never met and never spoken to?'

'That's about it, yes.'

Sam shook her head. 'That doesn't make any sense.'

Woody smiled. 'It does to me. I just want him to shake my hand and to thank me for all the good work I've done, and to promise me that he'll have my back if anything goes wrong.'

Sam nodded thoughtfully. 'How about a quid pro quo?'

'I'm listening.'

'I'll fix up a meeting with General Quintrell. But after I've done that, I'll need you to come clean.'

'About what?'

'About who you really are.'

'You know who I am.'

Sam shook her head. 'No, I don't. I know who you say you are, but I don't believe that you were born Marianne Donaldson. Yes, your details are all over various Government databases, and the photograph held by the Passport Office is definitely you, but something doesn't feel right.'

'Oh ye of little faith.'

'I'm serious. We can't find any school records for that name and date of birth. And we've checked every GP in the country and come up with no matches. Yes, there's an NHS number, but it's never been registered with a GP.'

'I was never sick as a child.'

'Except you were. You had seizures.'

Woody shrugged. 'My parents took a more holistic approach to health.'

'We could go back and forth like this for ever, but I know I'd be wasting my time,' said Sam. 'You're saying you don't trust me, but that you will trust General Quintrell. So I'm saying that if I open the door for you to meet him, you need to be honest with me. I want to know who you really are. Or at least for you to prove to me that you actually are Marianne Donaldson. Do we have a deal?'

Woody looked her in the eyes and slowly nodded. 'Okay, yes. We have a deal.'

# CHAPTER 68

MARIANNE woke up to the sounds of birds singing. It took her a few seconds before she remembered where she was. The Wimbledon safe house. She rolled out of bed and padded over to the window. There was a wooden bird table in the centre of the lawn and two blue tits were pecking away at something that Jason had presumably put out for them. At the end of the garden was a wooden summer house, open at the front to reveal a double-seater swing chair. A black cat was sitting under the swing and seemed to be staring right at her. She waved. 'Good morning, cat,' she said.

Jason appeared in the garden below. She smiled when she saw that he was smoking a cigarette. He probably wasn't allowed to smoke inside and had to resort to the occasional sneaky one in the garden.

She showered and changed into a pair of cargo shorts and a denim shirt, tying her hair back with a scrunchie.

Jason was back in the kitchen when she went downstairs. 'Coffee? Tea?' he asked brightly.

'Water is fine,' she said, taking a bottle of Evian from the fridge.

'I can't start the day without a caffeine kick,' he said.

'And a cigarette?'

'How do you…?' He broke off, laughing. 'You saw me?'

'From my window. Why do you smoke?' She sat down at the table.

'It's my one vice. And only half a dozen a day. A coffee and a cigarette kickstarts my morning. So what about you? Any vices?'

Marianne shook her head. 'I don't like alcohol, I've never taken drugs. Chocolate Hobnobs, maybe.'

'Who doesn't like a Chocolate Hobnob?' said Jason. 'But I still prefer Jaffa Cakes.'

'Ah, but is it a cake or a biscuit?'

Jason laughed. 'Ah yes, the eternal question. So, what can I get you for breakfast?'

'You know what I'd really like?'

'Ask and it shall be yours.'

'I'm pining for smashed avocado on toast.'

'Really? That's one of my specialities. I use sourdough bread that I get from a baker in the village, lime juice, sea salt and chilli flakes to add a kick.'

'That sounds amazing.'

'And if we're pushing the boat out, what about a poached duck egg?'

Marianne grinned. 'Yes, please.'

Jason opened the fridge and took out two avocados and a large white egg, then popped a slice of sourdough bread into the toaster.

'Can I ask you a question?' said Marianne as she watched him work.

'Sure.'

'Others have stayed here before me, haven't they?'

'It's a safe house,' said Jason. 'People come and go.' He poured water into a pan and placed it on the stove.

'Anyone like me?'

Jason chuckled as he began to peel an avocado. 'Darling, you're one of a kind.'

'In what way?'

'Well, you're not exactly a typical Sam operative.'

'Because I'm a girl?'

'Well, there's that. But there have been two women here before. But they were…' He shrugged. 'I don't want to be bitchy.'

'Oh, you can be bitchy with me.'

'Let's just say there were bigger and stronger than you.'

'I'm quite strong.'

'Yes, I was warned that you are stronger than you look. But these two, well, one would have passed for a docker in a poor light, the other had a shaved head and was tattooed all over. And they both had attitude problems.'

'In what way?'

'They were just mean. To me. To everyone. I also felt as if I was walking on eggshells when I was around them.'

'Where are they now?'

'Oh, no one ever tells me anything,' said Jason. The toaster pinged and he took out the slice of toast and drizzled some oil over it. 'People come, and people go.'

'So we can't be friends?'

'I'd love to be friends, darling, but we're not allowed to exchange phone numbers or even full names.'

'I could look you up on Facebook or Insta?'

'I'm not allowed on social media,' said Jason. 'I'm sorry, but we really are ships that pass in the night.'

Marianne sighed. 'That's sad. I'll miss you.'

Jason looked over his shoulder. 'I'll miss you, too, darling.'

Marianne sipped her water as Jason broke an egg into the pan of boiling water. 'So most of the people who stay here are men?'

'There's a standard profile, generally. Fit men between the ages of thirty and fifty. Most have lost their hair or are losing it - I guess that's stress related. I tend not to pry but I'd say that half had been in the armed forces and the other half had been inside. They always had the tidiest beds.'

'And how long do they stay, these men?'

'The longest was about three months, I think. Usually it's just a few weeks.'

'Do they all have sessions with Dr Carter?'

'They do, yes. That's part of the process.'

'The process?'

'People who stay here are in transition. They come in as one thing and then they move on as something else.'

Marianne chuckled. 'That's a very tactful way of putting it.'

'But you get my drift, darling?'

'Yes. I do. And Dr Carter sees them all? It's always him?'

Jason nodded. 'He's the resident shrink.'

Eventually he brought over a plate and put it down in front of her. 'Breakfast is served.'

Marianne looked down at a perfectly poached egg sitting atop a pile of glistening smashed avocado dotted with flakes of chilli. She grinned. 'Jason, that looks amazing!'

He sat down opposite her. 'Enjoy.'

'You're not having any?'

'I had breakfast when I got up, hours ago,' he said. 'I'm an early riser.'

Marianne cut off a piece of toast, then jabbed it into the yolk of the poached egg. She popped it into her mouth and moaned with pleasure.

Jason beamed. 'Good?'

'Kill me now,' she said.

261

# CHAPTER 69

MARIANNE pushed with her legs and started the swing moving back and forth. There had been no sign of the black cat when she had walked across the lawn to the summer house, but the blue tits were still squabbling at the bird table.

Jason was cleaning the kitchen. She had polished off her breakfast in no time but had refused his offer of seconds. She could see herself piling on the pounds with him as her personal chef. She sipped her water and looked up at the wisps of white cloud in the azure blue sky. It really was a perfect morning. A soft, cool breeze blew down the garden, bringing with it the smell of rosemary from the small herb garden that Jason was cultivating at the side of the house. She sipped her water. She was growing to love the house, but she knew that it would never be anything more than a stepping stone to somewhere else. She was still being tested, that much was clear. Sam probably still didn't trust her, not after she'd tried to run away. At least she no longer had to wear the shock collar. That at least was an improvement. But once she had proved her loyalty, what then? Where would they put her? Would she be allowed to live on her own, or would there always be a minder like Jason around?

Dr Carter walked out of the kitchen door and waved with his left hand. He was holding a coffee mug with his right. He was wearing a dark blue suit and the sun glinted off his glasses.

Marianne waved back.

He went around the edge of the lawn, sticking to a paved path, as if he feared getting his shoes dirty. 'And how are you this lovely morning?' he asked when he got closer.

'I'm good. Thanks.'

'Jason tells me you had his signature smashed avocado with duck egg. I envy you.'

'I'm sure he'd do one for you, if you asked.'

'I don't like to impose,' said Dr Carter. He looked around the summer house. 'This is nice. I'd love one of these, but my garden is tiny.'

'Where do you live?'

'Not far, actually. Beckenham. Well, outskirts of, as the estate agents say.' He gestured at the swing. 'Room on there for me?' he asked.

'Sure,' said Marianne, pushing herself to the side.

Dr Carter sat down next to her. 'There's something so relaxing about a swing, isn't there?' he said. 'It's as if you can swing all your cares away.'

'It's like that crystal you use for hypnosis. The swinging relaxes you.'

'I hadn't thought of that,' he said. 'You're absolutely right. Maybe I should try using the swing to put people in a hypnotic state. Do you want to try?'

Marianne forced a smile. 'Not really, no.'

Dr Carter sipped his coffee. 'How did you sleep last night?'

Marianne shrugged. 'Fine.'

'And no problems this morning?'

Marianne sighed. 'You don't have to fuss over me, Dr Carter.'

'That's what I'm paid for.' He sipped his coffee again. 'Jason said you were asking about previous residents of the house. Are you worried about something?'

'Not really. I just…' She shrugged. 'I guess I just feel happy here and don't really want to leave.'

'Oh, I can understand that,' he said. 'Who wouldn't want Jason on tap, twenty-four seven?'

'But this is temporary, isn't it?' It was interesting that Jason had reported her conversation to Dr Carter. Was everything she said reported back to Sam and Dr Carter?

'It's a safe house,' he said. 'People come and go.'

'But where do they go?'

Dr Carter frowned. 'What do you mean?'

'What's the next step?'

'For you?'

'For everyone. Where do people go from here?'

Dr Carter sipped his coffee. It felt to Marianne that he was playing for time, gathering his thoughts. 'It depends,' he said eventually. 'Some move on to another safe house, maybe in another country. Some are relocated in their own places, often with new identities.'

'And what about those who fail?'

'Fail?'

'The ones who aren't good enough. The ones who don't make the grade.'

'That's not something I'm involved in.'

'But you are, Dr Carter. If you decide that someone isn't psychologically suitable for your needs, presumably they're let go.'

'Well, yes.'

'And "let go" could mean a number of things, couldn't it? Allowed back to their old lives. Returned to prison if they were criminals. Maybe found alternative employment.'

Dr Carter looked pained. 'I'm not operational.'

'Yes, you've said that before.'

'You're worried that something bad might happen to those that don't make the grade?'

'Well you can see why I'd worry, right? Do you know what I've done for Sam already?' Dr Carter opened his mouth to reply but she

264

cut him short with a shake of her head. 'I know, you're not operational. But you must have some idea?'

'Well, yes, obviously.'

'So if for whatever reason I don't make the grade, what happens to me. We just all shake hands and bid each other a fond farewell? Sam would let me go, knowing what I already know?'

'I'm not sure that what you know would worry her.'

'Seriously? I know that she runs an assassination group that murders enemies of the state. I know that she recruits assassins from prison and the armed forces.'

Dr Carter smiled. 'Can you hear yourself? Do you think anyone would take you seriously?'

'If I told them what I did in Hong Kong. Or in Spain. I think they would, yes.'

'You mean you'd confess to murder to make life uncomfortable for Sam? I don't see the logic in that. And even if that did make some sort of sense, what proof do you have?'

'There are bodies. There'll have been police investigations?'

'I think you underestimate just how good Sam is at covering her tracks. She's been in this business a long time.'

'Have you ever followed up on people who haven't made the grade?'

'Actually I have. And I can assure you that the ones I have followed up are alive and well. Maybe not exactly leading productive lives, but alive none the less.' He flashed her what he obviously assumed was a reassuring smile. 'Don't overthink it. Sam is, as you say, in the business of eliminating enemies of the state. You most definitely do not fall into that category.'

She took another sip of water and she realised that Dr Carter was watching her closely. He was noting which hand she was using. She smiled. 'You're worried that it's Woody talking.'

'I can never tell,' said Dr Carter.

'It's me. Marianne.'

'Can I talk to Woody?'

'Are you bored with me?'

Dr Carter chuckled. 'No, not at all. I just have a few questions for him.'

'*It's okay, Marianne,*' said Woody. '*I'm up.*'

# CHAPTER 70

WOODY transferred the bottle of water to his left hand, and looked enviously at Dr Carter's coffee mug. 'I'd kill for a cup of coffee,' he said.

'Well there's no need to go that far,' said Dr Carter. 'I'm sure Jason will rustle up a cup for you.'

'Sounds like a plan,' said Woody.

They stood up and walked over to the house. The black cat was back, hiding in a flowerbed and staring at the blue tits on the bird table.

Jason was sitting at the table and studying his iPhone when they walked into the kitchen. The stove was gleaming and the pans and crockery were on the draining board by the sink.

'Any chance of coffees?' asked Dr Carter. 'You make the best cappuccinos in town.'

'Of course,' said Jason, getting to his feet.

'Can we have them in the sitting room?' asked Dr Carter.

'Of course.'

'Let's go through,' said Dr Carter, and he led Woody along the hall to the sitting room. He waved Woody to the sofa and dropped down onto one of the sofas.

Woody looked at him expectantly. 'You said you had some questions?'

'A few. I'm still trying to work out what makes you tick.'

'Because you want to help?'

'Exactly.'

Woody shook his head. 'Why do you think we need your help, Dr Carter? We've been getting along just fine on our own.'

'The life you have, it's not normal.'

Woody laughed out loud. 'Dr Carter, how is your life in any way normal? You spend you time vetting potential assassins.'

Dr Carter smiled. 'Well, yes, when you put it like that...'

'You're in the business of killing people, Dr Carter. Not operational, I get that you're on the periphery of it, but people die and you're part of that. I do what I have to do to survive. You do it to pay for your Hugo Boss suits and your house with a tiny garden. So which of us needs help?'

'I'm beginning to regret ever saying that,' said Dr Carter.

There was a knock on the door and Jason appeared, holding a tray. 'I forgot to ask if you wanted milk or sugar, so I brought both,' he said, placing the tray on the table in front of them. He smiled at Dr Carter. 'And a few Jaffa Cakes, just in case you're peckish.'

He headed out and closed the door behind him. Woody poured a splash of milk into his coffee and stirred it.

'I find it strange that you have different tastes,' said Dr Carter. 'Marianne only drinks water, but you love coffee.'

'Why should that be strange?' said Woody. 'We're different people.'

'But you're not, are you?'

Woody frowned. 'What do you mean?'

'Well, you are you. It's the same body. So why does Marianne only drink water and you drink coffee?'

'Because I like coffee. And Marianne doesn't.'

'And what about Sofia? What does she drink?'

'Usually vodka. Neat.'

'Really?'

'It's the Russian in her.'

'So Sofia is Russian?'

'She likes to think so.'

Dr Carter shook his head in bewilderment. 'I really do have trouble getting my head around this.'

'It's simple enough,' said Woody. He sipped his coffee.

'So can you tell me how many personalities are in there?' asked Dr Carter.

Woody looked at him for several seconds before nodding. 'I don't see why not,' he said. 'Including me and Marianne? Eight.'

'Can you name them for me? And do you mind if I take notes?' He took a small notebook and a pen from his jacket pocket. 'My memory sometimes lets me down.' He pushed his glasses further up his nose.

'Go ahead,' said Woody. Dr Carter flicked the notebook open and looked at him expectantly. 'There's Jasmine. She's the singer, She speaks Chinese. Sofia speaks Russian, and you know what Sofia does.'

Dr Carter smiled. 'Yes. Yes I do.'

'Jim is the parkour expert, the diver and the swimmer.'

'It was Jim who did the physical tests?'

Woody nodded. 'Jim is super fit. And fearless. If you need someone to jump off the top of a building, Jim's your man.'

'And the driver?'

'Liz. She can drive like a pro and she's one hell of a mechanic. Billy is the hacker. He can break into any computer system.' He smiled. 'And he plays a mean game of chess.'

'That's seven.'

'Last but not least is Karl.'

'And what is Karl's speciality?'

Woody grinned. 'Karl is a naughty boy. He's, shall we say, light fingered.'

'A thief?'

'Stealing, breaking and entering, shoplifting. There was a time, ten years ago or so, when we had nothing. Karl would get us food, whatever we needed. And he's a genius with locks and alarm systems.'

'So you all took care of each other?'

'No one else would.'

'What about Marianne's parents?'

Woody frowned. 'You know what the father did, right? And his bitch of a wife covered for him.'

'Marianne couldn't have gone to the police?'

'He said he'd kill her, and he meant it.'

'So what happened?'

'Once she reached her teens, the father lost interest. Then the wife killed herself. Accidental overdose, they said. But she killed herself. Maybe the guilt. Social services stepped in and took her away from the father.'

'Even though he was family?'

'Like I said, he lost interest once she got to thirteen. Puberty. So Marianne was put in a succession of foster homes, some good, some bad.'

'Was she still abused?'

'Sofia took care of that. Anyone who tried it, came to regret it. But abuse isn't just physical. Some of the homes were only interested in the money they got for taking care of kids. Their welfare came second. Or third, behind booze and drugs. Eventually we ran away.'

'We?'

'I tend to think of us in the plural. We moved to London when she turned fifteen. We lived in a succession of squats. Karl supported us but then Billy started to develop his hacking skills. Initially he broke into government databases and got her income support and disability payments, but eventually he was able to take money from banks and we could say goodbye to the squats.'

'So money has never been a problem?'

270

Woody grinned. 'Not for a long time.'

'And the father?'

Woody shrugged but said nothing.

'Do you want to talk about it?' asked Dr Carter.

'Not really.'

'But he's dead?'

Woody's eyes hardened. 'Why do you say that, Dr Carter?'

'Because I don't feel any resentment when you talk about him. It feels to me that he is a door that has been closed. If he was still alive, there'd be hatred. Contempt, maybe. But when you talk about him, it's matter-of-factly.'

Woody nodded slowly. 'I forget how clever you are, sometimes.'

'It's not about showing how clever I am, it's about me increasing my understanding of what you've gone through. And where you're heading. So can you tell me what happened to Marianne's father?'

'According to the police, he killed himself.'

'What was his name?'

'You don't know?'

'How would I know?'

'Because Sam checked Marianne's birth certificate.' He grinned. 'You're not trying to trip me up, are you, Dr Carter?'

'Sam doesn't think that you are Marianne Donaldson. If that's true, then everything we think we know about you is a lie.'

'Marianne is Marianne, you have my word on that.'

'But not Marianne Donaldson. That was just an identity that you used?'

Woody shrugged.

'Because the man shown as the father on the Marianne Donaldson birth certificate is alive and well and living in a retirement home in Bournemouth. His wife, former wife, died of cancer seven years ago.

There's no record of their daughter but the father, Noel, thinks she might be in Australia now. They didn't have the best of relationships.'

'You have been busy,' said Woody.

'Not me. Sam has people for that.'

Woody nodded. 'They can't be that good if they can't find out what happened to Marianne's real parents.'

'Agreed. But I think we both know that you're good at covering your tracks.'

'I'm not, but I know a man who is.'

'Billy?'

Woody nodded. 'Billy.'

'I would love to know who Marianne really is.'

'Well, if Sam comes through on her promise for me to meet General Quintrell, then you will.' He smiled. 'But not before then. It's my only bargaining chip.'

'That's fair enough,' said Dr Carter. He sat back in the armchair. 'Can you at least tell me how he died?'

'Just to satisfy your curiosity?'

'It's more than that. Much more than that. I think it's fairly obvious that Marianne's father is the key to what has happened to her. Getting to the truth might allow me to help her.'

'Because the truth always helps?' Woody laughed hollowly. 'We both know that's not true.' He sipped his coffee, and then put the mug down on the coffee table. 'Okay, how about this. Marianne's father fell from his apartment window and broke every bone in his body. His blood alcohol level was three times the driving limit, the coroner said suicide was unlikely but possible, but put it down as an accident.'

'Woody, I can sense there was more to it than a drunk falling out of a window.'

Woody grinned. 'Your Spidey sense is tingling, is it?'

'It's more your attitude right now. Sofia was responsible, was she?'

Woody held his look for several seconds, then he shrugged and smiled. 'That's Sofia's skill set.'

'And she has no conscience?'

'None that I've ever seen,' said Woody.

'What about Marianne? Does she regret what she's done?'

Woody wrinkled his nose. 'I think her bigger regret is all the shit she went through when she was a kid.'

'I hear you. But killing doesn't worry her?'

'She isn't the one who kills. That's usually Sofia. And Sofia doesn't give a fuck.'

'That must be useful,' said Dr Carter.

'Useful?' repeated Woody. 'How so?'

'Well, in effect you export any guilt that you might otherwise feel. You can say that Sofia is responsible for the bad things that happen. So the guilt doesn't fall on your shoulders.'

'I wouldn't feel guilt anyway,' said Woody. 'Zero guilt about the father and anyone else who abused us. I'm glad that they're dead and I'd happily dance on their graves.'

'And Boris Morozov. You tracked him down and killed him?'

'Billy did the tracking, Jasmine got us up close and personal, Sofia did the killing. Jim got us out of the house and Liz did the driving.'

'A team effort?'

Woody smiled. 'We all have different skills.'

'And how many more men have you tracked down and killed?'

'Not enough. And it's not just men. Women can be every bit as vile and abusive.'

'You're still looking?'

Woody nodded. 'Some are harder than others. Some go the Jimmy Savile route and hide in plain sight, others hide in the darkness.'

'And no guilt, obviously?'

'Not one iota.' Woody looked at Dr Carter and smiled. 'You've never been abused, have you, Dr Carter?'

Dr Carter shook his head. 'No.'

'Because if you had been, you'd never ask a question like that.'

'I'm sorry. You're right, of course.' Dr Carter drank his coffee. 'Jason does make a terrific cappuccino.'

'He does.' Woody smiled at the man's clumsy attempt to defuse an embarrassing situation.

Dr Carter put his mug down on the table. 'What about the operations that you're carrying out for Sam? Did they produce any feelings of guilt?'

Woody shrugged. 'They're a means to an end.'

'What end?'

'To get back to the life we had. Sam has us over a barrel. We don't have a choice, do wc? We do as she says, or our life is over.'

Dr Carter nodded. 'You're referring to yourself in the plural again.'

'Because you understand what's going on. We are plural. You are one of the very few people who know that.' Woody's eyes hardened. 'And obviously we'd like it to stay that way.'

'Can I ask you what it's like? With so many personalities in one body, doesn't it get confusing?'

'Sometimes, but we're used to each other.'

'So how does it work? How do you decide who's in charge at any one time? I mean, obviously there are times when you need Sofia's skill set, but who makes the decision that it's time for her to be in control? And what about when someone else is doing whatever it is that they are doing, what do the rest of you do?'

Woody chuckled. 'It's complicated.'

'Use simple words.'

Woody laughed out loud. 'Okay, I'll give it a go. It's as if we're in a car, driving down the road. A people carrier. Two seats up front and six in the back. Only the two up front can see what's happening and where we're going. In the back, you know what's happening but all you can really see is what goes by the side windows.'

'They see it as it happens? They don't know what's coming?'

'Exactly. And a lot of time, they're not even really aware of what's going on. Billy is probably playing chess with himself, or running through some coding. Jasmine might be singing. Everyone has their own thing.'

'And are you usually the one who's driving?'

'No, Marianne is usually in control. When we sleep, it's Marianne. When we shower or eat or do all the normal things, it's Marianne.'

'But you're in the front passenger seat, watching?'

'It has to be that way,' said Woody. 'In many ways she's quite naive. She doesn't spot problems heading her way. I do.'

'And you're able to minimise her stress levels, to avoid the seizures?'

'That's right. As soon as I see an issue that needs resolving, I resolve it. Either by myself, or by getting someone else to take over.'

'And what about the others? Do they ever take control on their own?'

'Like a mutiny?' Woody shook his head. 'It doesn't work like that.'

'They can't just grab the steering wheel?'

Woody laughed. 'No. They'd wait for me to okay it. They're sitting in the back, remember. With limited vision. They can't see the big picture.'

'But you can?'

'Yes. Because I'm up front.'

'Okay, so here is my question to you. Why don't you drive all the time? Wouldn't that be safer?'

Woody frowned. 'Why would I do that?'

'I just said - it would be safer.'

'But it wouldn't be fair to Marianne.'

'Because she was first? She was the original personality?'

'If it wasn't for Marianne, none of us would exist.'

'She's lucky to have you, Woody.'

'And vice versa.'

The door opened and Sam appeared. She was wearing a dark blue blazer over a white dress and carrying her iPad. 'Hello, Simon, I see you're the early bird today,' she said breezily.

'Did I misread the schedule? I'm sorry.'

'No, no, it's all good. It's just that something has come up that I need to discuss with Marianne. An operational matter.'

Dr Carter closed his notebook. 'No problem,' he said.

'How's it going?' Sam asked as she sat in the empty armchair.

'I think we're making good progress,' said Dr Carter. He looked at Woody. 'What do you think?'

Woody nodded. 'Slowly but surely.'

'And you've been feeling okay?'

'Right as rain,' said Woody.

'So the seizure was a one-off?'

The question was directed at Woody, but it was Dr Carter who answered. 'There's no physical cause, which is good news,' he said. 'It might well have been stress related, and we can work on that.'

'You were definitely under a lot of stress in Spain,' Sam said. 'I was wondering, do you think the jump into the water might have brought it on? And the breath-holding. You did stay underwater for a long time.'

'I've never had problems before,' said Woody.

'That's good to know,' said Sam. She smiled at Dr Carter. 'Okay, we won't keep you, Simon.'

Dr Carter nodded and stood up. 'I'll probably pop around to see you tomorrow,' he said. 'We can continue this conversation.'

'It'll have to be in the afternoon,' said Sam. 'I need Marianne to do something tomorrow morning.'

'Right, okay.' Dr Carter smiled and nodded at Woody. 'So, anon.'

'Anon it is,' said Woody.

# CHAPTER 71

WOODY sipped his coffee as Sam sat down next to him on the sofa and crossed her legs. 'So how is it going with Dr Carter?' Sam asked.

'It's fine. He asks a lot of questions.'

Sam laughed. 'I suppose he has to. It's his job.'

'How much of what we talk about does he discuss with you?'

'Broad brush strokes, really. Your mental health is his responsibility but obviously if there's a problem then I need to know about it.'

'So there's no doctor-patient confidentiality?'

'Are you worried about something?'

'No, not at all.'

'It's in your best interests to be open and honest with Dr Carter.'

'Oh, I am.'

'Because if there is an issue moving forward, we need to be aware of it so that we can deal with it.'

'You're worried about the seizure?'

'Of course! You've no idea how scary it was when you had the fit on the plane. I genuinely thought you were going to die.'

'I'm sorry I gave you a shock.'

Sam patted Woody on the leg. 'It's okay now. We know that there's nothing physically wrong with you.'

'I don't think it'll happen again. Dr Carter thinks it might have been an anxiety attack.'

'Yes, he said. But it does seem strange that the seizure happened after the operation was over. If you were going to have an anxiety attack, wouldn't it be more likely to have happened when you were on the ship with Van Niekerk? Or when you jumped off the ship and did that amazing dive.'

Woody shrugged. 'I guess so. Maybe I just stored up all the anxiety and it burst when I was on the plane.'

'Do you feel anxious when you're ....'

'Killing?' Woody finished for her.

Sam nodded. 'Yes. Does it worry you when you're doing it?'

'Not really. It's a job that has to be done. A task that has to be completed. I just focus on the job in hand, so there's no anxiety.'

'And no fear? And no guilt?'

'I just do what I have to do. Really, Sam, I think the seizure was a one-off. It won't happen again.'

Sam forced a smile. 'Let's hope not. Right, down to business. It's proving slightly problematic to get you a meeting with General Quintrell.' Woody opened his mouth to protest but Sam held up her hand to cut him short. 'It's going to happen, you have my word on that, but you can't just pop around to see him.'

'Likes his privacy, does he?'

'There's more to it than that,' said Sam. 'He made a lot of enemies during his time out in Afghanistan and Iraq. So much so that a senior Iraqi mullah issued a fatwa against him. The fatwa was subsequently withdrawn, but as Salman Rushdie discovered in New York, withdrawing a fatwa doesn't mean that the threat is gone. There have been four serious plots to kill General Quintrell over the past ten years, and only one was a lone nutter. There are several active terrorist rings that want him dead.'

'So he's well protected?'

'He doesn't go so far as to sleep in a different bed every night but he moves around and his whereabouts are a closely guarded secret.

The internet has been purged of most of his details, and there are no recent photographs of him online.'

'You've met him, right?'

'Not recently. But yes, of course. Several times over the past few years. Usually I'll get a phone call and be taken to a safe house, if a face to face is necessary,'

'So it's doable?'

'Yes, it's doable. But it will take time to arrange.'

Woody folded his arms. 'I can wait.'

'Yes, I know. But we'd like to move on the Sako thing.'

'Why the rush?'

'We have an opportunity tomorrow and having learned of your swimming skills, we'd like to take it.'

Sam opened the iPad and placed it so that Woody could see the screen. It began to run a slideshow showing scenes of an expanse of grey water. In some of the pictures there were blue pedaloes, in others swimmers were braving the water.

'Every Saturday morning, Sako goes for a swim in the Serpentine,' said Sam. 'The lake in the middle of Hyde Park. His bodyguards go with him but they don't go into the water. It's one of the very few occasions when he is on his own.'

Woody watched the photographs scroll by. In several of the pictures there was a long building topped by a four-sided clock tower. People were sitting on a terrace overlooking the lake. 'That's the Lido Cafe,' said Sam.

'You want me to kill him in the water? Or in the cafe?'

'The Serpentine is up to fifteen feet deep. If your swimming skills - and breath-holding ability -is everything it seems to be, you should be able to make it look as if he's drowned.'

'So you want it to look like an accident?'

'Sako's killing isn't about sending a message, it's about ridding the world of an extremely vicious individual.'

280

'And getting revenge for what happened to the NCA officers?'

'Exactly. I know you said that you wanted a face to face with the general before we go any further, but we have a golden opportunity tomorrow and it would be a pity to pass it up.'

'There's always next weekend.'

'He's flying back to Albania next weekend for his brother's wedding. He's pretty much untouchable out there so we'd have to wait for him to return.' She leaned towards him. 'I've spoken to the general, on the phone, and he's very happy to meet with you.But he's north of the border today and tomorrow, probably returning early next week. So can you do this for me?'

'As a favour?'

'If you like. But you will meet with General Quintrell, you have my word on that.'

The slideshow came to an end. Woody recognised the final picture - it was Sako. It looked as if it was a photograph taken in a police custody suite and Sako was staring at the camera with cold, lifeless pale blue eyes, his thin lips curled back in a snarl. Woody nodded. 'Okay, let's do it.'

# CHAPTER 72

MARIANNE looked out over the Serpentine. A gentle wind was ruffling the surface of the grey water, and several geese were bobbing around. There were six swimmers braving the icy water.

Sam was sitting next to Marianne in the rear of a white BMW SUV. She was holding a transceiver in her hand and listening through an earpiece. 'Roger that,' she said, clicking the transmit button. 'Over and out.' She turned to look at Marianne. 'Sako has just left, he should he here within twenty minutes.'

'It looks bloody cold out there,' said Murray, who was in the driver's seat with a flat tweed cap pulled down over his eyes.

'It'll be fine,' said Sam. She patted Marianne on the leg. 'Really, you'll be fine.'

Marianne was wearing a sweatshirt and jeans. Underneath she had on a dark blue long-sleeved Speedo bathing suit, partly as protection against the cold but partly to cut down her visibility in the water. There was a black nylon holdall on her lap containing a towel, a pair of swimming goggles and a dark blue swimming cap to match her bathing suit.

'So we have to stay within the roped off area?' she said.

Sam nodded. 'The further out you go, the deeper. So under the line of floats it's between twelve and fifteen feet.'

'There's a lifeguard,' said Marianne, pointing over at a young man in red shorts and a yellow t-shirt standing on the pier that jutted into the lake.

'I've arranged a distraction for him,' said Sam.

'A pretty girl?'

'A pretty boy,' said Sam. 'He's gay.'

'And Sako will enter the water from the pier?'

Sam nodded. 'He'll use the Serpentine Swimming Club changing rooms. He's a member. He usually swims for half an hour, changes, then sits on the terrace of the Lido and has breakfast with three of his men. Members are allowed in the water from seven thirty and the public can go in after ten. But Sako is always a late riser, he never gets here before ten.'

'What do his men do while he's in the water?' asked Marianne.

'Stand around smoking,' said Sam. 'They don't keep an eye on him, if that's what you're worried about. So, I figure you should get into the water just before him, swim out to the floats, and pull him down. Does that work for you?'

Marianne nodded. 'I suppose so.'

'I'd suggest you swim back to shore underwater. Assuming that his body is spotted, all attention will be on that. The lifeguard might at that point go to his aid, but I don't see that making any difference. Ambulance response times are pretty awful in the capital at the moment so I don't see them getting there within fifteen minutes. It'll have the appearance of being an accident so the cops will probably take even longer. I figure you'll have all the time you need to shower and change and get back here.'

Marianne nodded again. 'Sounds good.'

'You're okay?'

Marianne shrugged. 'I guess so.'

'Any issues?'

Marianne forced a smile. 'None that I can see.' She stared at the water as the minutes ticked by. Sam stayed on the radio and was in constant contact with whoever was watching the Albanians.

Eventually Sam nodded and looked across at Marianne. 'He's just entered the park,' she said. 'You should head over.'

'*Okay, Jim,*' said Woody. '*You're up.*'

# CHAPTER 73

JIM opened the door of the SUV and climbed out with his holdall. 'See you later,' he said.

'Break a leg,' said Sam. She and Murray were looking over at the black Audi that had entered the car park close to the Lido building.

Jim closed the door and walked over to the changing rooms. It had just turned ten o'clock and there were now a dozen swimmers in the water, most of them sticking close to the shore. More swimmers were walking along the narrow jetty that jutted out into the water. The jetty was covered with a blue non-slip rubber material and there was a handrail running along one side. A couple in their seventies were leading the way, grey haired but with trim bodies. He was wearing tight-fitting black trunks, she had on a black wetsuit that covered most of her body.

Following them were three middle-aged women wearing swimming costumes and caps. They were all staring sullenly at the old couple, clearly resenting their slow progress along the pier.

At the end of the pier there was a ladder with curved stainless steel handrails leading into the water. The old woman turned slowly and began to make her way down the ladder, smiling at her husband. The three women formed a queue behind the old man, shifting their weight from foot to foot. They had all folded their arms and were shivering. Jim smiled to himself. They would be even colder once they got into the water.

He reached the reception area, paid the fee in cash, and went through a turnstile to the coin-operated lockers. He pushed a pound coin in one, opened it and shoved in his holdall, followed by his clothes and shoes. He closed the locker and pulled out the key. It was attached to a red rubber ring which he pulled onto his left wrist.

As he left the changing rooms, he saw Sako and three Albanian men walking away from a black Audi. They were heading towards the swimming club's changing facilities. Sako was wearing a Versace tracksuit. One of his companions was carrying a Nike holdall, presumably containing Sako's towel.

Sako looked over at Jim, smiled and winked. 'See you in the water,' he said, in accented English.

Jim smiled back, then turned away, avoiding eye contact.

The lifeguard was at his station. He was in his twenties with curly blond hair and powerful thighs. Jim looked around but didn't see the distraction. Presumably he would hold back until Sako was in the water. He smiled to himself at the thought that it might be Murray who had been lined up to flirt with the lifeguard.

Jim reached the end of the jetty. There were a dozen people lined up to enter the water. The old woman was now swimming, a leisurely breaststroke, and her husband was moving slowly down the ladder.

Jim reached the end of the queue where two young men in wetsuits were arguing about something to do with foreign exchange. One of them looked at Jim, smiled, then made the sort of clicking sound that someone might use to attract the attention of a dog. Jim ignored him turned towards the water, and dived in. He went completely under, kicked as he surfaced, and then began a lazy crawl to take himself away from the jetty.

'Show off!' shouted the man.

Jim transitioned into breast stroke, and headed towards the line of white floats that marked the limit of the swimming area.

He stopped when he was midway, trod water, and turned to look back at the shore. A young man in tight-fitting Lycra shorts and vest was talking to the lifeguard, tossing his long chestnut hair as he laughed at something the lifeguard had said.

Soka stepped onto the jetty. He was wearing khaki shorts and swimming goggles. Jim kicked with his legs to get his head higher as he looked around for the Albanian's friends. He spotted them, walking towards the Lido Cafe.

Soka walked along the jetty until he reached the queue of swimmers waiting to enter the water. He touched his toes a few times, did six brisk star jumps, then dived into the water. He emerged a couple of seconds later doing a fast crawl. Soka was clearly an expert swimmer.

Jim started a slow breaststroke so that he could watch the man's progress.

Soka kept up the pace, taking a breath on every third stroke. He cut through the water like a shark. As he reached the line of floats he turned to the right and swam parallel to it for about a hundred yards and then turned right again heading towards the shore. He was swimming laps. Perfect, It made his every move predicable.

Jim took a deep breath, bent at the waist and swam to the bottom. Visibility was poor, he couldn't see more than about ten feet around him. He swam along the lake bottom, then rolled onto his back and looked up towards the surface. He could see the lighter patch that was the sky but that was all. He was about twelve feet down, which was more then enough. He kicked and headed back to the surface, and went back to his slow, lazy breaststroke.

Soka had turned again and was swimming parallel to the shore. The water was probably only a few feet deep there. Soka was slowing a little but his strokes were still powerful.

Jim kicked to get a better view of his surroundings. The old couple were both doing the breaststroke, close to the shore. The three women were also doing the breaststroke, keeping together like a flock of anxious ducklings.

The man in Lycra was still talking to the lifeguard, tossing his chestnut hair and flashing his pearly white teeth.

Soka made another right turn and swam back into deeper water. He was continuing to take a breath every third stroke and swimming like a machine.

Jim turned towards the outer line of floats, and then transitioned into a crawl, taking a breath every second stroke. He cut through the water easily. It was cold, but not unpleasantly so, and the vigorous exercise soon warmed him up. He looked over to his left. Soka was about fifty feet from the line of floats.

Jim reverted to the breast stroke. He was about twenty feet from the floats. He began to take slow, deep breaths, loading his blood with life-giving oxygen.

Soka made the right turn that took him parallel to the shore, the line of floats just six feet to his left.

Jim took a final deep breath, held it, ducked under the water and swam towards the lake bottom. He reached it with three strong strokes, then swam parallel to the bottom, his head back so he could see the surface.

In the distance he saw a dark patch, heading in his direction. Soka.

Even with the goggles, Jim doubted that the Albanian would be able to see more than a couple of metres at most.

Jim dropped his feet until they were touching the lake bottom, bent his knees, then he pushed himself off, towards Soka, his arms outstretched.

Soka powered through the water. His face disappeared as he took a breath, then reappeared. Jim was only ten feet away now, and about five feet underneath Soka. Jim kicked hard. Soka was directly overhead now. Jim grabbed Soka's right leg, just below the knee, and pulled him down.

Soka immediately started to struggle but he was underwater before he could cry for help.

Jim pulled again. Soka was now three feet under the water. His arms were thrashing around and he kicked out, trying to get away from Jim.

Soka was holding his breath but Jim doubted that he had much air in his lungs, he had pulled him under so quickly that he wouldn't have had time to take even a quick breath.

Jim yanked Soka down again, then turned him so that he was on his back. He put his arm around Soka's neck and kicked out with both of his legs, taking them deeper.

Soka clawed at Jim's face but Jim turned away. They were about six feet under the surface now. Soka was bucking around like a rodeo horse, but Jim tightened his grip on Jim's neck. He kicked again and they went still deeper.

Soka's cheeks were bulging in and out as he fought against the breath reflex. Without any training, the average person could only hold their breath for a minute, maybe a minute and a half if they were relaxed and not moving. Thrashing around as he was, Jim doubted that the Albanian would last thirty seconds. He kicked again and they sank lower.

Soka's struggling intensified. His arms flailed around and he twisted, trying to get Jim off his back. He had obviously realised that time was running out, this was his last chance. Jim wrapped his legs around Soka's waist and squeezed, then pushed his right hand against the Albanian's nose and pressed, hard. He felt the cartilage splinter and almost immediately air exploded from Soka's mouth in a foaming bubble. There was a final shudder from the Albanian and then he went still. Jim's own breath reflex hadn't even started to kick in.

Soka's arms went limp. Jim kicked to take them lower, keeping a tight grip on the man just in case he was faking it. He began counting off the seconds. He kicked again. And again. They were only a few feet from the bottom of the lake.

Jim wrapped his arms around Soka's chest and squeezed, forcing any remaining air from the man's lungs. He would still float, but it would take a while longer for him to reach the surface.

Jim's chest was burning now but he suppressed the urge to breathe. He released his grip on Soka. The Albanian's eyes were wide and staring. Jim used his hands to move away from the lifeless body. Soka's arms and legs spread out and his back arched. He was moving up towards the surface, but slowly.

Jim turned towards the jetty and began to swim, slowly and methodically, using the minimum amount of energy. The urge to breath was almost unbearable now but he knew from experience that the feeling would pass eventually.

He continued to swim, hugging the lake bottom. Several times swimmers passed overhead. Eventually he saw the jetty ladder ahead of him and he started to rise towards the surface. When he broke through he looked around. The nearest swimmers were twenty feet away and there was no one on the ladder. He took slow deep breaths as he swam slowly towards the jetty. He climbed the ladder and stood with his hands on his hips.

'How's the water today?' asked a plump lady in her fifties wearing a swimsuit and hat in a matching flower pattern.

'It's good,' said Jim. 'A bit cold when you get further out.'

'Oh, I'll be staying close to the shore,' she said. 'You have a great day.'

'You too,' said Jim.

The Lycra-wearing boy moved away from the lifeguard. Jim headed for the changing rooms. He had just reached them when he heard shouts from the Lido Cafe. The Albanians were standing and pointing at the line of floats in the distance. The lifeguard picked up a pair of binoculars to look at what they'd seen, then a few seconds later he put the binoculars on his chair, stripped off his jacket and jumped into the water.

Jim stood for a few seconds rinsing himself under one of the outdoor showers, then opened his cubicle and took out his holdall. He dried himself and changed back into his clothes. By the time he was walking back to Sam's SUV, the lifeguard had dragged Soka to the shore and was giving him mouth to mouth resuscitation. A small crowd of onlookers had gathered around him and most were using their phones to capture the moment. Jim knew that the mouth to mouth was a waste of time. The Albanian was dead.

As he climbed into the back of the SUV, he heard an ambulance siren in the distance.

'All good?" asked Sam as Jim closed the door.

Jim smiled. 'Couldn't have gone better.'

'*Nice job, Jim,*' said Woody. '*Okay Marianne, you're up.*'

# CHAPTER 74

MARIANNE was sitting on the swing chair watching a robin pecking at a ball of fat that Jason had left on the bird table. Jason made his own treats for the birds, using fat and birdseed which he rolled into balls and left to harden in the fridge.

The kitchen door opened. Jason waved at her. 'Sam just phoned, she's on the way to pick you up,' he called.

'Did she say where we're going?'

'I'm just the hired help, darling. She just said to make sure that you looked presentable.'

Marianne laughed. 'I always do.'

'Maybe run a brush through your hair.' He disappeared inside. Marianne stretched out her legs and let the sun play over her face. She loved the garden and would miss it when she eventually left. There was something so relaxing about being surrounded by trees and bushes and hearing birds sing.

She stood up and stretched. She was wearing a sweatshirt and baggy blue jeans and had tied her hair back with a scrunchie. There could be only two reasons for Sam coming to collect her - either there was another job for her to do, or she was finally going to meet General Quintrell. Either way, she was underdressed.

She went upstairs, stripped off and showered and washed her hair, then changed into a blue and white striped dress from Selfridges. She spent ten minutes on her make up and when she went downstairs Sam was just coming in through the front door. She looked Marianne up and down and nodded appreciatively. 'Very nice,' she said.

'I'm seeing General Quintrell, right?'

'Yes you are,' said Sam. She held the door open for her. 'Your chariot awaits.'

The chariot was a black Nissan SUV and Murray was in the driving seat. Sam and Marianne got into the back.

'No hood?' asked Marianne.

'I think we're way past that,' said Sam. 'Don't you?'

'Is it far?'

'Chipping Norton,' said Murray. 'It's a two hour drive. Any requests for music?'

'I'm easy,' said Marianne.

'Ed Sheeran?'

'Knock yourself out.'

# CHAPTER 75

MARIANNE looked at the two storey limestone cottage topped with a weathered tiled roof ahead of them. It was at the end of a narrow road with no other houses close by. 'Is that it?' she asked. 'It looks like something off a box of chocolates.'

'It's pretty, isn't it?'

'Doesn't Tony Blair live in Chipping Norton?'

'He does. And David Cameron. And the Beckhams have a place a mile down the road.'

'This is the general's home?'

'He doesn't have a permanent house,' said Sam. 'Not since the fatwa. This belongs to a friend. He's only staying for a few days.'

'Does he have bodyguards?'

'Only when he's travelling,' said Sam. 'His security comes from always being on the move. But whenever the security services get wind of a possible attack, he has armed bodyguards assigned to him. At the moment he's in the clear.'

There was a green Land Rover in the driveway so Murray parked in the road in front of the house and they all climbed out. Their shoes crunched on the gravel drive as they walked to the oak front door that looked to be more than a hundred years old. Sam rang the doorbell and it was opened by a grey-haired man in his fifties, wearing a green pullover, brown corduroy trousers and well polished brogues. He had gold-framed reading glasses perched on the end of his nose and had a copy of the Daily Telegraph under one arm. His cheeks and nose were flecked with broken blood vessels, which suggested he was either used to being in the open air or liked a drink, possibly both.

'Sam, pleasure to see you again.' He spoke with a clipped military voice, a voice that was obviously used to being obeyed. He nodded at Murray. 'You too, Sergeant.'

His face broke into a smile when he saw Marianne. 'And this must be the lovely Marianne,' he said. 'I have heard such good things about you. Come inside, please.'

He stepped aside and ushered them into a hall lined with framed fox hunting watercolours. 'First on the left,' he said, as he closed the front door. Sam led Murray and Marianne into a sitting room with an overstuffed leather Chesterfield sofa and two matching armchairs arranged around a fireplace. There was a bottle of malt whisky and a half-filled glass on a table next to one of the chairs.

'Would you like tea?' asked Quintrell from the hall. 'Or coffee?'

'Coffee would be lovely,' said Sam. She sat down on the sofa. Murray went over to the bay window and looked out over the front garden. Marianne could see a bulge in the small of his back. A gun.

'Let me help you,' said Marianne. She followed Quintrell down the hall to a large kitchen with oak ceiling beams. There was a green Aga cooker against one wall and a pine table with six chairs around it next to a leaded window that overlooked the garden.

Quintrell placed a brass kettle on one of the Aga hobs. 'So Sam said that you insisted on a face to face meeting with me,' said Quintrell, turning to look at her. 'Do you mind telling me why?'

Marianne's eyes narrowed. 'You don't remember me, obviously.'

Quintrell frowned as he looked at her over the top of his glasses. 'Remember you from where?'

Marianne's jaw tightened. 'It was a long time ago. And I was very different.'

'When exactly did we meet?'

'Fifteen years ago. You weren't a general, then, obviously. You were a major. I remember seeing photographs of you in your uniform. We came to your house. It wasn't as grand as this house, of course.'

Quintrell frowned. 'Fifteen years ago? How old would you have been then? Eight? Nine?'

'Nine. As I said, I was very different back then.'

'And your father, who is he?'

'Was. He's dead.'

'I'm sorry to hear that.'

'I'm not,' she said coldly.

Quintrell looked at her for several seconds without speaking, then checked his watch, a chunky Breitling. 'I'm afraid I'm really busy today, but it has been a pleasure meeting you. I'm sure you'll keep up the good work.' He took the kettle off the hob. 'We can have coffee another day.'

'I killed him, General Quintrell,' she said quietly. 'And now I'm going to kill you.'

Quintrell's eyes widened. 'Who the hell are you?'

'You raped me. My father took me to your house five times and every time you raped me. The last time, you had a friend with you. Roger Wainwright. A priest. The Reverend Roger Wainwright. You took it in turns to rape me. My father insisted you pay him double, do you remember? You laughed and paid.'

Quintrell frowned and shook his head. 'No.'

'I think you do. I killed Wainwright but he was easy to find. You were a lot harder. Wainwright didn't know where you were, I took off three of his fingers and an ear before I believed him. But that's water under the bridge. But I'm here now.'

Quintrell sneered at her. 'This is ridiculous. You clearly have mental health issues.'

Marianne laughed harshly. 'Well that's certainly true.'

'*Sofia, you're up,*' said Woody.

# CHAPTER 76

SOFIA took a step towards Quintrell and he put up his hands defensively. 'You need to go, now.' He turned to look at the hall and took a breath, obviously intending to shout for Sam. Sofia took two quick steps towards him and slashed her hand across his throat. He staggered back against the stove, his eyes fearful. His hands went up to his neck as he gasped for breath.

There was a wooden block with six knives sticking out of it on the counter. Sofia grabbed one but realised it was a bread knife and she tossed it into the sink. The next knife was shorter and sharper. Quintrell was still struggling to breathe and his eyes widened with fear when he saw the knife in her hand. She stepped forward and stabbed him in the stomach four times. None of the blows would kill him immediately. It would take time for him to bleed out. She wanted to know what was happening and why. The hands fell away from his throat as blood soaked into his pullover.

Sofia took a step back. 'I hope you burn in hell,' she said. 'I'm sure I wasn't the only child that you raped. This is for all of them. For every child you hurt.'

She stepped forward again and stabbed him in the chest, twisting the blade so that it went between the ribs and pierced his heart. His mouth fell open and the life faded from his eyes as he slid down the stove onto the tiled floor. Blood pooled around his corduroy trousers.

'Marianne!'

Sofia turned, the knife in her hand, to see Sam in the hall staring at her with horror in her eyes.

'What have you done?' said Sam.

Sofia moved towards her and Sam ran back into the sitting room. Sofia hurried down the hall. Murray appeared, pulling his gun out.

Sofia kicked the gun from his hand. It span into the air and Sofia kicked Murray again, this time in the stomach. He fell back into the sitting room.

Sofia picked up the gun. Murray was still on his feet but he was bent double. Sofia slammed the gun against the side of his head and he fell back, sprawled over the sofa then hit the floor and rolled onto his stomach. Out for the count.

Sam was standing by the fireplace. She reached for a brass poker but Sofia waggled the gun at her. 'Don't even think about it,' she said.

'Why?' asked Sam. 'What are you doing?'

'Kneel down, Sam,' said Sofia.

'You don't have to do this,' Sam whispered.

Sofia gestured with the Glock. 'On your knees.'

Sam slowly knelt down on the rug in front of the fireplace.

'Close your eyes, Sam.'

'Don't do this. Please.'

'Do as you're told.'

Sam bit down on her lower lip and closed her eyes. She was trembling.

Sofia placed the barrel of the Glock against Sam's forehead. Sam winced but kept her eyes closed. Sofia smiled, raised the gun and hit Sam across the temple, hard enough to knock her out but not so hard as to cause any permanent damage. Sam fell to the floor without making a sound.

She hurried over to Murray, who was still unconscious, and took the SUV keys from his pocket, then let herself out of the house.

'*Okay Liz,*' said Woody. '*You're up.*'

# CHAPTER 77

MARIANNE tapped in her four-digit code and the door clicked open. She took a quick look around, pushed open the door and walked into the lobby. There was already a lift waiting and she took it up to the top floor.

She had driven the SUV through Oxford to London, and abandoned it in an NCP car park close to the Embankment before walking over Westminster Bridge. They would almost certainly have a GPS tracker on the vehicle, but even if they hadn't, the Home Office's Automated Number Plate Recognition System meant that Sam would be able to track her. They'd know where she left the car so their next step would be to analyse CCTV footage in the area but Marianne knew where all the cameras were and she knew how to get to her building without being seen.

The lock on her front door had a fingerprint reader and she pressed her right thumb against it. The door opened and she went inside. It had been several weeks since she had been in the flat but she hadn't missed it. It was a lovely flat, two bedrooms, two bathrooms and a large terrace overlooking the Thames, but it wasn't a home. Marianne had really never had a home. She spent her childhood wanting to escape where she lived, then she had stayed in a succession of squats, and when she had finally been able to afford a place of her own she had always had to keep her identity a secret and there was nothing of a personal nature in the flat.

There was a low white sofa facing the window, two armchairs made from the same material, a circular glass and chrome dining table and a low sideboard with a Bang & Olufsen stereo system. Most of the walls were lined with book-filled shelves.

She pulled open the sliding window that led to the terrace and went outside. Across the river were the Houses of Parliament, Big Ben and

Westminster Abbey. A cool wind ruffled her hair and she closed her eyes. She heard the rumble of traffic far below. She missed the sound of birdsong. She smiled. And she was definitely missing Jason's cooking.

The door entry phone buzzed and she opened her eyes. She never had visitors. Ever. It was probably someone tapping in the wrong number, or a food delivery firm pressing buttons at random to gain entrance.

She went back into the sitting room and over to the open plan kitchen. She looked in the fridge. All it contained was bottled water. She had a sudden craving for Jason's smashed avocado on sourdough toast. As she closed the fridge door, the entry phone buzzed again, more insistent this time.

She walked across the polished pine floor to the entry phone. As she picked up the receiver, there was a knock on the door. She frowned and put down the receiver. The knock was repeated.

Marianne looked through the peephole and cursed under her breath when she saw who it was. Dr Carter. How had he found her?

'*It's okay Marianne,*' said Woody. '*I'm up.*'

# CHAPTER 78

WOODY opened the door. 'How did you know I was here?' he asked. He looked over Dr Carter's shoulder. The psychiatrist appeared to be alone.

'Let me in and I'll tell you,' said Dr Carter.

Woody closed the door, undid the security chain, and opened it wide. Dr Carter walked in and stood in the middle of the room. 'This is nice,' he said, looking around.

'How did you find me?'

Dr Carter smiled. 'That's for me to know, and for you to find out.'

'What does that even mean?'

'Do you think you're the first operative to do a runner?' asked Dr Carter. 'At some point, everybody runs. I would have thought you'd have learned your lesson last time.'

'Last time there was a GPS tracker in my shoe. This time there wasn't.'

Dr Carter shrugged. He pointed at the sofa. 'Okay if I sit?'

'Are you staying?'

'I think we need a conversation, Woody. It is Woody, right?'

'Yes, it's Woody. But any second now and you'll be talking to Sofia, and that is not likely to be a pleasant experience. For you.'

'I think it'll be more productive if you and I have the chat.' Dr Carter sat down on the sofa.

Woody stayed standing. 'How did you find me?'

Dr Carter waved his hand dismissively. 'It doesn't matter.'

'It does to me,' said Woody. 'This apartment is owned by an offshore company, all the bills are paid through an offshore bank, nothing is in my name. There's no way you could know this was my bolthole.' He frowned. 'You tracked me. That's the only explanation.'

'We need to talk, Woody.'

'We are talking. You need to tell me how you tracked me.'

Dr Carter looked away, unwilling to meet Woody's gaze.

'Fine,' said Woody. He pushed open the door to the bathroom.

'Just sit down and talk to me,' Dr Carter called after him.

Woody ignored him. He took off his shirt and went over to the sink to stare at his reflection in the mirror. No, that would be too obvious. He'd notice anything amiss every time he showered.

He twisted around and tried to see his back in the mirror. He could see some of his right shoulder but not much. He twisted the other way. Now he could see part of his left shoulder.

He opened a drawer next to the sink and took out a small mirror. He turned his back to the mirror over the sink and held up the small mirror to check his reflection. It was uncomfortable and his hand and wrist were soon aching but he gritted his teeth and ignored the discomfort. It took him almost two minutes to find it, a small healing cut just inside his left shoulder blade, secured with a single stitch. He cursed under his breath and opened the drawer again, this time taking out a manicure set in a black leather case. He unzipped the case and took out a metal nail file with a pointed end. He went back to the sink. He held the small mirror in his left hand and the nail file in his right. He used the nail file to pick away the stitch, then stabbed at the wound. A trickle of blood ran down his back. He put down the nail file and picked up a pair of stainless steel tweezers. Again he used the small mirror to get his bearings, then he eased the pincers into the cut. It was painful but he blocked out the sensation as he moved the tweezers around. It took him several seconds of eye-watering pain but then he found what he was looking for. He gritted his teeth as he pulled out a small piece of plastic, about the size of a SIM card but four times the thickness.

He examined it for several seconds, then stormed out of the bathroom into the sitting room. 'You chipped me?' he shouted. He threw the bloody chip at Dr Carter and it bounced off his shoulder and fell onto the floor. 'You chipped me like I was a dog.'

'It wasn't my idea,' said Dr Carter.

'It doesn't matter whose idea it was,' hissed Woody. He shook his head in disgust. 'I should never have trusted you.'

He went back to the bathroom and grabbed his shirt.

'You're bleeding,' said Dr Carter when he came back into the sitting room.

'Fuck you.'

'Seriously, you need a plaster on that.'

'It'll stop bleeding on its own,' said Woody.

'It could get infected,' said Dr Carter. 'Please, let me put a plaster on it for you.'

Woody glared at Dr Carter, then pointed at the bathroom. 'There's a first aid kit under the sink,' he said. Dr Carter went into the bathroom and returned with a small first aid kit. He unzipped it and took out a cotton wool ball and a tube of antiseptic. Woody turned his back on Dr Carter, who dabbed at the blood and applied some antiseptic to the cut.

'So you had it done in France, right?' said Woody.

'I wasn't in France, remember? You were there with Sam.'

Dr Carter picked up a plaster and pulled off the protective strips.

'So the doctor I met was one of her people?' said Woody.

'I assume so,' he said as he applied the plaster to the wound.

'What sort of doctor goes around putting GPS chips in people?'

'The sort that gets paid an awful lot of money. Okay, you're done.'

Woody put his shirt back on as Dr Carter went to throw away the bloody cotton wool ball and the protective strips in the bathroom. Woody sat down on the sofa, then stood up and began pacing up and down.

Dr Carter came out of the bathroom. 'You need to calm down,' he said quietly. 'We don't want you having a seizure.'

'I don't get seizures,' snapped Woody.

'Please, sit down. We need to talk.'

Woody sat down on a chair. Dr Carter sat down opposite him on the sofa. 'Why did you do it, Woody? Why did you kill General Quintrell?'

'Oh come on, surely you've worked that out already.'

'He was one of your abusers?'

Woody nodded. 'Got it in one.'

Dr Carter nodded thoughtfully. 'So, this was all about getting to the general?'

'The fatwa meant that he was in hiding. Billy did what he could, but he could never get a location for him. There was information on the dark web about him being involved with an assassination unit, but zero intel on his whereabouts.'

'You knew that Boris Morozov was a target for assassination? And you knew that if you got there first Sam would bring you into the fold?'

'I didn't know about Sam at the time, but Billy discovered that the unit was looking at Morozov. I ended up killing two birds with one stone.' He grinned. 'Literally. So, is Sam mad at me?'

'She's not happy.' Dr Carter sat back. 'And she has a very sore head. But having said that, she's not stupid. She's joined the dots. She understands what you did.'

'You know her name isn't Sam?'

Dr Carter shrugged.

'I know who she really is,' said Woody quietly.

'Really?'

'Really.' He smiled and his eyes sparkled. 'Her name is Charlotte Button and the organisation she runs is known as The Pool. Partly

302

because there's a pool of people she uses, but also because a lot of the guys on her team are from Liverpool.'

Dr Carter didn't react, he just stared without blinking.

'She used to be a cop, with SOCA, the Serious Organised Crime Agency, but then she joined MI5 but left under a cloud and went semi-freelance.' Woody grinned. 'Come on, you can't say that you're not impressed that I know that.' He frowned. 'Or is it news to you?'

'I suppose there's a lot of information on the Dark Web.'

'Tons of it. And Billy is an expert at retrieving it. So, Sam or Charlie or whoever she is, she accepts that Quintrell is a paedophile?'

'She accepts that you believe that Quintrell abused you, and that's why you killed him.'

'Just cause?'

Dr Carter shrugged. 'She might want to talk to you about evidence.'

'He abused us, Dr Carter. There isn't much in the way of evidence, but I'd hardly be making it up, would I?'

'I think that's the view she's taking.'

'Am I in trouble?'

Dr Carter chuckled. 'You killed a retired general in cold blood. Are you expecting a medal?'

'Not a medal. No. Just an acknowledgement that I was in the right.'

'You killed a man, Woody.'

'So killing the paedophile who abused me is wrong, but killing people on Sam AKA Charlie's list is in the national interest so that's okay?'

'Apples and oranges.'

'Quintrell deserved to die. You think I was the only child he abused? He was part of an underground paedophile ring with members all over the country. Cops, judges, politicians, captains of industry, you've no idea how deep it goes.'

'I understand,' said Dr Carter. 'I empathise and I sympathise.'

'So that's what you wanted to talk about? Me killing Quintrell?'

'Something else, actually,' said Dr Carter. He reached into his jacket pocket and took out a grey thumb drive. 'Do you know what this is?'

Woody frowned. 'Of course. It's a thumb drive. I'm not stupid, Dr Carter.'

'Oh, no one would ever accuse you of being that, Woody. But this particular thumb drive is special. It's the one the French doctors sent. The full body MRI scan.'

'Which showed that I don't have a problem, right? There's no physical abnormality causing Marianne's seizures?'

'That's right. No abnormalities in the brain at all.'

'Which is good news.'

'Very good news. But as I said, it was a whole body scan. And it did show up some abnormalities.'

'The doctors in France didn't find any.'

'That's true. Because they were looking at your brain and at your heart.' He put the thumb drive on the table. 'You know where this is going Woody, don't you?'

Woody's eyes hardened. 'Why don't you tell me, Dr Carter?'

Dr Carter flashed Woody a tight smile. 'Okay, I will,' he said. 'I took a closer look at the full body scan, and the important words here are full and body. What is fascinating isn't what the scan shows, it's what the scan doesn't show. It's what is missing that tells the story.'

Woody's jaw tightened and his eyes hardened but he didn't say anything.

'What's missing is a cervix, a uterus, Fallopian tubes, and ovaries. All the things that a woman would generally have. Even in this brave new world of gender self-identification.'

Woody continued to stay silent.

304

'You weren't born female, were you Woody? Sam has been wasting her time trying to track down Marianne's birth certificate. Marianne is your creation, isn't she?'

Woody slowly clapped his hands together. 'Kudos,' he said quietly.

'So I'm right?'

'I can't really deny it, can I?'

'You were born male? You were abused as a male?'

Woody nodded.

'And you created Marianne to help you deal with the abuse? Why? Why would you do that?'

'You're the one with all the answers, Dr Carter. Why don't you tell me?'

Dr Carter nodded. 'I think the abuse was too much for you to deal with. But if you thought that by taking the abuse you were able to protect someone else, then maybe it might be easier. You were stepping up as the white knight, offering yourself to protect her. Like a big brother.'

Woody sighed. He had a sudden urge to lash out and hurt Dr Carter, but he quashed the thought. Dr Carter wasn't trying to hurt him, he was still on his mission to help, misguided as that was.

'I'm guessing that after a while protecting Marianne wasn't enough, so one by one you created Jasmine, Sofia. Karl, Billy, Liz and Jim. But you were the first. Is Woody your real name?'

'It's what everyone calls me.'

'But that's not the name on your birth certificate?'

'I'm not him any more,' said Woody. 'I'm Woody. I'm hard, like wood. And like wood, I have no feelings. No emotions.'

'Maybe we can fix that?'

Woody shook his head. 'I don't want to be fixed. I am what I am, this is my life now.'

'And the changes you made to your body? Where did you get that done? Turkey? Brazil? Thailand? Whoever did it, they did an amazing job.'

'Bangkok,' said Woody. 'The hospital I went to is a world leader in transgender surgery.'

'And Billy was able to get the funds to pay for it?'

'More than enough. I spent a year in Thailand. And a small fortune. But it was worth it.'

'I don't understand why, Woody? You're male. Marianne is female, I get that. But Marianne isn't real.'

'No, she's real. They're all real. We are all real.'

'But you could be real in a male body.'

Woody shook his head. 'I hated being male.'

'Because of what happened to you?'

Woody grimaced as if he had a bad taste in his mouth. 'Don't psychoanalyse me, Dr Carter.'

'That's my job, you know that. And I'm right, aren't I? Being abused as a boy was more than you could take. But by transitioning to female, that boy is gone for good. You have a new start.'

'I'm happy the way I am now.'

'But you're fractured, Woody. Originally there was just you, now there are eight personalities sharing the same body. Wouldn't you prefer to go back to the way you once were?'

'That's not possible.'

'But it is. You created those personalities. They all stem from you. And if we work on it, they could be reabsorbed back into your core personality. You could become whole again. It will take time, and it will be hard work, but I believe we can put you back together.'

'And what happens to Marianne? And Sofia? And everybody else?'

Dr Carter frowned. 'They're not real, Woody.'

'But they are. And if you fix me the way you want to fix me, they won't exist any more. They'll be dead.'

'They were never alive, Woody.'

Woody shook his head. 'You're so wrong,' he said. 'And how do you think Sofia will react to the news that you want to kill her?'

'I don't want to kill anyone, Woody. I just want to help you.'

'You keep saying that. But you can't help me by killing seven other people, don't you understand that?' He gritted his teeth together. 'Maybe you should explain this to Sofia. See if you can persuade her that killing her is a good idea.'

'Woody, please...'

They both heard a noise at the door and turned to look at it. 'Did you come alone?' asked Woody.

Dr Carter opened his mouth to reply but before he could say anything the door crashed open. There were two men there, dressed in black and wearing gloves and ski masks. Behind them were two more masked men.

'*Sofia*...' Woody started to say, but he was cut short by the crackling sound of taser prongs embedding themselves in his chest and sending fifty thousand volts through his body. He went into spasm and fell back as everything faded to black.

# CHAPTER 79

MARIANNE opened her eyes. For a brief moment she thought she was in the Wimbledon bedroom and that she could hear birds singing in the garden outside. She blinked to clear her vision and her heart sank. She was back in the grey box with no windows, lying on the inch-thick blue plastic mattress, covered by a rough grey blanket.

She felt something around her neck. She reached up to touch it. It was the shock collar. Tears welled up in her eyes.

'*Woody, please, help me,*' she whispered. '*Please.*'

THE END

Printed in Great Britain
by Amazon

27502539R00179